McGARVEY

BY DAVID HAGBERG

Twister
The Capsule
Last Come the Children
Heartland
Heroes
Without Honor*
Countdown*
Crossfire*
Critical Mass*
Desert Fire
High Flight*
Assassin*
White House*
Joshua's Hammer*
Eden's Gate
The Kill Zone*
By Dawn's Early Light
Soldier of God*
Allah's Scorpion*
Dance with the Dragon*
The Expediter*
The Cabal*
Abyss*
Castro's Daughter*
Burned
Blood Pact*
Retribution*
The Shadowmen*+
The Fourth Horseman*
24 Hours*+

End Game*
Tower Down*
Flash Points*
Face Off*
First Kill*
McGarvey*

**WRITING AS
SEAN FLANNERY**

The Kremlin Conspiracy
Eagles Fly
The Trinity Factor
The Hollow Men
Broken Idols
Gulag
Moscow Crossing
The Zebra Network
Crossed Swords
Moving Targets
Winner Take All
Kilo Option
Achilles' Heel

WITH BYRON L. DORGAN

Blowout
Gridlock

**NONFICTION WITH
BORIS GINDIN**

Mutiny!

* Kirk McGarvey adventures
*+Kirk McGarvey ebook original novellas

McGARVEY

DAVID HAGBERG

A TOM DOHERTY ASSOCIATES BOOK

NEW YORK

This is a work of fiction. All of the characters, organizations, and events portrayed
in this novel are either products of the author's imagination
or are used fictitiously.

MCGARVEY

A Forge Book
Published by Tom Doherty Associates
120 Broadway
New York, NY 10271

www.tor-forge.com

Forge® is a registered trademark of Macmillan Publishing Group, LLC.

The Library of Congress Cataloging-in-Publication Data is available upon request.

ISBN 978-0-7653-9420-0 (hardcover)
ISBN 978-0-7653-9421-7 (ebook)

Our books may be purchased in bulk for promotional, educational, or business use.
Please contact your local bookseller or the Macmillan Corporate and Premium
Sales Department at 1-800-221-7945, extension 5442, or by email at
MacmillanSpecialMarkets@macmillan.com.

First Edition: November 2020

Printed in the United States of America

0 9 8 7 6 5 4 3 2 1

AND NOW FOR MARY

PART
ONE

Earlier

PART

ONE

Earlier

ONE

□

John McGarvey, pushing sixty-five, the age at which he and his wife, Lilly, who was the same age, planned to retire, sat back at his desk, scanning for a third time the results he'd just received from the Cray supercomputer.

It was late on Friday, and except for a few techs across the way in the cavernous Building F, which was the workshop for the Los Alamos National Laboratory's high energy and applied physics department, he was alone. But it was midsummer and still light out. He was excited by the results that the Cray had been chewing on for nearly three weeks—and vindicated. The concept was viable. The damned thing would work. And it was due in large measure to Lilly's progress with quantum information systems.

They'd met in their senior year at Garden City High School, in southwestern Kansas, she a town girl and he a rancher's son living ten miles northwest. They'd fallen instantly in love, both of them dubbed the school's brainiacs. She went to Caltech, where she earned her PhD in mathematics, while he went to MIT, on the opposite coast, earning his PhD in advanced computer design and applied physics.

They never took summers off, only snatching a week or so here and there to get together, and despite the strong advice of their major advisers, they got married in a brief ceremony in Garden City, followed by a one-week honeymoon in Paris, after which they went back to school for two more years of study and then two years of postdoc work. Both of them were hired by Los Alamos during the same week in 1956 and had worked there continuously, on a variety of projects, for more than thirty years. Eight years ago, the facility was renamed the Los Alamos National

Laboratory, and John knew that, in a lot of ways, after they retired they would miss the science, the day-to-day interactions with some of the brightest minds on the planet.

"Where to next?" Lilly had asked him a few years ago, when they'd decided to retire at sixty-five.

"The ranch, full-time."

"I hoped you'd say something like that," she told him, and he didn't think he'd ever loved her more than at that moment.

"Farmers at heart?"

She'd laughed. "What do you suppose the kids will think?"

"Joanne has her own life with Stan and the two grandbabies in Salt Lake, so I don't think she'd want to come back to help out when we get doddering."

"And Kirk's got a start at the CIA, so it's not likely he and his wife and the baby would come home."

"Spies retire early," John had told her.

"So we leave the ranch to him?"

"I think so."

"Me too."

Locking the printout in his safe, John went to the window of his third-story office and looked across what, in the past thirty years, had become a vast campus that no longer specialized in nuclear weapons design and testing but had branched out to a host of other disciplines, including Lilly's quantum mechanics, chemistry, energy systems, superconductivity, and all the earth sciences.

It was going to be strange to leave it, and yet some of the kids coming up were doing work that, five years ago, he'd never even dreamed about. Some of it was almost science fiction.

At six three, with a lean, almost lanky figure and a narrow face with what Lilly called the kindest, most expressive eyes on the planet, he looked more like a rancher than a scientist. And his wife liked that, too.

"We're just a pair of Great Plains country bumpkins, and that'll never change," she'd said just last week, when they were sitting on the porch of their ranch house having their usual sundowners—pinot grigio for her, a gin and tonic for him.

She was right, of course. As usual, he thought, turning away from the window. But they would miss the lab.

Her office was on the opposite side of the complex. When he phoned, she answered on the first ring.

"What do you think?" she asked.

"It's better than I thought it would be."

"I'm looking at it now, for the umpteenth time, and I think it'll work."

"Because of you."

"And it scares me just a little. The Russians get hold of this, they'll go even crazier than in eighty-three when Reagan came up with SDI. And God only knows what they'll do."

"That's up to the politicians."

"You mean the ones we elected?" she asked.

"Yeah," he said. Sometimes they would agree about something—especially politics—when anyone around them would swear they were having a knock-down, drag-out argument. "You ready to pull the pin?" The Fourth of July was on a Tuesday, so a lot of people were taking four-day weekends.

"Give me five minutes to lock up."

"I'll meet you out front."

Lilly, wearing jeans, a white, military-style shirt with the sleeves rolled up and fastened above her elbows, and a safari hat at an angle on her head, came out of the advanced mathematics building, jumped in the open-top Jeep, and gave her husband a peck on the cheek. She was all smiles.

She was tall for a woman. Though she was six inches shorter than John, she had the feminine version of his lean and lanky build. Her pretty face was oval, with green eyes so brilliant they almost looked unreal, and a short-cropped mop of blond hair with which she seldom did much of anything except run her fingers through it.

Even after more than thirty years of marriage, he couldn't keep his eyes off her. And for a longish moment or two, he just sat there.

"If we want to get home before it's time to get back here, you might think about putting it in gear and driving us over to the airport," she said.

"I called Tommy and told him to pull the plane out of the hangar and top off the fuel. We'll be in the air thirty minutes from now."

They had a ten-year-old Beechcraft Bonanza V-tail 35B that cruised in excess of one hundred seventy miles per hour, with a range of more than five hundred miles, plenty to get them to the well-lit, two-thousand-foot paved strip on the ranch, with a healthy reserve—and in time for sundowners.

A stocky man of medium height, who worked as a day shift maintenance man in the administrative and mathematics buildings, watched from Lilly McGarvey's office as she and her husband drove away in the Jeep.

All of the offices in which classified information was handled were swept for electronic bugs once per week. But in a typical American effort at efficiency, the sweeps in the math buildings were conducted only on Mondays.

Every Tuesday, the maintenance man, whose work name was Peter Lester but whose real name was Petr Lestov, an agent for the Russian KGB's First Chief Directorate, installed the Theremin bug in a half dozen offices here. He then usually took them away at the end of the workweek, but always before Monday.

His high-value target for the past three months had been the McGarvey woman, who automatically gave them access to her husband's work.

"You are to drop everything else and concentrate on these two." His control officer's order had arrived at the drop box in Santa Fe. "They are expecting results from a computer search. The moment that happens, you are to make contact at the emergency telephone number."

Lestov removed the bug from one of the electrical outlet plates, put it in his toolbox, and left the building by the rear entrance, near where he'd parked his battered Ford F-150 pickup truck.

In eight minutes, he was through the main gate and, taking great care not to exceed the speed limit on highways 502 and 64, made it to the phone booth outside a supermarket two miles from his apartment, where he made the long-distance call to a woman in Denver. It was answered on the first ring.

"Hi, sis," he said.

"Peter! It's nice to hear from you. It's been so long, I was starting to get worried."

"I'm thinking about taking the long weekend off, maybe come up to see you and the kids."

"Are you bringing presents for them?"

"You bet. And this time they're really good."

TWO

☐

Kirk McGarvey had been lucky to snag an exit row seat aboard the Boeing 747 from Moscow, which made traveling coach only slightly more palatable. But then, the Central Intelligence Agency never sent its agents first class. And especially not new recruits.

At twenty-seven, McGarvey—Mac to his few friends in the Company—was in superb condition, in part because of the luck of the genetic draw but also because he'd worked out just about every day of his life since he was old enough to help on the ranch. Then the air force's tough Officer Candidate School physical training, and then the much tougher physical demands that he aced at the Company's training facility, the Farm.

He was a little under six feet, and considered handsome in some circles, though that opinion had begun to sour somewhat in the past year for his wife, Katy, who had begun to complain that he was just a "bit over the macho edge."

"I almost hate to take you to any decent function," she'd told him, before he'd left for Moscow, where he'd set up an American dollar account at Arvesta Bank. The CIA wanted to funnel hard currency into the country, right under the noses of the KGB, to be used at first to fund relatively low-level intel ops. If that much went without a hitch, the level of operational sensitivity would be increased a bit at a time.

It was a little after three in the afternoon when they touched down at Washington's Dulles Airport, a light drizzle falling from a deeply overcast sky.

He'd called Katy yesterday from his hotel in Moscow, giving her the flight number and arrival time, but she was just heading to the private aviation terminal at National Airport, where her father's jet was to fly her and their two-year-old daughter, Liz, up to New York for the day.

"I'll try to make it back in time, but I can't guarantee anything, Kirk. You know how Daddy can be, and he and Mom haven't seen Elizabeth in ages. They want to show her off a little. Ed and Mario will be there for dinner, of course."

Ed Koch was the mayor of New York and Mario Cuomo was the governor. They were friends of Katy's father, who was the senior partner in one of New York's most prestigious law firms.

"No problem, Katy. I can take a cab," McGarvey said.

"Kathleen," she corrected him. This was also something new she'd been doing over the past six months or so. "It might be easier."

He was passed through customs and immigration with a single suitcase and a garment bag under the work name of James T. Parker, with a bulletproof CIA-generated passport. Outside, he'd half hoped that Katy would be there, but she wasn't, and he was disappointed but not surprised. He joined the queue for a cab, and when it was his turn, the cabbie, a tall heavyset black man, got out and put the bags in the trunk.

McGarvey gave him the address in Chevy Chase.

"Yes, sir," the cabbie said, pulling away. "And welcome home."

"Do I know you?" McGarvey asked. He'd packed the Walther PPK in his luggage, in a container secured with a diplomatic seal. He wished he had it now.

"No, sir. Don Parker. I'm with Housekeeping." The reference, borrowed from the British MI6, was the insider's term for CIA security, which was under the Directorate of Management and Services. "Mr. Danielle's office asked that you be picked up."

Lawrence Danielle was the deputy director of operations, answerable only to the deputy director and director of the agency. "They must want something," McGarvey said. It was the first thing that came to mind.

Parker laughed. "No free lunch these days. Anyway, I was told to tell you 'Job well done and you don't have to be back until Tuesday.'"

"Now I *am* worried," McGarvey said, but he laughed too, his mood a little lighter than it had been the past twenty-four hours. Three and a half days. Time enough to mend some fences.

McGarvey let himself in, dropping his bags in the entry hall, tossing his dark blue blazer on the padded bench, and headed back to the kitchen.

Katy was behind the center island, just finishing a glass of wine, and she looked up with a momentary flash of guilt behind her eyes.

"Oh, good, you made it in one piece," she said. "I just now walked in the door myself."

It was such an obvious lie, McGarvey didn't bother with it. Besides the wine, she was wearing lounging pants and a light sleeveless top, an outfit in which she would never travel.

He went around to give her a kiss, but she turned slightly away so it landed on her cheek.

"There's beer in the fridge," she said.

"Where's Liz?" McGarvey asked. He got a snifter from the wet bar and poured a Napoleon brandy, drank it straightaway, then poured another before he turned back to her.

"In New York with my mom and dad."

"For how long?"

"They haven't seen her in ages."

McGarvey said nothing.

"Look, you leave for weeks at a time with absolutely no explanations, so what are we supposed to think? We know that you work for the CIA, but you've never told us what you do. Or if you're in some sort of danger."

"Who is *we*?"

"You could be killed, and then what the hell am I supposed to do?" Katy demanded, her voice rising.

"Katy, it's important. Who is the *we* you're talking about?"

"My father. Who do you think I'm talking about?" she said. "He pulled some strings—important strings—but all he could come up with was that you were a spy. A fucking spy!"

"For Christ's sake, Katy, you could get me killed."

"My name is Kathleen," she screeched.

McGarvey put down his drink, picked up the phone, and started to dial.

"Who are you calling?"

"Your father."

"He's not in New York. He and Mother took Elizabeth to Grenada for the holiday."

McGarvey put down the phone and just looked at his wife. He thought, at that moment, that he didn't know who she was. What she had become.

Because of her father, and his money, and the financial support he'd given her all her life, she was independently wealthy. She sat on the boards of a half dozen charities, such as the Red Cross and the Easter Seals, plus the Smithsonian and a couple of other museums, including the Met in New York. She was a somebody, a distinctly separate person from her husband.

"You'd never send our daughter away without talking to me first," McGarvey said, taking great care to keep a reasonable tone.

"You were gone. What was I supposed to do?"

"Wait for me to come back."

"You're always gone. And one of these days you'll come back, but in a coffin or a fucking body bag! Then what do you want me to do? Write a letter to hell?"

McGarvey held up a hand. "Okay, let's call a truce. I'm going to unpack and take shower. Maybe you can change and we'll go somewhere to get a bite."

"I've already eaten."

"I thought you just got home."

"I had something to eat at the airport," she said. She was very wound up, her obvious lie showing on her face.

"Truce anyway, Kathleen. We need to get a few things straight."

"More than a few," she said.

He nodded.

"Go clean up and I'll fix you something."

"Let's talk first."

THREE

John was up at dawn, which was usual for him whenever he was at the ranch. Downstairs, Mary Jorgensen, their housekeeper/cook, was just finishing eggs, beans, steak, thick country toast, and sliced apples for the six ranch hands.

"Mornin', Mr. M. You're wanting something to eat?" Mary said, when he came into the big kitchen. The long table in the porch alcove could easily fit a dozen people and was set as usual for the staff.

"Just coffee. Bob around?"

"Down at the office. He's already had his breakfast," Mary said. She poured a large mug of coffee, strong and black. "Mrs. Lilly up yet?"

"Just stirring," John said, and he went out onto the long porch, which looked northwest across the vastness of the gently rolling hills that stretched in every direction for as far as the eye could see.

Setting his cup on the rail, he lit a Camel unfiltered and took a deep drag. A bad habit that would someday kill him, though, due to Lilly's nagging, he'd managed to cut down to a half a pack a day. But the best was the first, like this morning.

The ranch stretched twenty thousand acres, with the main house, barns, and other outbuildings at the northeast corner, just two miles from Highway 50/400, which followed the Arkansas River. In the distance, to the southwest, the hills were dotted with some of the five thousand head of cattle. Directly to the south were the landing strip, hangar, and gas pumps for the Beech as well as all the other ranch vehicles. And two miles directly east, well downwind from the house and bunkhouse, was the feed lot, with a spur up to the BNSF tracks outside of Garden City.

John was a scientist, yet in many ways he considered himself an old-fashioned man. The ranch was third generation, started by his grandfather, Patrick, just off the boat from Ireland as an eighteen-year-old immigrant hungry for a new start. John remembered the old man telling stories about the rigors of cattle drives. But it was only later that his father told him that his grandfather's stories were just that—whoppers. The old man had missed cattle drives by more than fifty years.

Taking his coffee, John headed down to the hangar, where the ranch office was housed in an enclosed balcony that looked down on the Beech and the fully equipped machine shop in which ranch manager Bob Wehr and one of the hands could fix just about anything on the ranch that needed fixing, including the airplane.

Most of the hands, dressed for work, were coming up the path from the bunkhouse to have their breakfast before they got started for the day.

"Mornin', Mr. M.," all of them said, tipping their hats.

"Mornin', guys. Bob still down at the office?"

"Yes, sir," one of the men said.

They were all good workers, three of them Mexicans from Texas whom Bob had recruited several years ago on the promise that the ranch's profits would be shared among them. The job was seven days a week, but operations could be conducted by four or five men, which meant everyone got at least one day a week off, and that schedule was left up to them, except in an emergency, when all hands were needed on deck.

No one complained. Ever.

Bob Wehr, dressed as usual in jeans, scuffed Tony Lama work boots, and a chambray denim shirt, was just coming out of the hangar, a work bag of tools slung over a shoulder, when John came around the corner.

Square jawed, with thick dark hair and a stocky build, Wehr looked more like a worker in some foundry than a ranch manager, computer expert, amateur painter in watercolors, handyman, and above all, superb judge of character and motivational expert.

"You're up early," Wehr said. It was his same greeting every morning.

"You too. Where you off to?"

"The water pump at seven B is coming up short. I'm going to saddle up and take a look."

Seven B was a spot about five miles southwest, one of eleven locations around the ranch that used windmills to pump water into long metal troughs from which the cattle drank.

"Mind some company?"

Wehr grinned. "If you think you can keep up."

"I'm old, not dead yet," John said. "And you do know who your boss is." It was their usual banter.

"You remind me every weekend. And, frankly, I'd rather have the missus ride out with me," Wehr said. When he'd come to them nine years ago, as a thirty-two-year-old man, he had just lost his wife to cancer, six months earlier, and he wanted to bury himself in work somewhere remote for a year or so. The McGarvey ranch filled the bill, and he never gave an indication that he was ready to move on.

"She's a terrible nag."

"A lot better looking than you."

It was nearly one in the afternoon when KGB deep cover operative Igor Klimov pulled the eighteen-wheeler around back of a warehouse that once had held mattresses, for an Ohio factory now long closed, and stopped just past a used dark blue Nissan Pathfinder. This was a mostly abandoned industrial section on Denver's south side, not far from Centennial and just a quarter mile off I-25.

He and his partner, Yevgenni Zimin, jumped down from the tractor. Around back, they opened the rear doors and manhandled a pair of ramps of the type used on car transporters. Zimin put on a pair of rubber gloves, got behind the wheel of the Pathfinder, and drove it around to the truck, where he carefully eased up the ramps and inside. He shut off the engine, set the parking brake, and, with Klimov's help, attached chains from the SUV's front and rear frame to strong points welded in the truck's floor.

A half hour after they'd pulled in, they were heading south on the interstate, the eighteen-wheeler with its Rocky Mountain Transport Service logo anonymous on the highway. Their bulletproof papers identified them as brothers James and Orville Heikkila, from Duluth, Minnesota. The bill of lading and trucking company papers that had been put in place six months ago also were bulletproof. They would have no difficulty passing inspection at any weigh station as they left Colorado and entered Kansas.

The activation call that they had been expecting for the last half year had finally come, last night.

"They've made the breakthrough, and I'm told it's potentially worse than anticipated, especially if they're allowed to continue."

"It is a go?" Zimin asked.

"Yes, you have the green light," their control officer—a man they'd never met—told them. "Do not fail."

"We will not," Zimin said, but the line was already dead.

It was just past one thirty when Lilly walked down to the hangar. John was late for lunch, as he sometimes was, and she figured that he and Bob Wehr had buried their noses in one piece of machinery or another.

The phone in the office upstairs started to ring, and she hurried to answer it. "Hello."

"Mrs. McGarvey?"

"Yes."

"Is your husband there?"

"May I ask who is calling?"

"Sorry. I'm William Cooper calling for Mr. Pittman. I'll be leaving Washington later this afternoon and I would like to have dinner with both of you. But it'll be late, probably not until sometime after nine."

"I'm sorry, I don't know Mr. Pittman either."

"He is the DOE's assistant secretary for international affairs. We were apprised just this afternoon about your recent breakthrough, and I was asked to speak to you. I can't tell you how excited we are here."

"I have no idea what you're talking about."

"I understand. Believe me that nothing classified would be discussed at our meeting—at least not in public. But let me give you the number for the switchboard. You can call and confirm who I am."

"I will," Lilly said, and she hung up. She immediately dialed the number. It was answered after two rings.

"Good morning, you have reached the Department of Energy, how may I direct your call?"

"I would like to speak with Mr. Pittman."

"Mr. Pittman is not in his office. May I put you through to his assistant, Mr. Cooper?"

"No, that won't be necessary," Lilly said. "Just give him the message: El Conquistador at nine. He'll understand."

FOUR

Mac headed up the last and steepest hill on the heartbreaker confidence course at the Farm, leaving all but one of the other runners well behind. This was the place along the York River, near Williamsburg, Virginia, where CIA recruits received their initial physical and spy craft training. Known as Camp Peary, it was officially an armed forces experimental training activity base. Sometimes, operational officers who worked at Langley headquarters or who had rotated home from an overseas posting made the hundred-and-fifty-mile drive down from Washington to get in shape, to hone their hand-to-hand or small arms skills, or, like Mac this morning, simply to get away.

Nothing had been accomplished between him and Katy yesterday, and she'd suggested that he spend the night in the guest room. She needed some time to think.

He'd hoped that she might come to him in the night, but she hadn't, and well before dawn he grabbed his bag, which he hadn't unpacked from Moscow, left a note for her on the kitchen counter, and drove here.

At the top of the hill, he pulled up short. From about three hundred feet above the river, he could almost see the Gloucester Point bridge from Yorktown, and south to the world's largest naval base at Norfolk.

A long way from Kansas, the unbidden thought came into his head. He'd not been out to see his parents in more than a year, though he usually talked to them once a week, unless he was out of the country. The last time was just before he'd been sent to Moscow. His mother had answered the phone and she'd sounded excited.

"Work going well?" he'd asked.

"You could say that," she'd said. "How about you, and Katy and Liz?"

Whenever they talked, she would steer the conversation away from what she and John did at Los Alamos, but he'd never heard her almost breathless like at that moment. "They're doing good."

His mother had hesitated for a beat. "Did you mean to say that *we're* doing good?"

He'd never been able to lie to her. "She doesn't like my job."

"Do you?"

He laughed. "Good question, but I don't think even the shrinks are sure about me."

She laughed too, but there was no humor in it. "I don't like not being able to share some things with you. But just try to stay safe, okay?"

"It's a deal," McGarvey had said.

"Good. I'll get your dad."

A very fit-looking woman in her midthirties, wearing an instructor's jumpsuit, came up from below, a light sheen of perspiration on her upper lip. McGarvey had seen her around the last time he was here, but she'd never been one of his teachers and he didn't know her.

"You're a tough guy to catch up to," she said, not out of breath. She was just a little shorter than McGarvey, with an oval face, freckles, and short, dark hair.

"You caught me."

She smiled. "Julie Madison. You're wanted back at Langley."

"Who wants me?"

"Mr. Danielle. I have a Jeep at the bottom of the hill."

McGarvey's heart quickened a little. "What's the urgency?"

"That part's above my pay grade. But they did say they wanted you by one. Gives you an hour to get out of here."

Katy, dressed in a fashionable white suit, left her Mercedes CLK convertible with the valet at the Watergate Hotel a few minutes after twelve and walked into Jean-Louis Palladin's busy upscale restaurant.

She'd phoned Tony Borman, her friend from the Red Cross board of directors, to have lunch and catch up with their girl gossip. Tony had been divorced for a little more than a year, and Katy wanted to know how she'd coped. Not after the divorce, but during the five years of her marriage to a man she'd described as a complete asshole. She felt like a kindred soul.

"I have reservations for two," she told the maître d'. "Kathleen Mc-Garvey."

"Yes, madam. Ms. Borman left a message that she was unfortunately tied up and would not be able to meet you for lunch. Do you still wish to have your table?"

"No," Kathleen said, and she turned abruptly to go, bumping into a tall man. She got the momentary impression he was handsome, and very well dressed. Armani, she thought. "Pardon me."

"Entirely my fault, Mrs. McGarvey," he said, his voice cultured.

Katy was a little flustered. "You know who I am?" she asked.

"I overheard," he said. "Permit me. I'm Darby Yarnell, a lawyer here in town." He held out his hand and she took it.

"Pleased to meet you," she said, and she started to step around him.

"The place is busy, you have a table for two, and I have no reservations. May I buy you lunch?"

Katy's immediate inclination was to say no, but she nodded. "I could use the company."

"Even the company of an attorney?"

"Especially an attorney."

McGarvey got to CIA headquarters and a young man met him in the lobby with a red badge for the third floor and above. "Thank you for being on time," the man said on the way up in an elevator. "It's a busy day, but Mr. Danielle wanted to have a word with you."

"The Russian op?" McGarvey asked.

"I wouldn't know. I'm just a runner."

At the seventh floor, McGarvey followed the escort to the CIA director's office, where the secretary dismissed the young man and asked McGarvey to go directly in.

Lawrence Danielle, the heavyset deputy director of operations, was seated across the desk from the DCI John Fasser, and they both looked up.

"Mr. McGarvey, thanks for coming up so soon," Fasser said. He was a short man, standing less than five six, with a serious expression and a fierce reputation. He motioned for McGarvey to take the empty chair next to Danielle's.

"Good job in Moscow," Danielle said.

"Thank you, sir. But it was fairly routine."

"Wouldn't have been, had you gotten yourself caught," the deputy director said. He took a file folder from Fasser and handed it to McGarvey. "Your latest psych eval. Is it accurate?"

"I expect so, sir," McGarvey said, handing back the file without opening it.

"How's your home life?"

"My wife doesn't like my job here."

"Does she know what you do?"

"I never discussed the details with her, if that's what you mean."

"But she knows that you're a spy."

"Yes, sir."

"Your parents have apparently made a breakthrough at Los Alamos," Fasser said. "Have they discussed it with you?"

McGarvey was instantly angry. "If this is a witch hunt, I won't be any help, sir. Yes, my marriage may be in some trouble, but my wife has never pressed me for details. She only wants me to quit. And yes, I know where my parents work, and I know my father is a brilliant physicist and my mother is a gifted mathematician, but they've never asked me about the details of my work, nor do I ask about theirs."

Fasser did not reply.

McGarvey got to his feet. "Now, gentlemen, if you'll excuse me."

"We think that you would be a good match for our black ops program," Danielle said. "And if you're interested, we may have something coming up soon."

FIVE

John was driving their completely restored 1952 MG TF 1500, the top down, at a sedate fifty miles per hour. He had a lot on his mind, not much of it good. He'd bought the car five years ago, and he and Bob had taken it down to the bare chassis and then rebuilt the old machine over a two-year period, bringing it back to as close to new as possible. It was their baby, and sometimes he had to fight Bob for the right to drive it into town.

"A penny," Lilly said, sitting in the left-side passenger seat.

"Timing's all wrong."

"The car's running great."

"I meant meeting the DOE guy," John said. "No one out there should have found out about our work so soon."

The light atop the Garden City water tower was in clear view just a few miles out, and the closer they got, the more worried he had become. It wasn't right. As soon as Lilly had told him about the call from Cooper, he'd tried to reach John Gray, LANL's director, but the man had already left for the long weekend and wasn't expected back until Wednesday. Nor was he reachable.

There was a William Cooper who worked for the department, that much he'd been able to verify, but the agency was shut down and the switchboard only gave an automated message that the DOE would be closed until Wednesday morning. There was no public access to an emergency number.

"Do you think we have a spy at the lab?"

"Well if it's a DOE snitch, he or she has access to the Cray's output."

"That's a hell of a lot of data to sift through. And whoever it is would have to be smart enough to understand what they were looking at."

"And the implications," John said, glancing over at his wife.

"That's what worries you the most."

"Yes."

"We could turn around right now and wait until Wednesday," Lilly said. "I'm serious."

"I want to find out what this guy wants and how he got on to it so goddamned fast."

"Well there is one good thing, anyway," Lilly said. "All they got from the Cray was raw data. It's still going to be up to us to translate it into hardware design. There's nobody else I know of who could do it. Which means we're still in the driver's seat."

Klimov slowed down just before the border with Kansas and pulled off the highway into a truck stop. They had purposely left Denver with less than a half tank of diesel so that when they stopped here they would need a fill-up and not just a top-off, which could have raised an eyebrow or two.

"I'll make the call while you fill up," he told Zimin, as he eased to a stop at one of the pumps.

He climbed down from the cab, went over to a pay phone, and fed it enough quarters for the Denver number. The call was answered on the first ring.

"Yes."

"We're fueling up."

"You'll have to hurry. They already left the ranch."

"We can be in position in under ninety minutes. Can you delay them?"

"Yes. But if you haven't made contact by ten thirty, cancel the op."

"I understand," Klimov said, but his contact had already rung off.

It was past nine thirty and the Mexican restaurant was full and noisy, typical for a Saturday night, especially one at the start of a long weekend. John ordered them another frozen margarita.

"He's late," Lilly said. "And I'm hungry."

They had delayed ordering until Cooper showed up, but John was becoming vexed, and he was hungry too. "Let's order. And if he isn't here by the time we're finished, we'll call it a night."

"Deal," Lilly said.

When their waitress returned with their drinks, Lilly ordered tamales with beans and rice and John ordered a chile relleno with salsa verde on the side.

A minute after the waitress left, she returned. "A Mr. Cooper just phoned, said to tell you that he was running late and that he was terribly sorry. But he wants you to wait here until ten thirty, if you would. Oh, and he promised to make it up to you."

Lilly raised her glass. "What do you want to do? Eat and run, or hang on?"

"I'd just as soon go home, but I want to know how the DOE found out so soon."

"And I want to know what he means by 'making it up' to us."

Just after ten, Klimov pulled the eighteen-wheeler off to the side of the all but deserted highway. He put out the danger triangles for a hundred feet in front of and then behind the truck, and Zimin opened the rear doors and manhandled the car ramps down by himself.

It was essential that no other vehicle pass them, especially not a highway patrol or county sheriff's radio unit, until the Pathfinder was offloaded and well away. But in the last ten miles, they'd seen only one pickup truck, heading west, and at the moment there were no headlights on the horizon in either direction.

Zimin put on rubber gloves. Inside the trailer, he unlatched the Pathfinder, started the engine, and, headlights off, backed down onto the side of the road.

"I'll start at ten thirty," Klimov said.

The timing would be incredibly tight, but their contact had assured them that the McGarveys were extremely punctual people. Remaining at the restaurant until ten thirty was exactly what they would do. And they would almost certainly be driving the small English sports car.

"Once I get it done, I'll head on foot back west, but if someone happens to show up, I'll hide in the ditch at the side of the road," Zimin said.

They were both well-trained and well-blooded First Chief Directorate professionals who knew how to adapt to just about any situation, foreseen or otherwise.

The highway was still deserted when Zimin drove away, heading the ten miles to Garden City, where, if they were lucky, he would wait at the El Conquistador for the McGarveys to leave in their little green sports car.

John looked at his watch. It was just about ten thirty and the DOE bastard had not shown up. The restaurant's bar was still going full swing, and would until after midnight, but everything felt off-kilter to him, almost like he was looking through a kaleidoscope, the images sharp-angled and jiggly.

"Let's get out of here," Lilly said. "We can straighten out whatever it is when we get back to the lab."

"I agree," John said, and he called for the bill. When it came and he'd paid, he and Lilly went out to the MG and headed out of town, back to the ranch. He decided that, in the morning, he'd sleep in later than normal and have the cook make up a breakfast tray, which he would take up to his wife. Maybe with some champagne. They deserved it.

Zimin followed the McGarveys at a respectful distance, keeping about a hundred yards behind them, until they were three or four miles out of the city. No one was coming from the west, nor were there any headlights behind.

He accelerated, catching up with the MG in under a mile, hung back for just a second or two, and then started to pass.

Just as the front of the Pathfinder was in line with the much smaller car's rear wheels, Zimin swerved sharply right, slamming into the curving rear fender.

He got the momentary image of the woman, her eyes wide, her mouth open, as if she were screaming something, and then the MG fishtailed toward the ditch.

The man overcorrected, sliding out of control into the ditch, where the front right wheel dug in, sending the car airborne, flipping end over end.

Zimin managed to stop well off the side of the road, thirty or forty feet away from the wreck, which had started to burn.

There still were no other headlights visible in either direction as he ran back to the upside-down car. The mangled bodies of the man and woman, lying askew, half in and half out of the car, were dead beyond any doubt, so battered that he figured it would have to be a closed-coffin funeral.

He lingered only for a moment, then he headed in a quick jog back toward the west to meet Klimov in the eighteen-wheeler. By morning they would be in Kansas City, where they would ditch the truck and pick up their very ordinary Chevrolet Impala for the drive down to Atlanta and the start of their trip home to Moscow.

PART
TWO

Present Day

SIX

□

The weather on the Greek island of Serifos in early fall was warm and brilliant, as usual. It had been only one month since the wedding, and Kirk McGarvey had taken his new wife, Pete Boylan, who worked with him at the CIA, to what had become his refuge from the world between assignments.

Six months ago he had purchased the old lighthouse, which he'd rented for several years. It was perched on a rocky promontory on the west side of the island's main harbor, and at great expense he'd had a construction team come over from Athens to build a swimming pool and the pipeline to bring saltwater up to it from the Aegean Sea.

The sun had just come up, and Mac did laps, his mind awash with what his best friend Otto Rencke called "premos"—premonitions. Something was coming. He had no idea what it was, but something in his head was warning him to keep a sharp eye over his shoulder lest something sneak up from behind and bite him in the ass. It was one of the first lessons the CIA drummed into the heads of new recruits.

He was in his early fifties, with the body of an athlete, and had been a black ops officer for the CIA for more years than he wanted to remember. He kept in good shape, working out every day despite the fact that he had lost his left leg just below the knee in an op a couple of years ago. And whenever he could get to the Farm, he pushed very hard on his tradecraft skills—including hand-to-hand combat, shooting with a variety of weapons, especially his favorite Walther PPK semiautomatic in the rare nine-millimeter version, and training with all manner of explosive devices.

The women in his life had all thought he was handsome, but in a rugged way—almost like the cowboy in the old Marlboro commercials. Those who didn't like his looks thought he was too macho, too arrogant, too self-assured.

Pete, who'd fallen in love almost from the first moment she'd laid eyes on him, was fond of telling anyone who'd listen something to the effect that when Mac walked into the middle of chaos, the waters parted and everyone—absolutely everyone—knew for a fact that everything would turn out just fine. He had that effect.

At just under six feet, his face was square, his jaw firm, and his eyes were sometimes a startling green and other times gray, depending on the gravity of the situation he was in.

Less than two months ago, a trip he and Pete had taken to Paris had gone terribly bad. They were having lunch at the Jules Verne restaurant in the Eiffel Tower, and he'd just asked her to marry him, when terrorists had planted bombs with the idea of bringing down the tower.

They'd stopped the attack, but Pete had been captured and terribly wounded and he'd had to give himself over to Pete's captors in exchange for her freedom. He'd been sold to the Russians for his operational knowledge of the CIA, but President Putin had sent him back to the States to unravel one of the most dangerous assignments he'd ever been involved with, one that had turned into a face-off between the American and Russian presidents.

"Care for some company?" Pete asked, coming out to the pool. She was ten years younger than Mac and, at five five, shorter. Her face was round, her eyes large and vividly blue, and her dark hair was cut boyishly short. Her figure was stunning, her body almost athletic, with healing scars on her left side and beneath both breasts.

McGarvey turned over onto his back. Pete was nude, a bottle of Dom Pérignon in one hand and pair of flutes in the other.

"Breakfast?" Mac asked.

"Only if we drink it before it gets warm."

"Sounds good to me."

She came into the pool and sat down on the second step, the water just below her breasts. McGarvey swam over and took one of the flutes, which Pete filled. She filled her own glass, set the bottle off to the side, and they clinked glasses and sipped the champagne.

It was crackling cold. "Good," Mac said. "So what do we drink to? Another month before we go back to the world?"

"What's eating you?"

He almost laughed. "I'm not going to dignify that remark."

She smiled. "I meant your black ass the last few days." She tapped the rim of her glass on Mac's forehead. "Something's going on inside there. What?"

"I don't know."

"A premo?"

McGarvey looked away for a moment. "Something."

"I talked to Otto the day before yesterday. He and Louise are coming in on the ferry from Athens. Should be here at noon. It was supposed to be a surprise."

"Are they bringing Audie?"

"She's at the Farm," Pete said.

McGarvey was instantly brought back to the deaths of his wife and their daughter, Liz, in an attack that had been meant for him. The only survivor was Liz's child, Audrey, who'd been just a baby at the time. Otto and Louise had taken in the girl and adopted her as their own. But whenever trouble came their way, they sent her down to the Farm, where she would be safe.

"What's going on?" he asked.

"Absolutely nothing. They're simply coming here for a vacation, something neither of them have taken in more years than anyone can remember."

It didn't sound like them, especially not Otto. "Christ," he said, half under his breath.

"Relax, sweetheart. Nothing's wrong that needs your fixing," Pete said. She got the bottle and refilled his glass. "Take a deep breath. I'm preggers."

He almost dropped his glass in the water. "You're kidding," he said, and in some distant way, he almost hoped that she wasn't kidding.

"Yes, but I got your attention. You need to take a deep breath, come down from your perch, and start enjoying yourself. I told Louise that I'd meet them at the dock and we could do a little grocery shopping. In the meantime, we're going to finish the bottle and then I'm taking you to bed. We have all morning, and I'm going to make damned sure that we use every minute of it."

The windows in the second-floor bedroom suite were open to the breeze from the sea, the curtains ruffling, but there were no noises, not even birdsong. Pete, lying beside him, her head on his chest, had fallen asleep after their lovemaking, but McGarvey was awake, his mind still alive with a kaleidoscope of memories.

Japan, Russia, Chile, North Korea, France—all places where he'd been involved in some black op. Each with its own distinct memories. Most of them satisfying, but none of them good.

He'd started out, what seemed like a century ago, as a second lieu-tenant in the Air Force Office of Special Investigations. The colonel had told him that he would almost certainly burn out by the time he was thirty because he had a chip on his shoulder. The unit's commanding officer was long dead now, and he'd been right about the chip on Mac's shoulder, but instead of burning him out, it had lit a flame in his belly that seemed to be just about the only constant in his life.

A few years after he'd joined the CIA, the deputy director of opera-tions at that time had told him he was an anachronism, that his dedica-tion to what he'd called McGarvey's Superman complex—truth, justice, and the American way—was sadly out of date. But then 9/11 had come along, and it turned out it was the DDO who was sadly out of date.

He gently disengaged himself from Pete, who mumbled something but then, still asleep, rolled over on her side. He got up and went to the window.

Something or someone was coming. He'd been trying over the past couple of days to figure out what it was, why his internal alarm system was banging like a sledgehammer on a giant gong. But he'd come up with nothing that made sense, which had only deepened the morose mood he was fighting.

He remembered the early morning call from Bob Wehr, telling him that his parents had been killed in a car crash. That had been more years ago than he could count, but the memories were still as vivid as ever. It was something he'd never been able to erase from his head.

He turned and looked back at Pete sleeping peacefully. None of it was fair to her. She knew that something was wrong, and she had almost certainly asked Otto and Louise to come out for a visit, to help lift his spirits. She wanted to do something for him. But he wasn't letting her in.

He didn't know if he could.

SEVEN

☐

McGarvey stood on the open deck at the top of the lighthouse as the Jeep crested the last hill, about a quarter mile away. Pete was driving, Louise was riding shotgun, and Otto was in the back. Until the construction crew had regraded the old dirt track from town so that they could get their equipment in place to build the pool, the only easy way up was either on foot or by helicopter.

Most of the time he'd been here alone, and he'd preferred the forty-five-minute walk. He'd liked the solitude. It was the same reason he'd never had a phone line put in, and he'd seldom turned on his sat phone. This was his private aerie.

The few times someone had come to see him, because of some trouble they wanted him to get involved with, they'd hiked up. Otto a couple of times, but once even Marty Bambridge, the former deputy director of the CIA's Clandestine Service, had made the climb. As a result, whenever Mac saw anyone coming up from town, his gut tightened a little.

It was the same now. Pete's story that she'd asked Otto and Louise here for a mini vacation didn't ring true. If that were actually the case, they would have brought Audie with them.

Dressed only in dry swim trunks, he went down to the bedroom, where he put on one of the bright Hawaiian shirts Pete had brought him, and a pair of deck shoes, and got downstairs just as Pete was pulling up.

Tall, gangly Louise, with a narrow face, eyes that never missed much, and a million-watt smile, jumped out of the Jeep, came over to him, and they embraced.

"Oh, wow, it seems like forever," she gushed, using one of her husband's expressions.

Pete got out, Otto right behind her. He was tall, but shorter than his wife, with an enormous head and long hair almost reminiscent of Einstein's, but tied back in a ponytail. He was actually dressed respectably, in khakis, a neat button-up white shirt, and soft, green low-top sneakers. He was McGarvey's best friend in the world, and the only man on the planet Mac respected and trusted with no reservations.

"Oh, wow, Mac, hi," Otto said, giving him a bear hug. "So how's your honeymoon coming along?"

"None of your business," Louise told him, and they all laughed.

She and Otto were geniuses. Before they were married, she was the leading photo analyst for the National Reconnaissance Office, which was responsible for every U.S. spy satellite in orbit. Ultimately, it was she who designed the flight paths of every spy bird to maximize their intel potential. And she was sorely missed there and at the National Security Agency, where she still had many friends and pulled a lot of weight.

Otto, who worked in his own intel analysis department at the CIA, was considered by just about everyone in the know, just about everywhere, to be the smartest computer expert on the planet. He'd designed all the computer systems for every U.S. intelligence agency, plus the FBI's. And it was he who kept all of those systems relatively free of hackers—especially the government-backed hackers in Russia and China.

On the other hand, he also was one of the most feared computer geniuses in the world. It was unspoken knowledge that under the right circumstances, and for the right reasons, he could destroy just about any system on the planet.

More than once, he'd become the target of an assassination attempt. Before he'd met Mac he'd hid out in France. But a number of years ago McGarvey had brought him in from the cold, got him his own department in the Company, and watched his back.

Otto stepped back. "You're right. He does looked stressed out," he said. "So what gives, *kemo sabe?* Someone creeping up in your six?"

They'd unloaded the groceries, and Pete shooed her husband and Otto poolside with two glasses and a bottle of Kourtaki, the Greek retsina wine.

"Do we get a hint for dinner?" McGarvey asked. He was trying to keep the mood light, at least for the moment.

"Lobster, a light salad, linguini with butter, parmesan, and squid ink, and a good baguette," Pete said. "Now, see if you can get him to open up," she told Otto. "I can't."

McGarvey poured the ice-cold wine, and Otto sat back and took a sip. "I always hated this wine, until you showed up and explained it to me."

"You still don't like it."

"No, but I should. Like tennis or soccer or horse racing."

"Then why drink it?" McGarvey asked, but they weren't talking about wine.

"That's what friends do for friends who've asked for help."

"I haven't asked."

Otto smiled a little sadly. "Sure you did," he said. "What's up?"

"Your darlings picking up anything? A little lavender around the edges?" McGarvey asked.

Otto's "darlings" were his special computer programs that were keyed into just about every intelligence information resource in the world, especially satellites, and even bits and pieces of the mainframes of some of the opposition's intelligence agencies. When a threat seemed to be looming on the horizon, the background color on his monitors turned lavender. The more intense and imminent the threat, the deeper the shade of color.

"Nothing for you to worry about. Even North Korea has quieted down for the moment."

McGarvey said nothing, lost in his own thoughts. This morning, before Pete left to pick up Otto and Louise, she'd pecked him on the cheek. "Maybe you're getting yourself bummed out because nothing's on the table. You have no real idea how to do nothing."

He'd shrugged.

"Take a deep breath. Relax, for Christ's sake. Or are you getting tired of the married life already?"

"No, but I do worry about you," he'd said.

"I can take a hit now and then," she'd said, kissing him on the cheek again.

"See you in a bit."

She got behind the wheel and started the engine. "Practice your smile while I'm gone. Looks good on you."

Otto was staring at him. "Is it your past catching up with you?" he asked. He nodded toward the open sliding doors to the kitchen. "Guilty because Kathleen is dead and you figured out how to fall in love again?"

The question stung, because in part it was true. "I worry because she damned near bought it."

"Because of you."

"Because of what I am."

Otto took a serious moment to reply. "Feeling sorry for yourself is something new, *kemo sabe*, I shit you not. Pete's a fine woman."

"She is."

"But beyond that, she's a damned good operative."

"Yes."

"And as I recall, she's covered your back a couple of times."

"And damned near got killed doing it."

"You're right, Kirk, but you're going to have to deal with it. From my ringside seat, she's head over heels for you. So either dump her now, minimize the damage, or get your head out of your ass."

McGarvey was startled for just about a nanosecond, but then it was as if some impossibly high dam had broken inside of him, and he laughed so hard tears almost came to his eyes.

Pete came to the open slider. "There's a sound I haven't heard for a while. If I'd known that some vile-tasting Greek wine was the magic bullet, I would have had a tank car of the stuff brought up here."

Louise was there, smiling at her husband. She winked.

"Airline food is crap," Otto said. "So, if you don't mind, get back into the kitchen. We're starved, and we still have a ton of shit to hash over."

EIGHT

☐

McGarvey woke at dawn to the smell of freshly brewed coffee. Pete was asleep, turned away from him on her side, the sheet pulled up under her chin, her hair tousled. Last night had been as marvelous as it had been troubling for him. Marvelous because he was with old friends, but troubling because Otto had dwelled pretty hard on the past.

He got up, pulled on a pair of shorts and a T-shirt, and went downstairs. He poured a cup of coffee and went outside, where Otto, wearing only swim trunks, his long hair wet, was sitting at the poolside table, a file folder in front of him.

"Good morning."

Otto looked up. "Are there any more lighthouses for sale around here? I think Lou and I could get used to this."

"You'd get bored in five minutes," McGarvey said, sitting down.

The morning was gorgeous, slightly cool with the nearly constant light breeze off the sea. They were isolated up here, but whenever he flew to Athens, took the ferry across, and hiked up to the lighthouse, it was as if he had tucked himself in and pulled the covers over his head. Until Pete, he was always lonely here, but each time it was what he needed to get his head straight. A week, sometimes a month or even two, and he was ready to return to the world. Having Otto and Louise here made him realize that dwelling on the past was doing him absolutely no good, and he almost wished that they had brought him some bad news.

"We'd have to have a pool, but a real one, with chlorinated water," Otto said. "I like the smell."

"We could always have a truckload of seaweed brought up and spread around. When it started to rot, you'd have the same smell."

Otto smiled. He pushed the file folder across. "Pete said I should dig this up and bring it over. Said you were talking in your sleep."

"What is it?" McGarvey asked, reaching for the folder.

"Your parents."

Mac stayed his hand. "That's twenty years ago."

"Twenty-eight, this month. I checked."

McGarvey looked away. He'd thought a lot about Katy, and about the other women in his life who had been killed because of him. But each year around this time, he was brought back to the early morning phone called from Bob Wehr, and the aftermath.

"No way to make this easy, Kirk, but your parents were killed last night in a car accident," the ranch manager had said.

McGarvey had been unable to grasp what Bob was telling him. The news was so far out of any sort of reality that it was impossible to comprehend.

"The cops said it looked as if a Pathfinder evidently clipped the rear end of the MG. It went off the road and flipped over. No seat belts."

"What about the SUV driver?"

"The car wasn't badly damaged, still drivable, but whoever was behind the wheel evidently took off on foot."

"Plates?"

"Colorado. The cops are checking."

"I'll catch a flight to Dodge City."

"I'll come pick you up."

"Stay at the ranch, in case the cops come up with anything," McGarvey said. "I'll rent a car."

Katy had woken up. "Who was it?"

"Bob Wehr. My parents are dead."

"Oh, my God, Kirk."

The remainder of that week, including the funeral, had been surreal. No trace had been found of the other driver, nor had any evidence been found in the SUV. It had been an accident, plain and simple. The driver had panicked and walked away, possibly hitching a ride with someone. But there was nothing else.

"The Company got involved because you were an employee training for black ops," Otto said. "I pulled that file, plus what the Garden City cops and Kansas Highway Patrol had, but it wasn't much. Your parents had dinner at a Mexican restaurant in town, and the accident happened when they were headed back to the ranch. They'd had a couple of drinks, but their blood alcohol numbers were within the limits. They weren't drunk."

McGarvey nodded.

"But there were a couple of other things that caught my attention. They came well after the accident, and you might not have been told. The first was that there was no physical evidence in the SUV. No fingerprints inside or outside that were in the Bureau's database. And no fingerprints whatsoever on the driver's side door, the key still in the ignition, nor on the steering wheel. That side had been wiped clean."

"Either that or the driver wore gloves. I knew some of it."

"The between-the-lines implication—at least from my perspective— was that your parents were murdered by professionals."

"Why?"

"They'd made a significant breakthrough at Los Alamos. Something that eventually led to our countermeasures to the Russian laser pulse antisatellite weapons. It was possible they were killed to stop the development."

"If it was the Russians, they were too late."

"Yeah, and it was hushed up at the time because it was thought that if the Russians had ordered the hit, we wanted them to believe they had succeeded in stopping the project."

"My control officer lied to me," McGarvey said.

"He knew that you would have moved heaven and earth to find their killers, which would have blown the whistle on the project."

"'To better serve the interests of the nation,'" McGarvey said. The eight words had covered a multitude of sins over the years, and were still being used today.

"Nothing's on my radar for now."

"Meaning?"

"If you want to take a run at this, Lou and I would help out. And I already checked on a couple of the details. As it turns out, Bob Wehr has retired and is living in Sarasota. You guys are practically neighbors."

"I didn't know."

"Neither did I, until yesterday."

"What about someone down at Los Alamos who might have worked with my parents?" McGarvey asked, but he really didn't know why, because if he went through that door it would be like opening an old, very deep wound.

"No one on that project. Anyway, none of them would talk to you."

"How about someone at the DOE?"

"Same thing. The satellite defense system is buried deep. We're not supposed to know anything about it."

McGarvey had another thought. "If they were murdered, whoever did it wanted to stop their project."

"The Russians."

"But if that was the case, someone was working deep cover at the lab. Someone close enough to understand what was being done."

"It's been nearly thirty years, so we might not come up with anything."

Something from his last op came to McGarvey. The one in which Pete had been taken and he had been traded to the Russian SVR. He'd had a face-to-face with Putin, who was in a power struggle with the head of the spy agency. It was something the Russian president had said during their brief conversation.

A Russian nuclear warhead was supposedly missing, and Putin had asked for McGarvey's help in finding it. He said that they were kindred spirits in many respects. He had been an officer in the KGB as Mac was in the CIA.

"We were adversaries," Putin said.

"Still are," McGarvey had countered.

NINE

☐

Yevgenni Zimin, who had retired from the KGB seventeen years ago as a full colonel, finished dressing in his uniform and was about to leave his upscale apartment in Moscow's tony Khamovniki District when his telephone rang. It was still fifteen minutes before noon, and the Rossiya Club, where every Friday he met some fellow retired intelligence officers, was just around the block.

He answered the phone. "*Da?*"

"Colonel Zimin?"

"This is he. Who the hell are you?"

"I'm calling for General Raskopov. He wishes to speak with you immediately." Anatoli Raskopov, who had just returned from leading Russian operations in Syria, had been appointed by President Putin to head the SVR, a position that often was held by a civilian.

Zimin was impressed. "Put him on."

"He wants you in his office. A car is waiting in front of your building."

"I'm having lunch with friends."

"Now, Colonel," the secretary said, and he was gone.

"Fuck," Zimin said, putting the phone down. He was impressed, but being called to meet with a man so high up the food chain was also intimidating. He couldn't imagine what the head of the entire fucking SVR would want with him. "Fuck," he said again.

He checked his appearance in the hall mirror, something his wife of forty years had done for him until she died of cancer two years ago. She had been a patient woman who nevertheless spent sleepless nights when he was off somewhere on assignment. He never told her what he did, nor had she ever asked.

It had been for the best. Trying to explain the necessity of what was called *mokrie dela*, or wet work, the spilling of blood, assassinations, to a naïve girl from the sticks would have been more than upsetting.

The car outside was a black Mercedes-Maybach. The driver held the rear door, and when Zimin was settled in they headed south, away from the city center, crossing both ring roads, until they were out in the heavily wooded Yasenevo District where the SVR's sprawling complex, with an impressive skyscraper all its own, was located. In fact, the headquarters compound was known sometimes simply as *kontora*, "the office," or more often as *les*, "the forest."

They pulled into an underground VIP parking lot, where a young woman in a dark business suit waited at an open elevator door as Zimin got out of the car. He thought that she was very attractive.

"If you will come with me, Colonel, the general is most anxious to speak with you," she said.

"About what?"

She smiled. "I couldn't say. I'm just an escort."

Zimin nearly laughed out loud. The word meant something different in English.

Upstairs, the top floor was quiet, no sounds of phones ringing or computers bleating, not even muted conversations. Zimin was shown into the palatial inner office of the director of the SVR. The general, standing behind his desk as he talked to someone on the phone, was a tall, slender man, his build un-Russian but his manner brisk and to the point.

"Yes, Mr. President, he's here now," Raskopov said, and he hung up.

Zimin came to attention and saluted.

The general did not return the salute. "I'm reactivating you with the rank of brigadier general, only for the pay grade, no uniform."

"Sir, I'm retired."

"No longer. Do the names John and Lilly McGarvey mean anything to you?"

Zimin nodded. He and Klimov, who, ironically, had died in a car crash a few years previous, had been given the Order of Lenin for killing them.

"Because of you, the work they were involved with was delayed nearly two years, giving our scientists time to come up with a counter-measure—a thing that, to this day, the Americans are apparently un-aware of. All these years, they have believed that they were safe from a nuclear strike."

"Yes, sir."

"Quite possibly that may be coming to an end. And your country once again needs your help."

Zimin was flattered, but he'd enjoyed his retirement—or at least that's what he'd been telling himself all along. Yet, once a week, he put on his uniform and met with friends at the Rossiya, where they rehashed some of their old operations.

"Am I being asked to go to Syria?"

"You're not being asked anything; you are being ordered. But not to Syria. You're to lead a small team on an operation in the U.S.," the general said. "How is your English?" he asked in English.

"Passable," Zimin answered in kind. "I've been told I sound as if I am from London or one of their former colonies."

Raskopov picked up the phone. "Has Captain Lukashin arrived?"

Zimin couldn't imagine what would be expected of him, and he was certain that he'd rather be going to Syria than back to the States.

"Good," the general said, and he hung up. "Come with me, General."

Zimin followed him through a connecting door, into a small confer-ence room with a table and seating for six. A small, wiry man with dark hair and a swarthy complexion was seated next to the escort from the parking garage. Like the woman, the man was wearing an American-cut business suit, the tie properly knotted. He was dressed like a banker, but he looked more like a used car salesman.

"This is General Yevgenni Zimin, the man I briefed you on," Rasko-pov said. "I have temporarily assigned him to Directorate KR for the operation that has been code-named 'Follow Up.'" Directorate KR was the SVR's external counterintelligence division.

The man and the woman got to their feet and started to salute, but

Zimin waved them off. "We won't be wearing uniforms, so military courtesies will not be practiced."

"Yes, sir," the woman said, and they both sat down.

"These two are your team. No others will be involved, though you will have a control officer in the States, reachable only by phone. Captain Petr Lukashin is from Directorate S and Captain Larissa Anosov works in Directorate X. They are extremely capable officers, and their English is flawless."

S was illegal intelligence, responsible for planting and working deep cover agents abroad, and X was the division responsible for gathering scientific and technical intelligence.

"May I learn now what our specific goal is?" Zimin asked.

"I have the operational planning files, General. We can go over them in detail with you," Larissa said.

Zimin had directed his question to Raskopov.

"Does the name Otto Rencke mean anything to you?" the general asked.

"Vaguely. I think he might work for the CIA, in their Science and Technology directorate."

"And the name Kirk McGarvey?"

"That one, yes, definitely. He is the son of John and Lilly, and he briefly held the same office in the CIA that you do here, sir."

"He was a junior officer for the agency at the time of the Kansas operation. Now he's supposedly been retired for several years, but in actuality he is still very active, with mostly extrajudicial operations and others not sanctioned by the White House or Congress—and very often even not sanctioned by the agency itself."

"Are we keeping a watch on him?"

"Of course," the general said. "He and Mr. Rencke are reported to be the best of friends. And it came to our attention six days ago that Rencke started digging into the McGarveys' deaths. We've kept a loose watch on several locations, including the western Kansas ranch where the original operation was concluded, and of course on Los Alamos, where it began and continues to this day."

"Whatever he may have found can have no relevance today, sir. Technologies have certainly advanced by quantum leaps."

"Technologies have changed, but methodologies have not. In any event, we still have two well-placed operatives inside Los Alamos, and their product is very important to us."

Zimin was mystified. "What exactly to you want us to do, sir?"

"Until four days ago, I would have said 'nothing.' But the president himself ordered me to get involved."

"Sir?"

"Kirk McGarvey and his new wife were on their honeymoon at an abandoned lighthouse that Mr. McGarvey purchased on the Greek island of Serifos. Rencke and his wife, who herself was a highly placed officer in the American NRO and NSA agencies, came to visit. Two days later, Rencke returned to Langley, while McGarvey and his wife—who was a CIA field officer—flew back to the States. The president thinks, as I do, that the four of them are investigating the deaths of John and Lilly McGarvey. If their efforts succeed, it would jeopardize not only our assets at the laboratory but also those still in orbit."

"What has led the president to suspect such a thing? People travel all the time."

"Mr. Rencke has made certain inquiries—most of which we can't decipher. But there has been something of a pattern."

"I'm sorry, sir, but that doesn't add up."

"It's the anniversary of the McGarvey operation. Sometimes sons develop the need for closure."

It was still thin, in Zimin's mind. There had to be more. But he was a man who'd always followed orders. "Our orders?" he asked.

"Kill them all."

TEN

□

McGarvey and Pete were having breakfast in the gazebo in the backyard of Mac's house on Casey Key, down the coast from Sarasota, Florida. This had been Katy's favorite spot, where she could watch the boats passing in the Intracoastal Waterway and the various seabirds on the densely overgrown strip of wildlife preserve on the mainland, just a couple of hundred yards away.

He'd brought Pete down here before, and they'd spent a couple of months together before their Paris trip, but it had been difficult sharing the gazebo with her.

"I've always liked your house," she said.

A boat whistle sounded, a long and then a short blast, signaling the Blackburn Point Bridge just around the bend to open.

"Our house, now," McGarvey corrected, and she smiled.

"So what's next? We've been here for two days and you haven't tried to contact your parents' ranch manager."

"I wanted to get us settled in first."

"It's me you're talking to, Kirk. What's the hesitation? Are you afraid that you're going to find out something you don't want to know? Like how strange it was that Bob moved here from Albuquerque after you started teaching at New College and bought this place?"

It was no coincidence, of course. Bob had stayed on at the ranch until Mac sold it, and then he had moved down to New Mexico. He'd turned down a cash bonus, asking instead for the Beechcraft, which Mac had gladly given to him.

He'd gotten his FAA certification as an airplane mechanic and had opened a shop at the airport, doing a steady business because he was good and his prices were fair, according to what Otto had found out.

McGarvey had not kept track of the man after that, busy with his own issues, going to ground in Switzerland after Katy had given him the ultimatum—quit the CIA or get out.

There'd been many operations over the years, and finally he and Katy had gotten back together and had this place built. But it wasn't until Otto had brought the news that Bob had retired and lived outside of Sarasota now, on a forty-acre ranch with its own airstrip, had he given much thought to the man.

"His phone number, email address, property and income tax records are all listed under the corporate name of Todd Consulting, whose president is a man whose tax ID and Social Security number are identified as Todd Lundgren," Otto had said. "Odd. Like he's hiding from something."

"But why Sarasota?" Pete had asked.

"You'd have to assume it was because Mac was there," Otto said.

"Then moving to Florida under a fake identity means something not good," she'd pressed. "What's he hiding?"

"I'll ask him," McGarvey had interjected.

After breakfast, Pete drove into town to buy groceries and McGarvey walked down to their Whitby ketch, docked on the Intracoastal Waterway fifty feet below the gazebo. The charger that normally kept the bank of batteries topped off had gone bad sometime over the past couple of months. Yesterday, McGarvey had bought a new charger and connected it.

Going aboard, he opened the hatch to the engine compartment. Overnight the charger had brought the batteries up to one hundred percent.

Topside, he sat down in the center cockpit and watched as a thirty-foot flybridge fishing boat glided smoothly north up the ICW toward Sarasota. A man was at the helm, and two bikini-clad women—one of them older—sat on lawn chairs on the foredeck, their feet up on the rail. They waved, and he waved back.

Time, he supposed, to take Pete sailing over to the Abacos for a month or so before the hurricane season started up. He'd put off the trip because it reminded him of the trips that he and Katy had taken on this boat, to those same islands. In fact, he'd not gotten around to renaming the sailboat from *Kathleen*.

He got a cold beer from the fridge in the galley below and went up on deck again. Too many things had been put on the back burner since Paris, and since he and Pete had gotten married. Was it time to jump back on the train before it got too far away for him to catch?

He used his cell phone to call Bob Wehr's number. It was answered on the third ring.

"Kirk! It's good to hear from you, finally. It's been a long time."

"Too long a time. How are you enjoying your retirement?"

Wehr laughed. "Probably as much as you are. Anyway, congratulations on your marriage."

"How'd you know that I married again?"

"I keep up with things, especially friends. It's an old habit I picked up from your mother."

McGarvey hadn't blocked his caller ID because he wanted to see if Bob would pick up when he saw who it was. That, and the fact that Bob knew about the marriage, and of course that he was living here in Sarasota, and that he mentioned Lilly were conclusive of nothing. And yet Mac had never believed in coincidences, nor in long strings of seemingly innocent bits.

"I've been thinking about them a lot lately, and I was wondering if we could get together for lunch soon."

"I'm free today," Bob said, a little too quickly, as if he'd not only expected the call but even the invitation, after all this time.

"Crow's Nest down in Venice?"

"I know the place. Noon in the downstairs bar," Wehr said. "It's more private."

Pete got back around eleven, and Mac went up to the house as she was putting away the groceries. "We keep eating like this and we'll get fat," she said. She looked up. "What?"

"I called Bob Wehr. We're having lunch today."

"Was he surprised?"

"No."

"Call Otto, let him know what's going on," Pete said. "Do you want me to tag along?"

"No. But talk to me, Pete. What are you thinking?"

"The fact that he moved here to Sarasota just after you and Katy did, that he never once contacted you, and when you called this morning he wasn't surprised. . . . Nothing's adding up."

McGarvey went upstairs and changed out of his shorts into a pair of crisply starched jeans, a long-sleeve, lightweight fisherman's button-up shirt, and boat shoes.

Back downstairs, he used the encrypted phone in his study to call Otto, who was in his suite of offices at CIA headquarters outside Langley.

"I phoned Bob Wehr this morning."

"How'd he sound?"

"He was expecting my call, and he congratulated me on getting remarried."

"Didn't hit the papers or the internet," Otto said.

"He said he kept up with things, that it was a habit that he picked up from my mother. Which was an outright lie. My mother was brilliant, but keeping up with things—other than my dad and her work—was never a part of her routine."

"Well, if he works for the opposition and was sent to Florida to keep track of you, he'd have to be suspicious of your calling him after all this time," Otto said. "Unless . . ." He let it trail off.

"Unless what?" McGarvey asked.

"I haven't been covering my tracks, didn't think there was a need for it," Otto said. "Wehr said he kept up with things. You and Pete. What about me?"

"Could be coincidental," Mac said, playing devil's advocate.

"I'll know better by this afternoon."

T E N

"Call me soon as."

"Kemo sabe?" Otto said.

"Yes?"

"Carry your Walther."

"I'd planned on it."

ELEVEN

McGarvey parked his restored '57 Porsche Speedster in the Crow's Nest parking lot. The car was a recent replacement for the same model that had been destroyed by explosives in an assassination attempt a few years ago. The restaurant was on the entrance to the channel out to the Gulf of Mexico and was a very popular spot with tourists and locals alike, especially in season—Thanksgiving to Easter.

The bright dining room upstairs afforded a spectacular view of the gulf and of the ICW. The much darker bar downstairs, and what was essentially a small menu restaurant, was the place a lot of the local fishermen and boaters gathered for a couple of beers and a dozen raw oysters.

Bob Wehr, older and grayer than the last time McGarvey had seen him, was seated at a booth by one of the small windows that looked out at the marina and gas dock. He had a Budweiser in front of him, and as soon as Mac walked in the door the waitress brought over another.

"You don't look too worse for wear," Bob said.

Mac came over and sat across from him, and they shook hands. "A few aching joints sometimes, with the weather. But you haven't changed much."

Bob laughed. "Bullshit. But thanks for the compliment. Pushing seventy ain't for sissies, as the people around here like to say."

Mac poured his beer and raised the glass. "Thanks."

"Curious as to how you got my phone number," Bob said. "It's unlisted."

"A friend of mine up at Langley watches my back. Mentioned a few days ago that you'd moved here a while ago. A blast from the past, he called it."

"Otto Rencke. A good friend to have."

McGarvey's hackles were up. "How the hell do you know Otto's name? And how the hell did you know that I'd moved here?"

Bob chuckled again. "You think I'm a spy?"

"The thought crossed my mind."

"From what I've read, Otto is a very good man at finding out things. Secret things, interesting shit. But he apparently has the same blind spot that you do. A lot of folks in your profession share the same fault."

"I'm listening."

"Tell him that he ought to do a global search on himself, and on you. You guys might be surprised at how famous you are."

"You still have my attention."

"Look Kirk, you've heard the name Julian Assange, and the website WikiLeaks? You and Otto aren't exactly afterthoughts. Tell him to check the Russian entries dating back maybe ten years ago. Pissed off their intelligence people something fierce, from what I could gather. I'm guessing that it's one of the reasons they put a lot of rubles and effort into building their cyber security and hacking division. Threw the last election into a tailspin."

"I don't know if I believe you," McGarvey said. He'd come here to trip the man up and find out something that would tell them who Wehr actually was. But the man had all but told him straight out that he was an intelligence officer.

"I'm sure that Otto is checking it out even as we speak," Wehr said. He pulled a device about the size of a pack of cigarettes out of his pocket and laid it on the table. A small red light was illuminated. "You're carrying an active cell phone in your pocket. Encrypted, it looks like. So I have to assume that Otto has been listening in."

McGarvey took his cell phone out and switched it to speaker mode. "Anything yet?"

"My darlings are just getting their first hits, but so far it's mostly old news," Otto said. "There's a huge amount of data to get through, so it's going to take some time. But it looks like the son of a bitch is right. I'd just shoot him and get it over with. The only way to be sure."

Bob laughed for the third time. "Fair enough, but not until you find out what you guys came to find out about John and Lilly. Were they assassinated by the Russians? I'll give you the same answer I gave the *fede-rales* when they came snooping around after the accident: I don't know, but my guess was and still is yes."

"I'm on it," Otto said. "But watch yourself."

Mac took the phone off speaker mode and put it in his back pocket. "Okay, first round is yours. But let's start out with your scanner."

"Your dad gave it to me when I came to work the ranch for him. I had to go through a pretty thorough background check before they could hire me. A couple of security officers from Los Alamos came up and spent damned near three days talking to me. Sodium thiopental, lie detector tests, just plain old feet to the fire. Good cop, bad cop. In the end I was cleared. Another team came up and taught me all about weapons and explosives—and this gadget, which was originally meant to detect bugs on landlines. But it worked just fine when the first bulky old cell phones came on the market, not long after, and still does."

"Did you know what my parents were working on?"

"Not in any detail, of course, but I knew it was top secret, and I knew that the Russians and Chinese and a bunch of other people were being kept in the dark."

"How did you know?"

"Your mom and dad told me, of course."

"Why wasn't I told?"

"You were just a junior officer in the Company, and what they were into was way above your pay grade. Even the Bureau guys who came out to take a look knew only that your folks worked at the lab, but not what they did. None of the investigators even knew how important their work was."

"But you did?" McGarvey asked, still a niggling suspicion at the back of his head. Wehr's explanations had the ring of truth, but they were too pat.

"Just the importance."

"Did you tell any of that to the FBI?"

"No."

"Why not?"

"For the same reason the CIA wasn't even told. A couple of guys came up from the lab to sanitize your parents' files and computers and made it extremely clear that I was to keep my mouth shut."

"Which you apparently did. But why did you move here from New Mexico?"

Wehr looked away for a moment. "Do you want an answer you'd like to hear, or the truth?"

"Both."

"I sold my airplane business and decided to retire where just about every old son of a bitch retires. I traced you here, so I thought what the hell. I've been around McGarveys for a long time."

"I didn't publicize the move."

"No, but New College lists you as a philosophy professor. You were something of an expert on Voltaire, your mother once told me. She was proud of you. You'd dropped out of sight, so I plugged in a Voltaire search. I figured if you were involved it'd be at some school around DC, but of course it was Sarasota. I also figured that, if you had a place in Florida, you might be into boating, so I checked registration files. A documented Whitby ketch named *Kathleen*."

All of Wehr's answers were way-over-the-top too pat for McGarvey. Yet everything the man said had been said with sincerity and a ring of truth. He finished his beer, and Wehr motioned for the waitress to bring them another round.

"I was sorry to hear about your wife and daughter. So many losses."

McGarvey waited until their beers came and the waitress was gone. There were only a half dozen other people in the barroom, no hum of conversation, no white noise.

"I don't know what the hell to make of you," he said.

"I understand. My answers are a little too glib—always have been. It's called the truth. I know too much about things I shouldn't know too much about. Makes me a prime suspect for spyhood." He shrugged. "I've always been a curious person. I got along with your parents for that, and for a lot of other reasons."

McGarvey said nothing.

"I loved them, you know. I think that they were murdered because of something they'd come up with at Los Alamos. And I figured that, you being in the CIA, sooner or later you'd take the time to find out what happened."

"And you wanted to be around when I did."

"Yes," Wehr said. "And because I think that, once you start digging into it, you're going to be the next target. You and your new wife. I figured that maybe you could use all hands on deck. So, sign me up."

TWELVE

□

Wehr ordered a dozen raw oysters each for them, and another round of beers. When the food came, he looked at the tray for a moment before squeezing a little lemon juice on one of the oysters. Before he ate it, he sniffed it.

"I'm originally a Hill County Texan. Out there, we never knew much about raw seafood. But when I got here, it seemed like the thing to do. A waiter out at the Crab and Fin on Saint Armand's Circle warned me not to eat the things until they passed the smell test. Said I'd never forget if I put one that had gone bad into my mouth."

"Good advice," McGarvey said.

They ate in silence for a bit, while Mac asked himself how far he was willing to trust the man. Otto had exhausted what little there was in the police and Bureau files on the accident, and there'd never been much in the CIA's database. At the time, the Department of Energy—which was the department that had run Los Alamos, and still did—had been a big force in Washington. Interdepartmental conflicts had always been around in Washington. No one wanted encroachments on their baili-wicks.

Otto had done a soft hack into their mainframe but had come up with nothing more than the facts of what was classified as an accident. The work that John and Lilly had been doing at the lab was highly classified, and Otto hadn't tried to dig into it for the time being.

Wehr put some horseradish on a saltine, an oyster on top, and ate the thing whole, chasing it with beer. "You came to me, Kirk, which I figured you'd do sooner or later, so I expect you want to pick my brains."

"You said that you didn't know what they were working on."

"Not the details, but I got the impression that it was something for the military."

"They weren't bomb designers."

"No, and especially not your mother. She was a pacifist."

"They both were, but Dad was more of a pragmatist than her. Truth, justice, and the American way."

"Superman's motto."

"I picked up something of that."

"Guess you did," Wehr said. He ate another oyster and drank a little more beer.

McGarvey followed suit. He didn't want to trust the man, but he found that he liked him. His manner was as easy as it was direct. His parents had always spoken very highly of him.

"It was a four-day weekend. The Fourth of July wasn't until Tuesday, so they flew the Beech up Friday afternoon, traded their lab clothes for jeans and boots, and settled in. But they were just about as excited as I'd ever seen them in the eight years I worked the ranch."

"They didn't discuss it with you?"

"No, but I could tell they wanted to, especially your dad," Wehr said. "They were both like kids at Christmas." He looked away. "Christ," he muttered half under his breath.

Still, nothing was adding up for Mac. Wehr was either a wonderful liar or he was sincere. "Was there anything else special about that weekend?"

"Your dad helped with the ranch chores, and your mother lent a hand to Mary in the kitchen with the lunch and dinner fixings for the hands. Busywork, they called it. Nothing out of the ordinary, until they got the call from Washington. Made them a little nervous."

"Do you know who called?"

"Some guy from the DOE, but I'm not sure about that part."

"What *are* you sure about?"

"He was flying out to talk to them that night. Saturday. Wanted to meet them somewhere public, I guess. So they drove into town to the El Conquistador—their favorite restaurant—around nine. They were killed on the way home."

"Did you tell all that to the Bureau?"

"Yes, and the local cops, and the team that came up from the lab. But none of them ever came back to tell me anything."

McGarvey had run some of that down himself, after the funeral. According to the FBI, a man by the name of William Cooper worked for the DOE at the time, but he denied ever making the call. But then he admitted that, even if he or someone else from the DOE had in fact talked to Mac's parents by phone or in person, they would deny it.

"Because of the sensitive nature of my parents' work?" McGarvey had pressed at the time.

"DOE policy," Cooper had said, and hung up.

It had been a dead end for McGarvey in part because he still was a rookie in the Company, and because he didn't have Otto.

Wehr was looking at him.

"His name was Cooper. Did he ever show up at the restaurant?"

"I don't know."

"Did you try to find out?"

"I was told point-blank to stay out of it," Wehr said. "I expect that you were told the same thing. It was an accident."

"People don't wipe the prints off their cars after an accident."

"The highway patrol said it was rare, but it happens. Someone's been drinking, gets into an accident that's their fault, and takes a runner."

"The SUV had Colorado plates."

"Stolen, I was told, just before I left the ranch."

"Told by who?"

"Jerry Rudner. He was a Garden City cop."

"Retired?" McGarvey asked.

"He was, until he put a pistol in his mouth and blew his brains out."

"How soon after the accident was that?"

A funny look crossed Wehr's face. "Two days ago. But I thought you knew that and it was why you called me."

It was another bit that didn't add up. "How'd you find out?"

"I still get the *Telegram*. Old habits. That's the Garden City newspaper. It was reported as an accidental shooting."

"What makes you think that he killed himself?"

"We were old friends," Wehr said. "Definitely not his style."

"People change."

Wehr shrugged. "Do you want another beer?"

"No," McGarvey said. He laid a fifty-dollar bill on the table and got up. "Thanks for talking to me."

"Do you still think that I'm a spy?"

"Jury's still out," McGarvey said, and he turned to leave.

"At least call me. I want to know how it all turns out."

McGarvey phoned ahead and Pete was waiting for him in the gazebo. She'd been in the pool, her hair still wet, the beach jacket over her bikini, damp.

"How'd it go?"

Mac sat down across from her and she offered to pour him a glass of the wine in the ice bucket, but he declined.

"I don't know," McGarvey said.

"That bad?"

"He's the Bob Wehr I knew before college and the air force, just older." Mac shook his head.

"But?"

"His answers seemed rehearsed to me. Like he'd been planning for my call for a long time."

"He probably was. What's next?"

"I'm going to Garden City, then Los Alamos, and you and Otto are going to find Cooper, if he's still alive, and you're going to camp on his doorstep. Somebody might have answers that make sense."

"What about Wehr?"

"He offered to help."

"With what?"

"He thinks my parents were murdered because of their work at Los Alamos. He told me that if I started to dig, I'd be the next target—that you and I would be the next targets."

THIRTEEN

☐

Zimin and his captains had been assigned temporary offices and a small conference room in the counterintelligence directorate located in the SVR's old headquarters building, which was modeled after the CIA's headquarters. He was at his desk, plowing through a stack of old paper files on the operation in Kansas, when Larissa walked in with another armful of files. She was dressed in civilian clothes, as were Zimin, Lukashin, and everyone else in this directorate.

"None of this has been entered into our mainframe," she said. "Not only that, there's still tons of it, none of which was written very well."

Zimin had to smile. "Igor and I were never much good at writing. We were primarily field officers."

Larissa blushed. "Sorry, General. No offense intended."

"None taken. Where is Petr right now?"

"Down in the archives, trying to pull out files that might still have some relevance."

"We're not getting anywhere with this bullshit," Zimin said. "Put what you have in the conference room and tell him to meet us there."

"Yes, sir. When?"

"Now."

Both captains were waiting in the conference room, the table stacked with files, when Zimin walked in and added the half dozen he'd been working on for most of the day. It was coming up on three. They jumped to their feet, but he waved them back.

"We're civilians now, and we'll be going to the States with our new cover identities. If any of us are caught, we'll go to jail, even if we haven't completed the assignment. So, let's none of us get caught. If something happens, or you believe something may be about to happen, drop everything and get out of the country any way you can and as quickly as you can."

"How far can we go?" Petr asked.

"Whatever it takes."

"Including harming civilians?" Larissa asked.

"Whatever it takes. Are we clear?"

Both of them nodded, and Zimin sat down across from them.

"Mr. McGarvey has begun his investigation, as we hoped he wouldn't, but as we expected he would. We have resources on the ground in New York, Washington, and elsewhere who are keeping track of him, his wife, and Mr. Rencke and his wife. You've studied their dossiers, memorized their photos and the few video clips."

"Are we to be given the identities and contact information for our resources?" Larissa asked.

"Not unless it becomes necessary. Our new contacts have been assigned to me and to me alone."

"But what if you are taken into custody?" she pressed.

"I won't be."

"Or killed?"

"Drop everything and get out," Zimin said.

"Yes, sir," Larissa said.

"You're taking the remainder of the day off. You've already been given your packages and travel documents. We'll meet at Sheremetyevo at six in the morning. We'll be flying first class to John F. Kennedy Airport, but not together. Nor, at any time until we reach our hotel, the Grand Hyatt on Forty-Second Street, will we acknowledge each other."

Zimin had put together the operational details over the past twenty-four hours, and his captains had been briefed and given their packages this morning.

"The next morning, we will take the train to Washington, separate cars, where we will go individually by taxi to three different locations in Georgetown, all of which are within walking distance to our safe house. At that point I'll give you the operational details."

Larissa looked serious, but Petr seemed too anxious, like a puppy straining at its leash.

"If you have questions about our travel and rendezvous arrangements, tell me now."

Neither of them spoke up.

Zimin had remained at his desk last night, only going down to the cafeteria for something to eat around midnight. There'd be plenty of time to sleep tonight. And dream.

"Both of you have been trained in *mokrie dela* affairs, though neither of you have participated in any such operation. Nor have either of you been to the U.S. Those were two of the reasons, along with your intellects, why you were chosen for this mission. But I want to make a few things very clear to you before we head toward badland. The first is that I have serious reservations about the wisdom of this operation."

Petr sat forward. "Sir?"

"We have our orders, which we shall carry out, but I believe that our chances of success are actually quite small."

"You think that this is a suicide mission?" Larissa asked.

"Not at all," Zimin said. "What you need to understand is that Otto Rencke and his wife, Louise, are geniuses. They see and understand things faster and at a deeper level than we do. It's a fact we cannot alter. So when we kill them, the strike will have to come silently, swiftly, and out in the open, where we'll have plenty of room to maneuver. We'll make it seem like a random act of terrorism."

"There will be collateral damage?" Larissa asked. "Civilians?"

"Possibly. A part of the war against the West by Muslim extremists, not an operation by Russian intelligence. It's the only way in which we will be able to get close to Mr. McGarvey and his wife."

"Was that in your orders, sir?" Larissa asked.

"The hits were supposed to be clean. Surgical, I was told. But the details were left up to me."

"Then why this?"

"If you understand—completely understand—who Kirk McGarvey is, you wouldn't have to ask that question."

"We've read the files, sir. We know his background. And a friend of mine actually met the man, and spent some time with him, at the Spetsnaz base in Novorossiysk."

"Yes. An operation in Istanbul had gone wrong for him. He was captured and turned over to our people, who were bringing him by boat, but he jumped overboard. One of our patrol boats fished him out of the water and a helicopter was sent out get him. I read the file. Raya Kuzin, one of President Putin's aides, is your friend?"

"We went to school together. She and I had a very long talk about McGarvey. He actually saved her life, and she admired him. Maybe fell in love a little."

"Extraordinary."

"That she would tell me things?"

"No, that Mr. Putin had McGarvey released, and now he has personally ordered McGarvey and his wife and friends to be assassinated. Maybe I could have her transferred to our operation and she could be used as bait."

"She was robbed and murdered on the street outside her apartment last year," Larissa said. "She told me that he is an extraordinary man, but contrary to what his files have to say, he's just a man after all."

"I hope that you are right."

At home, Zimin packed a Western-cut business suit, underwear, a pair of shoes, and the toiletry items that an international traveler would be expected to carry. There were more things for them, including weapons, one-time-use cell phones, and clothing, at the Georgetown safe house.

The first crack in the operation was President Putin's aide, who had opened her mouth about McGarvey to a friend. A silly woman in love with an American CIA assassin who, in Zimin's estimation, was possibly the most dangerous man on the planet.

Killing him would be formidable, and he had no idea why the president wanted him and the others dead. It made no sense to him.

FOURTEEN

⬜

Pete arrived at Washington's Dulles Airport a few minutes before noon and, wheeling her single carry-on bag, her purse slung over her left shoulder, went directly down to the Arrivals doors and the driveway where Louise was waiting with Otto's battered '78 Mercedes diesel four door.

"Good trip?" Lou asked.

"Traveling is always too long without Mac."

"I know what you mean. Anyway, we're going out to Langley. Otto's come up with a couple of things, but first we're going to have lunch, unless you've had something?"

"No, I'm starved."

A cop who'd been eyeing them and the police sticker on the dash of the beat-up old wreck, came over. "Anything I should know about?"

"We're undercover. I just used the sticker to avoid the hassle while I was waiting for my partner."

"Have a good one," the cop said dubiously.

When they were away, Pete couldn't help but laugh.

"Well, we are partners," Louise said.

They rode in silence until they were on the airport access tollway. The day was bright, and even warmer than Serifos, but Pete had forgotten the humidity, which was just as bad in the summer as in Florida. She didn't miss this place one bit.

"How's Mac taking all of this?" Louise asked.

"It's hard for him, all the memories. But I think he's been bothered for a very long time about what happened. And now that it's almost certain his parents were murdered, there's nothing on earth that'll stop him from finding out who was involved and why."

"Otto says it had to be the Russians, because of their work at Los Alamos."

"Has he been able to find out anything else about what they were working on? Something big enough to get the Russians' attention?" Pete asked.

"I'm not sure."

"Bob Wehr told Mac that they acted like they'd made some major breakthrough. They were over-the-moon happy."

"What about the guy? Does Mac trust him?"

"No."

"Neither does Otto."

They got off the highway that led into McLean, and Louise drove directly to J. Gilbert's, a steak and seafood restaurant that was one of her and Otto's favorites. The place was nearly full, but the greeter had saved them a window booth, and immediately a waiter came over with two glasses, a bottle of merlot, and one of pinot grigio.

"Steak or fish, Mrs. O.?" he asked.

"The merlot. I think my friend has had enough seafood for a while," Louise told him, and he poured their wine.

"Half a Reuben and a small Caesar salad?" Lou asked.

"Sounds good," Pete said.

When the waiter left, she and Louise clinked glasses and took a sip.

"Good," Pete said.

"Otto has a couple of things for you, but I wanted us to talk about Mac first. Otto said he didn't sound like himself when they talked on the phone. He's worried about him, and so am I."

"I don't think Wehr will cause much trouble. At the worst, even if someone sent him to Sarasota to keep watch, Mac didn't think the man was a shooter."

"I don't mean Wehr. I mean Mac. How is he doing?"

"Fine," Pete said, but she knew exactly what Louise was getting at. She shook her head. "Not fine. He was getting pretty jumpy on Serifos."

"We saw that much. He was obsessing about his parents' deaths."

"He wasn't sleeping very well, drinking more than usual, and pushing himself physically. He would run on the road down the mountain into town every morning. I followed him in the Jeep. We'd have lunch, and afterwards he'd run back up the hill." Pete shook her head. "It was like demons were chasing him."

"Premos."

"Yeah. He told me more than once that something was coming. He could feel it, but he had no idea what."

"He didn't seem surprised when we showed up out of the blue," Louise said.

"No. And it was a good guess on Otto's part, bringing the file."

"Otto thinks it made things worse."

"He's right, but it made Mac focus on what was bothering him," Pete said. "Gave him something to do." She wanted to cry.

When she was sixteen and no one had asked her to the junior prom and she was in her bedroom crying, her dad, who had named her Pete because he'd always wanted a boy, had told her to get it out of her system. Her mother had died the year earlier, so Pete didn't have her to share her sorrow with.

"Big girls don't cry," he'd said.

"You're right."

"Your mother would have, of course, but in the end she would have agreed with me. You have a soft, loving heart, but a backbone of steel. Whatever you end up doing or becoming, neither of those things will ever leave you."

She remembered gazing up at him, the concerned look in his eyes, the set of his mouth. She'd only ever seen him cry once, at her mom's funeral, and it had frightened her to the core.

"You'll have some tough times. All of us do. Learn to go with them or you'll break."

Louise reached across the table and gave Pete's hand a squeeze.

"Sometimes he won't let me in," Pete said.

"It's the business. Otto's that way sometimes. Just wait him out, be there, and he'll open up when he needs you."

"He's afraid for me."

"Understandable, considering that every woman he's even gotten close to was killed," Louise said. "Because of him."

Pete was frustrated. "He didn't kill them," she almost shouted.

"No. And he knows it in his head, but sometimes not in his heart."

"Complicated man."

Louise smiled. "Aren't they all?"

After lunch they drove out to CIA headquarters, using the back gate adjacent to Langley Fork Park. They didn't talk much, except about the meal and about Pete staying with them at their McLean safe house.

"First I need to get something from my apartment in Georgetown," Pete said.

"I didn't know you still had it."

"Actually, I bought it a few years ago and I've never gotten around to clearing out my junk and renting it."

"We can do it after Otto tells you what he's come up with."

"I need a day or two on my own. Before I can be much help to Mac, I have to get my act together."

"I understand, but watch your six."

Pete had to smile. "That's what Mac told me."

FIFTEEN

☐

Pete had been off the CIA's payroll for two months, but Otto had visitors badges for her and Louise waiting at the back gate. He met them in the VIP parking garage beneath the old headquarters building. His hair was a mess, his sweatshirt with the old KGB logo soiled and the laces on his left sneaker undone. He had the bone in his teeth, and there were no other considerations for him.

"Good trip?" he asked, when they got out of the car.

"Okay," Pete said.

Louise was looking critically at her husband. "You've found something not good."

"Yeah, but let's wait until we get upstairs."

"Something critical?" Louise pressed, as they got on the elevator and started up to the third floor.

"A couple of things, but I haven't talked to Mac yet. I was waiting for you guys."

Upstairs, Otto's lair was actually three interconnected offices that had once held a logistics team of eight people, whose main task had been creating flowcharts for training and equipping deep cover agents heading out into the field. It included the creation of identities, sometimes disguises, travel arrangements, and everything necessary to help the operator survive.

The entire department had been enlarged and moved to another building on campus a number of years ago. Otto had taken over the suite, setting up a state-of-the-art computer center complete with two-hundred-inch OLED monitors mounted on the walls, a pool table–size horizontal monitor that could be manipulated by touch or by voice control, and a half dozen workstations.

In addition, there were piles of older magazines, books, and newspapers in a dozen foreign languages that had not been digitized yet. He mined them, sometimes for a single word or sentence or photograph that fit into something he was working on. And Otto never threw anything away. His wastepaper cans were always empty, as was the shredder.

The door was keyed to facial recognition. It opened as soon as Otto came into view of the pinhole-size camera.

"Hello, Otto," the computer-generated voice of one of his darlings greeted him. She sounded exactly like Louise.

"Any updates I should know about?"

"Nothing significant at this time," the computer said. "Good afternoon, it's lovely to see you again, Mrs. McGarvey."

"Were you expecting me?"

"Of course."

"Do you know where my husband is at this moment?"

"He is currently driving a rental Jeep Cherokee west on U.S. Highway Fifty/Four Hundred, from the airport at Dodge City, Kansas. His probable destination is Garden City, which he should reach in approximately twenty minutes."

"Is he in telephone range?" Otto asked.

"I can link with his satellite telephone. Do you wish for me to do so?"

"Not yet," Otto said. "What is the current state of our security systems here and at my home?"

"Fully operative."

"Thank you."

"You're welcome, dear."

Otto took them into his inner office, where they pulled chairs from three workstations and sat facing each other.

"We'll start from the top down. Mac's parents were developing an antipulse weapon that could be piggybacked onto all of our defense and intel satellites that the NRO was putting up. They were proposing that ground stations be constructed at our old air force base at Thule, Greenland, at the Pentagon, and at one of our military installations on Hawaii.

They'd be disguised as ordinary radar facilities, but they could send elec-tronic pulse signals to satellites already in orbit."

"A weapon for what, specifically?" Pete asked.

"To protect our communications and spy birds from attack by Rus-sian laser weapons."

"I never knew," Louise said.

"The need-to-know list was extremely tight. It was leaked that John and Lilly were at least three months from finishing their work, because it was thought that the Russians probably had spies at Los Alamos."

"Were they tagged?" Pete asked.

"Nobody knew who the spy or spies were, but John and Lilly were warned about the possibility," Otto said. "LANL was and still is an ex-tremely compartmented place."

"The point was to hide the fact that the system was nearly ready, and maybe even fake a failure, to keep it from the Russians," Louise suggested.

"That's right. We wanted the Russians to believe that their satellite killing systems would be effective enough to block us from detecting nuclear missile launches until it was too late for a response."

"Bob Wehr told Mac that when John and Lilly came up to the ranch for that weekend, they were excited," Pete said. "Could he have been working for the Russians?"

"It's possible, but I haven't come up with anything solid yet. And my darlings have a fairly high confidence that the man is nothing more or less than he says he is."

"But whoever was at Los Alamos knew that they were getting close," Louise said. "So that's why John and Lilly were assassinated. To keep them from finishing their work, which would have given the Russians the advantage."

"But there were too many hands on deck to keep that sort of a thing secret," Pete objected. "The techs at Thule and Hawaii and here had to know what they were installing. Not to mention the people putting the devices on the NRO's satellites. Or the people actually manufacturing the equipment in the first place."

"New radar gear, for all they knew," Otto said. "In any event, it seemed to have worked, because so far as I can tell, our Kremlin watchers never detected even a hint in any policy shift."

"But then there's Wehr in Sarasota, Mac on his way to Garden City—and he said that he was going down to Los Alamos next—and me here storming the DOE's gates, which is bound to get someone's attention in the SVR," Pete said. "If we dig deeply enough and come up with even a hint that the Russians believed that the system hadn't been completed, we'd be sending up a red flag. Damned near telling them that the system had been up and running for the past twenty-plus years. Otherwise, why are we looking so hard?"

"But there is the other possibility, that the Russians knew all along," Louise said, playing devil's advocate.

"Are you saying that John and Lilly could have been killed just to make us think that the Russians had stopped the project?" Pete asked.

"Something like that."

"Decoys," Pete said. "Christ. If Mac finds that out, God only knows what he'll do."

Otto was morose. "I know," he said.

"Are you going to tell him?" Pete asked.

"As soon as we're in agreement."

"He has to be told," Louise said. "But you said that you had a couple of things."

"Bill Cooper did work at the DOE, but he's retired now. I have his address up in Chevy Chase, by the golf club. Ironically, it's not far from where Mac and Katy used to live. For now, he's our best bet, because no one at the DOE will want to cooperate with us."

"Hack their mainframe," Pete said. Mac's safety was at stake here, and she wasn't feeling particularly charitable at the moment.

"Government cutbacks. Most stuff from that era was never transferred over to the new computer system. Not enough money in the budget."

"But this was a vital program," Pete objected.

"The facts of life in DC. The department might run the lab, but it doesn't necessarily mean they know everything going on down there."

"Shit," Pete said.

"Yeah," Otto agreed.

SIXTEEN

◻

Zimin had arrived first at their safe house on the third floor of a brownstone building just down the hill from Georgetown University, on P Street Northwest, and he'd just finished checking for bugs or any other signs that the apartment had been tossed, when Larissa showed up.

He was standing in a corner directly across from the door, a ten-millimeter Glock 29 Gen24 subcompact pistol in his left hand.

She stopped in her tracks for just an instant, then came the rest of the way in and closed the door.

"Petr is right behind me, I think," she said.

"Did you have any trouble through customs and immigration?" Zimin asked, lowering the weapon.

"No, sir. You?"

Zimin shook his head. "We don't fit the Americans' profile of Muslim terrorists."

"From what I saw coming across the river, Washington is better than I expected."

"We're not tourists. Never forget we have a serious job to do," Zimin said. "The back bedroom has twin beds and its own bathroom. You'll share it with Petr. I'm going out for an hour or so. I want the two of you to remain here. When I get back, I'll brief you."

"Do we have a fallback?" Larissa asked. "In case you don't return?"

"Your exit papers are with your things, in the bedroom. If I'm not back by six this evening, I want the two of you to check into a hotel as a married couple and take the first flight to London. Your tickets are open-ended."

Larissa nodded.

"No one has been here, and no one suspects that we've come, so relax a little," Zimin said. "I'll be back."

Zimin changed into a pair of khaki trousers and a dark blazer, and exchanged his wallet for one filled with an international driver's license and other documents, plus a passport that identified him as Charles Wiggins, a New Scotland Yard detective with a permit to carry a concealed weapon.

Downstairs, he walked two blocks to Thirty-Third Street, where he caught a passing cab that dropped him off at the end of O Street where it jogged north at the edge of Rock Creek Park.

McGarvey owned a third-floor apartment a block away. When Zimin had phoned his control officer from the airport, the anonymous man had assured him that the American was not currently in Washington, though his wife had arrived this morning.

When the cab was gone, Zimin walked down the block and strolled past McGarvey's place. It was a weekday and traffic was moderate, though he'd passed only two pedestrians. The weather was too warm and humid for his taste, but the hot, dry summer of western Kansas had been worse.

At the end of the block, he suddenly turned as if he had forgotten something and walked back to McGarvey's building. Luck was with him, and the front door was not locked.

He hesitated in the tiny lobby, six mailboxes set in the wall. The one for 3A, McGarvey's apartment, was listed under the name of Paul Wiggins, which was the reasoning behind Zimin's cover name. He and McGarvey were distant cousins.

The building was quiet; there were no sounds of conversations or music playing or a television set on. Taking care to make as little noise as possible, he took the stairs, stopping for a moment at the second-floor landing, and again on the third.

Still there were no sounds, and he went to 3B and put his ear to the door. The rear apartment was silent. He did the same at 3A. McGarvey's place was quiet as well.

He had the lock picked in under thirty seconds, and drawing his pistol, he eased the door open.

"Kirk?" he called softly.

No one answered. Zimin stepped inside, closed the door, and engaged the dead bolt.

The apartment was small, just a living room, looking toward Dumbarton and the park, a kitchenette and dining area, and the bedroom and bathroom at the rear.

No one had been here for some time. The place was clean and tidy but smelled slightly musty.

He cocked an ear to listen again, but the building remained quiet.

Holstering his pistol, he started with the bedroom.

There were two schools of thought on tossing an apartment. The first was to leave no trace, especially not fingerprints, and nothing disturbed, nothing out of place. The problem with that approach, when it came to a professional's place, was telltales, little things that might not be noticed and would be inadvertently moved. Like a bit of dust, an out-of-place hanger in a closet, the condition of a bed pillow—touch it and there would be no way to return it to its previous state. Or a tiny bit of dust or powder on the floor that, if stepped on, could not be fixed either.

The second school of thought was to leave behind just a couple of subtle traces. It would send a message that the place had been searched by a pro. The mark would have to react, in many cases flushing themselves into the open. A first move had been made against them, and they would almost certainly make the next move, which could be telling. It was almost like a game of chess, the opponents jockeying for control of the center of the board.

The closet was half-filled with a couple of blazers, a tuxedo and shirts, trousers, and four pairs of shoes on the floor—one pair for running. A corner of rug on the closet floor was slightly folded over. Zimin lifted it away to expose a small floor safe. He didn't have the electronic device that would have helped find the combination, so he replaced the rug, making the fold slightly smaller.

Nothing else of any particular interest was in the bedroom or the bathroom, nor was there anything obvious in the kitchen or living room.

The fridge had been cleared of spoilable foods and had been cleaned. McGarvey was a tidy man. A bookcase in the living room held a dozen volumes, mostly on Voltaire. The stereo system was tuned to a local classical music station, and the television was tuned to CNN. The man was not only tidy but also his tastes were on the intellectual side, and Zimin decided that, under other circumstances, he would have been friends with the American.

Ten minutes after entering the lobby, Zimin was back on the street. McGarvey's new wife, Pete Boylan, had her own apartment nearby, on N Street Northwest, but when he got there and tried the front door it was locked. Like her husband's building, this was another three-story brownstone, typical for this part of Georgetown.

A gate on the north side was not locked, however, and Zimin went through to a back garden area, a small fountain bubbling in the middle of the yard.

A delivery entrance was not locked, and Zimin let himself in. The mailbox for 3A was listed under the woman's maiden name. He went up, listened at the door, and had the lock picked in under half a minute.

He was just letting himself into the apartment when someone started up the stairs from the lobby. He closed the door quietly, drew his pistol and screwed the silencer onto the threaded muzzle, and stepped back, knocking a low coffee table slightly askew.

McGarvey's wife was here in Washington, and with any luck it was her on the stairs. He would kill her now, one-fourth of their assignment completed on their very first day in the field.

Whoever was on the stairs stopped on the second floor. By the sound of the footfalls, Zimin guessed it was probably a man.

He put away his pistol and the silencer and quickly went through the apartment, finding about the same amount of clothing and other things as he'd found at McGarvey's place. Even though they were recently married, they maintained these apartments, evidently as separate pieds-à-terre.

It was likely that she would be coming here, possibly even staying here for however long she was in Washington. He would have Larissa move in here and wait for the woman to show up.

Which would leave the Renckes, who had a house in McLean, for him and Petr to take care of. The three deaths, especially of McGarvey's new wife, surely would bring the man back here, where they would be waiting.

SEVENTEEN

Louise found a parking spot across the street, a few doors down from Pete's building. They got out of the car just as a man who was heading their way turned and walked in the opposite direction.

Louise didn't catch it, but Pete did.

"Are you carrying?" Pete asked.

"What?"

"Do you have a pistol?"

"Yes. Otto has made me start taking one any time I leave the house. Why?"

"See that man in the blue jacket, across the street?"

Louise looked just before he disappeared around the corner. "What about him?"

"Get back in the car. I want to follow him."

"I don't understand."

"Get in the car, now. And give me your gun."

Louise got behind the wheel, started the Mercedes, pulled the subcompact Glock from the belt holster under her jacket and handed it to Pete. Waiting until a taxi passed, she pulled out and headed to the intersection with Twenty-Ninth Street Northwest. She turned north, in the direction the man had walked. But he had disappeared.

"He might be trying for the park," Pete said. "Go up to Dumbarton and take a right."

Louise did it, but there was only some light traffic and a woman walking a dog. No sign of the man.

They tried Twenty-Seventh Street Northwest, then circled the block to O Street and back to Pete's apartment, but the man was gone.

Pulling into the still open parking spot across the street, Louise shut off the engine. "What are you thinking?"

"I don't know," Pete admitted. "Except that when he spotted us he did a one eighty and just vanished. I'm jumpy. The situation doesn't feel right."

"I have to trust your instincts. I push satellites around, not people—except for Otto."

Pete had traveled light. "I have a gun upstairs in my apartment," she said. "I'll keep yours until we take a look." She stuffed the pistol into the waistband of her jeans, at the small of her back, beneath her shirt.

They got out of the car and went across the street, Pete's head on a swivel. Mounting the steps to her building, she inspected the door lock for any signs that someone had used a pick set—a tiny scratch, maybe a minute speck of metal shaving. But the lock looked mostly clean, and she let them in with her key.

The building was quiet, as it usually was on a weekday, when just about everyone was at work.

"We'll take the stairs," Pete said, pulling out the pistol again.

She went up, moving on the balls of her feet, trying to make as little noise as possible. Almost certainly she was being paranoid, but Mac had told her more than once that, in their business, paranoia was often a lifesaver.

"You have good instincts," he'd said. "Trust them."

Upstairs, at her door, Pete inspected the lock to her apartment. She couldn't be certain, not without a magnifying glass, but it seemed as if a pick set had been used. There was a tiny scratch in the lower left corner of the opening, as if someone had finished their business and had gotten just a little sloppy removing the pick.

An amateur, she had to wonder, if she was seeing what she thought she was seeing, or a pro who was leaving their calling card? Suspecting things like that had been part of her training at the Farm.

"Never assume that you're smarter than the opposition," more than one instructor had told the class.

Pete opened the door but motioned Louise to stay back. She went in low and fast, leading with the pistol in a two-handed grip as she swept left to right.

For a second or two she remained in a half crouch, but the apartment was clear except for the coffee table in front of the couch. It had been moved very slightly to the left. The indent in the carpet from one of the legs was exposed.

The man on the street who had made a sudden U-turn when they'd shown up and then had disappeared, had he been here? She was almost certain of it. The minute scratch in the door lock. And now the coffee table.

"Is it okay?" Louise asked.

"Someone's been here, but they're gone now."

"Are you sure?"

"Yes," Pete said, straightening up. "But stay back for a minute."

"What if he suddenly shows up?"

"Scream bloody murder," Pete said. She went through the apartment, which was only slightly larger than Mac's. The place was clean, except for the scratch on the door lock and the coffee table's position.

She got her Glock—the same model as the pistol Otto made Louise carry—checked the magazine and the action, making certain that a round was in the firing chamber, then went back to the living room. The Glock 29 Gen4 was the latest favorite weapon for field officers because, though it was a subcompact conceal-and-carry pistol, it fired a ten-millimeter cartridge and could hold either a ten- or fifteen-round magazine.

"It's okay, Lou," she said.

Louise came into the apartment and took her pistol, holstering it under her shirt. "I'll call Otto."

"Put it on speaker mode," Pete said. She checked the corridor, then shut and locked the door.

Otto answered on the first ring. "Everything okay, Lou?"

"Pete thinks we could have a situation."

"When we parked across from the apartment, a guy in a blue blazer and khaki slacks was heading our way," Pete said. "But he suddenly made a one eighty. Ordinary build, nothing distinguishing. Square face I think, though I only saw it for a moment, forty feet away."

"Hair?"

"Short, salt and pepper. No mustache or other facial hair."

"His gait?"

"He didn't limp, and if I had to take a WAG, I'd stay military or ex-military," Pete said. WAG—wild-ass guess—was a term CIA field officers and analysts used. "But my apartment has been tossed. Could have been a pick mark on my door lock, and the coffee table in my living room was moved."

"Anything else out of place?"

"My pistol, along with a couple of spare mags, plus a silencer in its case on the closet shelf, hadn't been moved or tampered with, so far as I could tell."

"Did you and Lou try to follow him?"

"Yes, but he'd disappeared."

"If it was the guy you saw on the street who tossed your apartment, he was a pro," Otto said.

"But the coffee table had been moved," Pete said. "It was sloppy."

"Nothing else was out of place?"

"No."

"You've been sent a message: 'We're interested in you, so we left a calling card.'"

"Dumb," Pete said.

"Besides calling me, what are your instincts telling you to do next?"

"Call Mac, of course," Pete said, and then she saw it. "Someone wants Mac to come back here. But it means they know that he and I didn't travel together. They knew I was here, and it's possible they know Mac is in Kansas."

"The Russians," Louise said.

"That's right," Otto said. "Somehow they know what we're looking for. Something from the DOE's records at the time of John's and Lilly's murders, something from Garden City and then the LANL."

"I don't understand what they want," Louise said.

"They want to herd me and Mac, plus you and Otto, into one place," Pete said.

"And kill us all," Otto finished.

EIGHTEEN

□

McGarvey checked in at the Best Western Plus, Garden City's best hotel, a little after three local. He had just brought his single bag up to his third-floor room when his cell phone rang. It was Otto.

"Looks like we have trouble coming our way."

McGarvey's gut always tightened when Otto said something like that. It had happened too many times over the past dozen or so years. "Is Pete with you?"

"She and Lou are on their way to our place, and I've sent forensics crews to your and Pete's apartments. Looks like hers was tossed, most likely by a pro. I'll know for sure once our people have taken a look."

"Start at the beginning."

"Lou met Pete at Dulles and they had some lunch on the way here. Girl talk, Lou said. Anyway, when they finally showed up here, I told them what I'd come up with, including Bob Pittman's name and address. Before he was retired he was the DOE's assistant secretary for international affairs; his number two was William Cooper, the guy we think set up a meeting in Garden City with your parents the night of the car crash. The police records say that they were on their way back to the ranch from a restaurant called El Conquistador."

"I know most of that," McGarvey said. He didn't like the off note in Otto's voice. But his old friend had never been good at hiding his emotions, especially when it came to bad news.

"Anyway, we know that they had made a breakthrough at the lab, and we think that the Russians knew about it."

"Okay."

"The problem is that the lab and your parents were making it very clear that any breakthroughs were months in the future. They were looking for a Russian spy or spies they were sure had penetrated their security, on the chance that Moscow had gotten word that your parents were close but not done with their research."

McGarvey understood the implications at once. "My mother and father were murdered so that they would not complete the project, is that what you're saying?"

"Yes, but there's more."

"You're goddamned right there is. The Russians were just as good as us—maybe even a little better—at disinformation campaigns. If there was a spy in the lab, they might had been in the right place at the right time to realize what the breakthrough meant. So my parents would have been killed to make us think that they were being eliminated *before* they were done."

"That's what I think," Otto said, his tone of voice even heavier now. "I can't think of any other reason. We thought all along that our nuclear missile defense system was a secret from the Russians and therefore bulletproof."

"But it wasn't."

"Looks that way. I think that Bob Wehr could have been one of those spies, and that he was sent to Sarasota to keep an eye on you. When you started poking around the deaths of your parents, he made his report to Moscow. And they just might have sent someone to take you down before you found out the truth."

"Me, and Pete," McGarvey said. "And you and Louise. It's the reason they tossed Pete's apartment and made it obvious, so that I would come running back to Washington. Take care of all four of us in one tidy package."

"Yeah. And if they find out you're in Garden City poking around, they'll come after you there."

"Not if, but when," Mac said. "And I hope it happens."

"Watch yourself."

"Take care of the girls."

"Will do," Otto said.

McGarvey drove over to the *Garden City Telegram* newspaper, which was housed in a low building with windows in front. The young woman behind the desk just inside the front door looked up and smiled. "Good afternoon, sir," she said. "May I help you?"

"My name is Kirk McGarvey. I used to live here with my parents, on their ranch."

Behind her, a half dozen desks with computer monitors occupied the newsroom. Two men and one older woman at work stopped what they were doing and looked up.

The girl nodded. "Yes, sir. Someone asked about you this morning. Said you might be showing up."

"Are they here in town?"

"No, sir," the receptionist said. "But they left a number." She got a sticky note from its pad and handed it across. "I think that's a Washington area code."

The number was 202. "Did they leave a name?"

"No, sir. The man just said that if you showed up to give you his number."

"Thanks. But I'm here because I want to take a look at your back files."

"Yes, sir. Mr. Evans figured that if you showed up it would be about the accident. He said that we were to give you anything that you needed." She smiled shyly. "You're something of a local hero, Mr. McGarvey."

One of the reporters got up and came to the desk. He was a stocky man in his late thirties, with a five o'clock shadow and a pleasant smile. "Brian Watson," he said, sticking out his hand. "Welcome home, sir."

McGarvey shook his hand. "I'd like to use one of your computers to take a look at what you guys had about the accident."

"That's back twenty-plus years. Still on microfiche. But I've already pulled up the dates. Front page on the first day, but inside on the second and third days—mostly backgrounders on your folks. Then, ten days later, we ran the official police report, plus a piece on Bob Wehr. He was the ranch manager and a close friend of your parents."

Watson led him around the counter to a back corner of the newsroom, where a microfiche reader was set up on a desk. A dozen file cabinets, including several with long, flat drawers, lined much of the rear wall on either side of a door into an office behind glass.

"Bob Evans, our managing editor, is out, but he asked that we give you whatever help we could."

McGarvey sat down at the reader, switched it on, and pulled up the first file, which was an image of the newspaper's front page the day after the accident. Under the banner headline "Tragic Accident Kills Local Ranchers" was a photograph of the mangled MG lying in a ditch, upside down.

McGarvey had seen the photograph before, along with others so graphic that they could not be printed in a newspaper, but looking at this one again caused his heart nearly to break. At the same moment, his anger spiked so sharply it nearly took his breath away.

"I'll just leave you, then," Watson said softly, and he left.

For a long time, Mac could not take his eyes off the photograph, let alone read the story that accompanied it under Bob Evans's byline. But when he could focus again, he did read the story, which told him nothing he didn't already know.

He started flipping through the rest of the newspaper, looking for stories not related to the accident but maybe important. He had no idea what he was looking for, but he suspected he would know it when he saw it.

Two days later, his name and his sister's appeared under "survived by" in the obituaries of John and Lilly McGarvey, but no mention was made anywhere about his parents' jobs at LANL. They were prominent ranchers, nothing else.

One short piece on the eighth day after the accident was about Mary Nordstrom, a waitress at El Conquistador. She said that the McGarveys had been expecting a guest to show up. He'd called to say he was running late, but after a couple hours John and Lilly got tired of waiting and drove away.

After going back two weeks in the files, McGarvey phoned Otto. It was well after six thirty in Washington, and Otto answered on the first ring at home.

"We're buttoned up here, how about you?"

"I'm just finishing up at the newspaper."

"Anything new?"

"No. But the opposition—if it's who I think it is—knows I'm here, and they unzipped their fly again," McGarvey said. He gave Otto the phone number he'd gotten from the receptionist.

"Just a mo."

Watson reappeared. "I'm headed out now. And unless you have other plans, we can go over to El Conquistador for a bite. It was your parents' favorite restaurant here in town."

"Sounds good. Just give me a minute."

"Sure."

Otto came back. "It's a throwaway cell phone. It was sold at a Better Image kiosk out at Dulles and activated this morning. Do you want me to hack it?"

"No. See if there are any security monitors at the airport that might have picked up something."

"I'm on it," Otto said. "You okay?"

"Frosty," McGarvey said, though he felt anything but.

NINETEEN

Larissa was at the window, staring at something down on the street, and Petr was in the tiny kitchen drinking a beer, when Zimin got off his secure phone with his Washington contact.

"What do you see?" he asked Larissa.

She turned around. "University students," she said. "No worries in their lives yet, except for their grades."

"And getting laid," Petr said.

"Simpler times," Zimin said, remembering his own Moscow university days. "McGarvey's definitely in Kansas."

"He returned your call?" Petr asked.

"I think Rencke called, probably from Langley. The number was a blind and was cut off in the middle of the first ring."

"Then they know that we're here in Georgetown."

"But not in this apartment," Zimin said. After his call to the newspaper in Garden City, he'd dropped the phone in a Dumpster four blocks away. Next he'd established a link with his case officer, using another throwaway cell phone. It was a secure number in DC proper but well away from the Russian embassy.

"One of us will have to go to Garden City to take him out," Petr said.

"Do you think you could do it?" Zimin asked.

"We don't have any other choice. He just might stumble onto something the previous team overlooked."

"You mean me?"

"Sorry."

"If there's anything left, it would be at the ranch, but we didn't have time that night to conduct a search. In any event—in any unlikely event—that the FBI missed something when they sanitized the place, whatever's left wouldn't be of any significance."

"Are you sure, General?" Petr asked.

"Just as sure as I am that if you were foolish enough to go head-to-head with Mr. McGarvey we would have to ship your body back to Moscow."

Petr bridled, but Zimin motioned him off. "We want him here, with his wife and their friends."

"We're only three, against four," Larissa said.

"Three against two. The Renckes are not trained field officers."

"How are we going to do this?" Larissa asked.

"If Rencke knows that we're here in Georgetown, then McGarvey knows as well," Zimin said. "We're going to make sure he comes running to protect the people he loves."

"Again, how?" Larissa asked.

Zimin called a Sarasota number, which was answered on the first ring.

"Is it time?" a man answered.

"He's in Kansas, I need him to return to Washington."

"He'll be going to the newspaper, and certainly to the ranch."

"Call his Casey Key house, his Georgetown apartment, and then the CIA. Make waves."

"Shall I call his cell phone?"

"You're not supposed to know the number yet. But call the ranch first thing in the morning."

"Shall I identify myself?"

"Your work name, of course."

The phone was silent for a long moment, until the deep cover agent came back. "It's almost over?"

"Yes," Zimin said. "When it's finished you can come home."

The agent chuckled. "Twenty years ago I would have said not a chance in hell. Moscow was a shithole."

"But now?"

"It'll be a relief to finally be with my brother and sister and their kids. Family has always meant a great deal to me."

"Family and the state?"

"Family and the *rodina*," the agent said, and the connection was broken.

The word literally meant "motherland"—the rich black soil, the people, the folk songs, even the long, fractured Russian history. It was slang for Russia, but it had never meant simply the state.

Zimin hung up, and for a longish time simply stared at nothing. Like most Russians—especially those from his era—the word was more than simply a word. The Russian memory was stronger and longer than in any Western soul, so much so that only another Russian could understand it.

"Is everything okay, General?" Larissa asked with concern.

Zimin nodded. "*Da*," he said, and he smiled. "Both of you get your bags. You'll leave here separately ten minutes from now. Larissa will walk directly to Wisconsin Avenue, where she will hail a cab. If none are available, then telephone for one. Petr, you will walk onto the university grounds, where you will call for a taxi."

"Where are we to go?" Petr asked.

"Both of you to Reagan National Airport—Larissa to the Hertz counter and Petr to Avis. You'll rent cars and check into separate hotels here in the city." Zimin pulled up Expedia on his phone and searched for cheap hotels Washington, DC. "Larissa will stay at the Club Quarters on Seventeenth Street Northwest. Petr, you'll stay at the Pod DC on H Street Northwest."

"For how long?" Petr asked.

"I'll pick you up at midnight and we'll come back here."

"What are we to do?"

"Petr will drive to the Renckes' safe house in McLean at eight. But before he gets within sight of the man's surveillance systems, he'll take off the plates and then park down the street for twenty minutes, unless someone approaches his position sooner, in which case he'll immediately drive away. Larissa will do the same at nine. And I will be there at ten."

"It will start to get dangerous by the time I show up," Larissa said.

"This is badland, not Gorky Park."

"The point being?" Petr asked.

"We're going to keep upping the ante until McGarvey has to come running to save his people," Zimin said.

After Larissa and Petr were gone, Zimin found a bottle of vodka in the fridge and poured a drink. It was Stolichnaya—not quite Russian enough for his tastes, but close enough.

Sitting to one side of the front window, in a position where he could look down onto the street but wasn't likely to be spotted by anyone below, he waited to see if their position had been compromised. But there were no windowless vans slowly passing, no cars with government plates, no one cruising past on a motorcycle or ordinary bike, no one on foot—a man walking a dog or a woman carrying a bag of groceries or pushing a baby carriage—lingering.

He powered up his iPad, entered McGarvey's extensive file, and went to the subfolder of photographs. Some of them showed the man in various spots around the world—Paris, Pyongyang, even Moscow—but most of them were taken either here in the Washington, DC, area or in and around Sarasota over the past ten years or so.

The point of commonality in each image was the man's eyes, the set of his mouth, his stance, and most of all a raw power, a determination that radiated from him like a solar wind, against which nothing or no one could remain standing.

He was a dangerous man, and Zimin had no illusions that taking him down would be easy or that the entire operation couldn't possibly explode in their faces. But if they wanted to go home, to resume their old lives, they would have to succeed. There were no other options.

TWENTY

□

It was a weekday evening, and El Conquistador was busy but not jammed. McGarvey picked a booth with good sight lines to the kitchen and front door, and Watson sat across from him.

"Nothing big town about this place, but your folks were comfortable here," the reporter said.

"When I got out of the air force, I came out to spend a weekend, and they took me here for dinner."

"Good times."

"Yeah," McGarvey said. Being here like this brought a lot of memories back—most, but not all of them, good. Garden City was home, but from the time that he was in high school, and maybe a bit before that, he'd felt that he didn't fit in. A square peg in a round hole. Just a little out of step with the crowd.

One incident, when he was a junior in high school, stuck out in his mind. It was something he'd carried with him all of his adult life. He was a good if sometimes a little overzealous quarterback on the football team. He'd never made it as a big man on campus because he had the reputation of being standoffish, but he'd been kept on the team because he helped win games.

After practice on a Friday night, he walked over to the El Conquistador to have dinner with his parents and his sister. Two blocks away from the restaurant, just before dark, he'd heard what sounded like a commotion behind the old Higgins Hardware Store. A girl was crying, so he went back to see what was going on.

Four of the BMOC football players had the sophomore girl's jeans off and her panties ripped away. Three of them were holding her down while the other one, his trousers down, was about to rape her.

McGarvey rushed in and beat the four boys so badly that three of them had to spend the night in the hospital. The police never believed he had singlehandedly beaten them, and though he'd never been prosecuted—the entire affair had been hushed up—he was kicked out of school and had to spend the rest of the year finishing his courses at home.

When his father had asked him why he had beaten up the boys, his answer had been simple: "It wasn't right."

Their waitress came. McGarvey ordered a Dos Equis with a piece of lime and Watson had the same.

"I was just a kid when your parents died," Watson said. "But I heard about it—everybody in town did. So when Bob said that you were coming to poke around, I did my research on you and on and John and Lilly."

"Bob Evans, the managing editor?" McGarvey asked, a little tickle nagging at the back of his head that something was off.

"Yes."

"How'd he find out?"

"I don't know. But the man has been around the business forever. He knows stuff."

The waitress came back with their drinks. "You gents know what you're going to order?" She was a middle-aged woman, tall and lean and fairly attractive.

"Not yet," Watson said. "Is Doris in tonight?"

"She's in back, cooking the books."

"Tell her that someone would like to have a chat, if she's not too busy trying to screw Uncle Sam."

Their waitress laughed and went away.

"Doris Gustafson was the head waitress that night," Watson said. "She and your folks went back a ways. She owns the place now. Maybe she can tell you something."

A woman, easily in her eighties, with a dowager's hump between her shoulders, came from the back, a huge smile on her narrow face. She wore a bright red blouse over skintight black pants and high heels. Her dark hair was pushed back off her forehead and her makeup was thick.

"Kirk McGarvey, what a sight for these old eyes," she said, her voice booming. She bent over and hugged him. Her breath smelled of bourbon.

"It's been a long time," McGarvey said. His parents had mentioned her, and he remembered her from the funeral—a lone woman in the back row, quietly sobbing.

"I guess," she said. "Scoot over a bit and let me in."

McGarvey slid aside and she sat down next to him. She smelled strongly of cheap perfume. But her smile and attitude were genuine.

"Mr. McGarvey is here to find out whatever he can about the accident," Watson said.

"'Mr. McGarvey,' my ass. He's Kirk—Mac to his friends," Doris said. "I figured you'd be back sooner or later, because the police report was purely bullshit."

McGarvey felt as if he was in some surreal dream where nothing was as it seemed. No one was supposed to know he was in town, or why. And only a very few people in his life had called him Mac. No one in Garden City—his parents, his sister, or anyone else—had ever called him that.

"What do you mean?"

"They came up with something down at Los Alamos, and they were killed for it. The FBI knew all about it, but they didn't say a thing to anyone."

"How do you know all that stuff? Their work was supposed to be top secret. And sure as hell they never talked about it."

"Didn't have to. The ranch hand they had knew more than they thought he knew. He used to come over and spend the night from time to time. He was never married and neither was I. And I was sorry to see him go, after your parents were killed. Never heard from him again. Probably dead by now."

"Do you mean Wehr?"

"Yeah, Bobby Wehr. Have you heard from him?"

"No," McGarvey said. "You?" he asked Watson.

The reporter shook his head, and McGarvey thought he was lying.

"What do you think happened that night?" Doris asked. "Just an accident?"

"I don't know," McGarvey said.

"Then what are you doing here?"

"I want to find out. Just like I want to know how you know my friends call me Mac."

"Shit," Doris said. "You're the most famous person ever lived in this town. You were the director of the CIA. You lost family to the bastards. You oughta google yourself."

McGarvey had never looked up his name, but years ago Otto had sanitized as many references as he could without raising suspicions.

"Can't erase the fact that you were the DCI," Otto had said. "And I had to keep some personal details in your bio, but nothing that could turn around and bite you in the ass. Honest injun."

"Anyway, you're not here tonight because of our refried beans," Doris said. "You want to know what I know about that night, right?"

"You're a start."

"Your folks came here that night to meet someone from Washington. Some mucky-muck, from what I figured, because he never showed up and your parents hung around waiting. Something they never would ordinarily have done, unless this guy was important."

"Did they mention a name?"

"No. But I talked to the guy on the phone. Said to tell John that he was running late, so just to hold on a bit."

"He never gave you his name?"

Doris shook her head. "No, but I figured that he was a wimp."

"What made you think that? What'd he say?"

"It's not what he said, it was how. He was weak in the knees, you know."

"No, I don't know," McGarvey said.

Doris laughed. "I had a boyfriend in high school who talked with a lisp. He turned out to be a fairy. After that, I could never trust a guy with a lisp, like the pansy on the phone."

TWENTY-ONE

Pete had settled in with Otto and Louise as best she could at their house in McLean. They'd had an early dinner of Lou's spaghetti and meatballs, and Otto was cleaning up while they sat at the kitchen counter finishing a bottle of very good Chianti. But it was driving her nuts, doing nothing while Mac was out in Kansas looking around.

"Brooding never helps, you know," Louise said, reading Pete's thoughts.

"You're right. But Christ only knows what's coming his way."

"Our way," Otto said, loading the dishwasher. "And in the morning you and Lou will drive up to Chevy Chase and have a talk with Bill Cooper. No telling what skeletons might jump out of the closet."

"I'd be surprised if he's the one who was supposed to fly out to Kansas to meet Mac's folks," Pete said.

"Maybe it was him, after all, and he'll remember something."

"Otto could be right. If someone does take notice of us talking to Cooper, it might kick over an anthill," Lou said. "We're going in armed, and between us, we're not pushovers."

Pete smiled, but she wasn't settled—nor would she be, she knew, until Mac was at her side.

"We have an anomaly, darling." The computer-generated Lou voice came from a cell phone on the counter.

Otto looked up. "What is it?"

"A one-year-old silver Toyota Camry has just pulled up at the entrance to our street."

"What is the anomaly?"

"The headlights were extinguished, and although I caught only one frame of the front seats, I have a ninety-three percent confidence that the driver is male and is the only person in the automobile."

"Is there anything else?"

"There is no front license plate," the computer program at Otto's office said.

"Sometimes people refuse to show a front plate," Lou said.

Pete slid off her stool. "I'll check it out."

"I'll come with you," Louise said.

No," Pete told her. "I'll take my phone, so give me a heads-up if something changes."

She went to the hall table, where she'd left her cell phone and her Glock, which she unholstered.

Louise was at the kitchen doorway. "Watch yourself, for Christ's sake. This could be the start."

"Yeah," Pete said. She flipped on the porch light and, concealing the pistol at the side of her right thigh, went outside. She hesitated for a moment and then headed down the driveway, walking directly toward the Camry.

The houses along this street, which ended in a cul-de-sac, were all two-story colonials, some with brick facings, some with two or three fireplace chimneys. Lights were on in most of the downstairs windows, but only a couple of garage doors were open. No one was out or about, though she could smell smoke from backyard barbecue grills. This was a pleasant, somewhat upscale neighborhood of mostly young families.

"It was a perfect choice for a spook's safe house," Otto had explained.

"You mean a geek's lair," Louise had chided.

"Yeah, that too," Otto had said.

They had laughed, but this now was serious, and Pete wished that Mac were here. "Is the Camry's engine running?" she asked.

"Yes," Lou answered from her phone.

Twenty-five yards out, Pete stepped onto the street. Almost immediately the car shot forward, and she started to bring her pistol up and to drop into a shooter's stance, in case the bastard meant to run her over.

But the car made a sudden U-turn and, within moments, had disappeared around the corner.

Pete straightened up and started back, hoping that no one had been watching out a window at some crazy woman in the middle of the street with a gun in hand, ready to shoot it out with a car.

"No rear plate," Otto's program said.

"Is anyone on the phone with nine eleven?" Pete asked.

"No, you're clear," Otto said.

Louise was waiting at the open door, and Pete put her phone and pistol on the hall table.

"It was spooky," Pete said.

"We were watching. You looked solid."

In the kitchen, Otto was on the phone with McGarvey. He handed it to Pete.

"Are you okay?" Mac asked.

"It could have been nothing," Pete said.

"No. They just opened the conversation. 'We're here, we know what you're all about, and we just want to know what's next.'"

"Okay, what's next? Are you coming back?"

"That's what they want. But you guys will be okay for the time being. My guess is they want to take us down in one op."

"They'll come after you, then?"

"I hope so. But if they do, it'll mean that they're willing to divide their forces."

"What forces?" Pete asked. "There was only the one guy in one car."

"There'll be more, tonight. Different car, no plates, one driver, no passengers."

"Dumb. Two cars, two people. Three cars, three people. They're going to show us their strength. That makes no sense."

"It does if you think that you're smarter or faster than the other guy," McGarvey said. "Or younger."

"That'd be a very big mistake on their part," Otto broke in.

"No one's perfect," Mac said. "But we've already learned what they're after."

"A cover-up," Pete said.

"Yeah, and they're doing a piss-poor job of it."

"Someone in Moscow is nervous," Otto said.

"They think that they're about set to blow a twenty-eight-year advantage."

"So what do you want us to do?" Pete asked.

"Button up and sit tight."

No one was in the lobby at a few minutes past midnight, when McGarvey left the motel, got into his rental Jeep, and headed west out of town on Highway 50/400. Two other cars without plates had shown up down the street from the Renckes' McLean house. They'd stayed twenty minutes and then drove off.

Otto had done a quick search of car rental outlets around the city, especially at Dulles and Reagan airports, but had come up with nothing definitive on any video feeds. It had been the same as his search at the outlet where the throwaway phones had been purchased.

The luck of the draw or professionalism—there was no way to tell.

McGarvey passed the town's water tower and then was outside the city limits and on the open highway, heading toward the Colorado border sixty miles away. He had the windows down, the air-conditioning and radio off. The night was soft and nearly silent. No cars or trucks were on the road at the moment.

According to the police report, the crash had occurred 8.3 miles west of the city limits sign. When the odometer showed that mileage, Mac pulled over, parked, and got out of the car.

A billion stars were flung across the sky, but there was absolutely nothing to mark the exact spot where John and Lilly had died. No trees, no distant sharp rise in the landscape, no curve in the road. Yet McGarvey could feel them.

It was the same as standing at their graves on the ranch. They were dead and buried, but they were alive in his mind.

TWENTY-TWO

Zimin sat in his rented Chevy Impala, parked on the street directly behind the Renckes' house. It was a few minutes before two thirty in the morning. Three Google Earth satellite photos showed the house, the street in front with the cul-de-sac, and the large backyard, which was separated from the street in the rear by seventy or eighty meters of trees.

No one was out or about at this hour, though he understood that he risked the possibility that a patrol car might come along and the police officer ask what he was doing here. He would have to kill the man, which would complicate the situation, though not impossibly so.

McGarvey's wife had come out to confront Petr, and he had left immediately. But no one had come when Larissa had showed up, nor when he had pulled up.

They knew that someone was watching them, "goading them into some kind of a reaction," as Larissa had put it. But if word had gotten to McGarvey, it was having no effect so far. As of an hour ago, the man was in his hotel, after driving a few miles out into the country to the spot where his parents had been killed.

Zimin could remember that evening in full detail—the smell of the night, the feel of it, the crash, and later the exhilaration of an operation successfully completed.

Back in Moscow, he and Klimov had received the Order of Lenin and were promoted. There'd been other field assignments, but nothing of the same importance as the McGarvey file. Eventually, they'd become instructors at what had been created as the KGB's School 1, but standing on that remote highway in western Kansas, tasting not only the night air but also the success, had never gone away.

Zimin checked his rearview mirror to make sure the road was still clear, then got out and headed into the woods.

"A man is approaching the house from the woods." Otto's darling spoke softly, waking him immediately from a light sleep.

"What is it?" Louise asked from beside him.

"More company." Otto got up and went to the window.

The night was dark. Only a dim light filtered around the side from the streetlight down the block in front of the house. Nothing moved, so far as he could see.

Louise came to him. "Shall I wake Pete?"

"Yes," Otto said, and she left. "Do you have any details?" he asked his darling.

"I have a seventy-eight percent confidence that the man in the woods is the same as the man in the third car."

"Is he still approaching?"

"Yes, but slowly. He has not yet used a source of illumination."

"Is he armed?"

"I have insufficient data at this time."

"How near is he to my property line?"

"Forty meters."

Pete, dressed in jeans and a T-shirt, her feet bare, her Glock in hand, came across the hall with Louise. "How many of them?" she asked.

"Just the one," Otto told her.

"I now have a ninety-six percent confidence that the man is the same as from the third car this evening," the computer reported. "He has taken out what is almost certainly a large-caliber pistol of a so far unknown make, because of the indistinct nature of the thermal imaging."

The metal of the weapon radiated almost no heat compared to the heat coming off a human body. The outline of the pistol appeared as a shadow in front of the infrared from the gunman's body.

"He won't be expecting me," Pete said. "I can go out and take care of at least this one."

"He doesn't want you. He wants all of us, Mac included," Otto said.

"Goddamnit, Otto."

"Listen to him," Louise said. "He and Mac have been together a lot longer than you or me. And survived."

"We'll sit tight and see what the asshole does," Otto said. "Anyway, it'd take at least a quarter kilo of Semtex to get inside."

"We could call Housekeeping," Pete said. "Let them deal with it."

"Lights, please," Otto said.

The entire backyard was bathed in flashes of red light just within the threshold of visibility to the human eye. It was as if the strobe lights of a camera were popping off.

The intruders had sent their message—actually four messages this night: *Would you like to come out and play?*

We've heard you, but no thanks for now, Otto had replied.

Pete was frustrated. "I'll call Mac," she said.

"We'll let him get his sleep," Otto said. He turned around.

Pete was moving from foot to foot, as a prizefighter would, shifting her weight. She wanted to fight right now. "They're herding us."

"You're right."

"So what the fuck are we supposed to do?" Pete raised her voice. "Just sit buttoned up here?"

"These are just opening moves. I've seen it before. Tomorrow, you and Louise are going out to talk to Cooper. Nothing's going to happen until Mac gets home and we're all together in one place."

"That doesn't make any sense!"

"That would depend on your perspective," Otto said.

Zimin pulled up short. That a man of Otto's mettle would have surveillance systems protecting his house had been a foregone conclusion. Here in the Wild West, it had become almost necessary for self-protection not from the state but from fellow citizens.

He wasn't particularly surprised by the level of sophistication; in fact, he was pleased. The house still wasn't visible from where he stood, but there was no doubt he was being recorded in the infrared, which unless he was mistaken could detect merely body shapes and not recognizable facial features.

Holstering his pistol, he turned and headed back to his car. The message had been sent: *We are here*. And the reply had come: *We know*.

Now McGarvey had to come home to rescue his wife and friends.

But if he didn't, the ante would be raised.

In the meantime, Petr and Larissa would be watching the house, but from a safe distance.

"The intruder is leaving," Otto's darling announced.

"Thank you," Otto said. "You may discontinue active infrared surveillance in five minutes, and return to the passive mode."

"Yes, dear."

Pete was beginning to come down. She shook her head. "I don't know where this is going."

"That'll depend on what Mac finds out in Kansas," Otto said.

"If there's anything to be found," Pete said.

Louise had been sleeping in nothing more than a nightshirt. She pulled on a pair of jeans and shrugged. "It's too late to go back to sleep, and anyway, how about breakfast?"

"First round: one for the cowboys, zero for the Indians," Otto said.

"Yeah, but who are the cowboys?" Pete said.

TWENTY-THREE

☐

McGarvey got up, showered and dressed, and was downstairs for break-fast at eight, which was late for him. Only a few people were seated at tables, and none of them bothered to look up as he got a cup of coffee and the *USA Today* newspaper. But he couldn't concentrate.

Otto had called just as he was getting out of the shower, and outlined what had happened last night.

"As soon as the guy in the woods knew that he was being watched, he did a one-eighty and boogied out of there."

"Did you call the cops?"

"I thought about it, but the three of them were doing nothing illegal and they didn't pose any immediate threat. They were just letting us know that they were there. Waiting."

"For me."

"Yeah."

"What about Pete?"

"She wanted to go out back and kick some ass. But I convinced her otherwise. There was this guy and two others in the cars, and there was no telling if they were waiting in the woods just outside the range of my systems."

"I'm going over to the newspaper to see what's been happening at the ranch, and then drive out and pay a visit," McGarvey said. It would be odd, going out there, knowing where his parents were buried—unless their bodies had been moved, in which case he didn't know how he would react.

"I can pull up something for you."

"No, I want to find out what's happened from a townie's perspective over the past twenty-eight years."

"I understand perfectly, but you do realize that the place has changed hands three times since you sold it."

"Yes, but I especially want to know what's been happening out there over the past few months," McGarvey said. "And maybe it'd be a good idea to keep Lou and Pete with you until I get back."

"I don't really think that anything's going to happen until then. Anyway, keeping either of them locked up here would be impossible."

"They're already on their way to talk to Cooper?"

"Left fifteen minutes ago."

It was about what McGarvey had figured would happen. "Let me know as soon as they call or get back. And ask them if Cooper spoke with a lisp."

"Okay," Otto said. "Also, two of the cars were probably rented at Reagan. I got the tag numbers and VINs and told DC Metro that they had probably been stolen. They might come up with something, but I doubt it, if this is a professional op."

"An SVR op," McGarvey said.

Watson was getting set to leave when McGarvey showed up at the newspaper. "Just need a minute of your time."

"No problem, 'cause I can guarantee that whatever it is you want will be a hell of a lot more interesting than the Ladies Garden Club of Greater Garden City."

"I'm going out to the ranch and I wonder if you could tell me something about the current owners."

"Sam and Chance Pickering. Good people. He retired as a CFO for Grollier Pharmaceutical Distribution and she taught economics at a community college in one of KC's burbs. They bought the place eight years ago and leased out the land to Jake Tomlinson. He owns the adjacent ranch to the southwest, just outside the Finney bison refuge."

"They get along with the town people?"

"I never met them, so I couldn't really say. They're gone a lot. Kids are married I think. No one else out there except for Jake's hired hands."

"Are they at home now?"

"I don't know. But I could give you their phone number."

"Not necessary," McGarvey said. "How is it that you know so much about them?"

Watson shrugged. "I'm a newspaperman. When I heard you might be coming to town, I did my homework."

Nothing added up in McGarvey's mind. He nodded his thanks and turned for the door, but then came back. "You said that they travel a lot. Any idea where they go?"

"Not a clue."

On the highway west of town, McGarvey phoned Otto. "Grollier Pharmaceutical in or near Kansas City."

"Just a mo," Otto said. He was back even before Mac had reached the spot where the accident had occurred. "It's a medium-size distribution company for a number of manufacturers here and in a couple of other countries."

"Including?"

"I'm just checking," Otto said, and then he drew his breath.

McGarvey could hear it over the phone.

"NovaMedika and COTEKC—Russia," Otto said.

"See what you can find out."

Nothing had changed since McGarvey had last been on the road that led two miles from the highway to the ranch, except for a security gate with a phone.

He got out of the car and picked up the phone. It was finally answered after eight rings by a man with a very deep Hispanic accent.

"I'm at the gate. Are Mr. and Mrs. Pickering at home?"

"No Pickerings here," the man said, and he hung up.

McGarvey considered calling the house again, but he got back in his car, drove out to the highway, and turned west toward what in his time had been called the Finney Game Refuge. As a kid, when he wanted to leave or return to the ranch in the middle of the night without having to go through the main gate and pass the house, he'd found a dirt track from the ranch, through the corner of the refuge, and up to the highway.

He'd always thought he'd gotten away clean, because his parents—especially his mother—had never mentioned it to him. But years later his sister, in a fit of pique over something, had admitted they'd known, because she had told them.

As kids, he and his sister, who was a few years older than him, had been mostly indifferent to each other. But when they'd moved away and gotten married, the distance had broadened. And when their parents had been killed and the ranch had gone to him instead of her, she'd become actively angry at him.

One time, in a rage, he'd called her a shrew—which he later regretted. It was at the Salt Lake City International Airport. He'd driven out to visit with her and his nephew and niece, and on the way out to where she had parked her car, she'd told him that Katy had called and complained about his work as a spy for the CIA.

"That's the dirtiest job anyone could do. Worse than being a pig farmer."

"Worse than being a fucking shrew like you?" he'd shot back.

He'd walked back into the terminal to get a return ticket to Washington.

They'd never had a civil word since.

He had to wait until an eighteen-wheeler passed before he could make the turn south onto the dirt maintenance lane that led back to what was now called the Sandsage Bison Range. A series of narrow tracks led through the refuge and onto the ranch just south of the airstrip, near which were his parents' graves.

There were no gates between the refuge and the ranch.

TWENTY-FOUR

□

William Cooper's house was a low-slung ranch in an L shape with a two-car garage on the left, at the end of a curved driveway, at the rear of a heavily wooded lot. The town of less than six hundred people was very quiet this morning.

As Pete and Lou pulled up, Otto called. "Where are you?"

"In Cooper's driveway."

"Just talked to Mac. He wants to know if Cooper speaks with a lisp. Or ever has."

"Did he say why?" Lou wanted to know.

"No."

"How is he?" Pete asked.

"So far, so good," Otto said. "He's on the way out to the ranch now, but we found out that the current owner used to work for a pharmaceutical company in Kansas City that does business with two drug companies in Moscow."

"The plot thickens," Pete said. Mac had felt from the beginning that nothing in the situation seemed to be adding up. This was just another brick in the load. She wanted him back here with her, but most of all she wanted him to be careful.

"He'll be okay," Otto said. "How about your six? Still clear?"

"Clear," Lou said.

"Just find what we need and get the hell out of there."

"Will do," Pete said.

She and Louise walked up to the house, but before they could ring the bell an older man, slender, slightly stooped, his white hair thinning, opened the door.

"What do you want?" he demanded. His voice was shrill, but there was no trace of a lisp, at least not in those four words.

Pete held up her visitor's badge. "We'd like to have a word with you, Mr. Cooper."

"The Los Alamos thing with the McGarveys. I wondered when someone would finally get back to me."

Larissa, driving a Chevy Impala she had stolen from long-term parking at Dulles, stopped just around the corner from Cooper's house. The general had suspected that someone would come out to speak with the old man, and he had sent Larissa to keep watch.

She used one of the throwaway phones. "They just went inside," she said, when Zimin picked up.

"We have a problem, so our timetable has changed, but the objective remains the same."

Larissa's gut tightened. "Yes, sir?"

"McGarvey is showing no signs that he's coming back this afternoon. Apparently he's on his way to the ranch, and there's no telling how long he'll be or what he'll find."

"*Da?*"

"Is it just the two of them?"

"Yes."

"Too bad," Zimin said after a brief pause. "I would have liked to take all three of them down. But for now it'll just be the two women."

"What about Cooper?"

"Kill him, too."

"Both women will be armed," Larissa said. She had no compunction about carrying out the wet work; such assignments were among those she'd been trained for. But she also wanted a reasonable chance of getting free afterward.

"Report when you're finished. If there are complications, you will go to fallback Alpha."

Alpha was the Jefferson Memorial, Beta was Union Station, and Gamma, the most extreme because of its distance from their safe house, was the Baltimore/Washington Airport.

Zimin rang off, and Larissa put the phone aside. She checked the load in her pistol, attached the suppressor to the SIG's muzzle, and made sure she had two spare magazines of nine-millimeter Parabellum ammunition.

She got out of the car and, keeping the pistol out of sight, approached the house through the trees on the west side.

Cooper brought iced tea and chocolate cookies out to where Pete and Lou were seated in a glassed-in kitchen alcove looking across a broad backyard and a sloping putting green guarded by a fairly deep sand trap. He was angry, but he was a gentleman of the old school: he had two ladies in the house, and he treated them with chivalry.

He sat down. "The point is, why me, after all these years?"

"The point is, was it you who told John and Lilly McGarvey that you were coming out to talk to them about their breakthrough?" Pete asked.

"The FBI pushed hard on that issue, but my answer now is the same as it was then: No. I did not call them, for the simple fact I knew nothing about their work—except in the vaguest of terms. The LANL, along with Sandia and the others, were under the auspices of the DOE, but in reality they were independent—or at least their scientific work was." Cooper waved a hand as if he were dismissing the idea. "In any event, we had no one on the staff who would have understood what they were doing. We were the bureaucrats, the money people. They were the scientists."

"Then someone impersonated you. Who do you suppose it was?" Louise asked.

Cooper laughed dryly. "The Russians, of course. Even I knew that much."

Pete had another thought. The KGB never fielded stupid officers, and they seldom made big mistakes. "I have an off-the-wall question for you, Mr. Cooper. Probably means nothing."

Cooper shrugged, waiting for it.

"Did you ever speak with a lisp?"

Cooper chuckled. "No, but my boss Bob Pittman did. Why did you ask something like that?"

"It's not important," Pete said. A simple mistake on the part of the

KGB, mixing up one man's speech impediment with another's—or another bit of misdirection?

She was about to thank him for his time and end the interview when, out of the corner of her eye, she caught a motion in the backyard.

A figure, dressed in jeans, had darted from behind one tree and to another less than twenty feet from the windows behind which they were seated. She got the impression that it was a woman, holding something low and to the left in her right hand. A pistol.

"Jesus Christ, down!" she shouted.

She was out of arm's reach from Lou, but she managed to shove Cooper aside as a small red hole appeared in the side of his head, six inches from Pete's.

At least three more holes starred the windows as Pete drew her weapon and dropped to the floor.

Lou was already under the table.

Pete scrambled to the rear door, yanked it open, and, keeping low and moving fast, crossed the backyard at a diagonal, away from the shooter.

The slight figure in jeans swiveled from behind the tree, her aim concentrated on the alcove windows, and Pete fired one shot, catching her in the neck just below the jaw on the right side. Blood bloomed as the woman went down.

Pete approached with extreme caution, her Glock in a two-handed grip. But the slightly built woman was choking on her own blood and nothing could save her now.

She died.

Pete lowered her pistol and walked slowly back to the kitchen.

Cooper was down, and Lou was on her knees, slumped forward, her forehead on the tile floor. An impossible amount of blood was pooled around her head.

Pete set her pistol aside, took Lou in her arms, and tried to lift her up. But Lou's head lolled loosely to the side, and her eyes were open and filled with blood.

Cooper was dead. The assassin in the backyard was dead. Lou was dead. And Pete began to cry softly, with no idea whatsoever how she would ever be able to face Otto.

TWENTY-FIVE

□

McGarvey stood at his parents' graves, thinking about how and why they had died, his anger controlled for the moment. It had been the last dregs of the overt Cold War, which had slowly morphed into a more subtle battle, one that had been raging for the last ten years in cyberspace.

Several years ago, Otto had warned that the situation was starting to spiral beyond even his control.

"Is it something we need to be worried about?" McGarvey had asked him.

They were sitting in the CIA's cafeteria, looking through the floor-to-ceiling windows across the corridor onto an enclosed courtyard. Several sculptures, including one called *Kryptos*, which had figured in one of the bloodiest operations in the history of the Company, were in plain view and always brought back a lot of memories.

"I just have to learn how to pick my battles," Otto had said. "Leave the small shit for someone else."

"Do you have anyone in mind?"

"Lou has offered to be my one-girl mop-up crew. And she's damned good."

McGarvey had never seen his friend more happy—more consistently happy—since he and Louise had gotten together. In his mind at that time—before Pete—there'd never been a more perfect couple. He'd envied their happiness.

There always seemed to be a wind out here on the plains in the middle of nowhere. It had been necessary to power the water pumps, but very often, like now, the wind was lonely. He had the overwhelming urge to get back to his people. Now. Immediately.

He walked to his Jeep and, sitting behind the wheel, he looked at the ranch for what he figured was his last time. He'd seen none of the hands, and the pavement of the airstrip was cracked, grass growing out of control. The entire place seemed devoid of life, of hominess. It had become nothing more than a factory farm. Graze the cattle until they were grown enough to be sent to a feedlot, from where they would be shipped to an abattoir to be slaughtered for their meat.

He started the car and was about to head back to the dirt track through the refuge and up to the highway when his phone rang. It was Pete, and she sounded like a total stranger.

"They're dead and I don't know what to do."

Instantly, McGarvey was calm, though every fiber of his being was on peak alert. "Who is dead?"

"The woman. I killed her. Russian probably."

"Are you okay?"

"Everyone is on their way now," Pete said. Her breath caught in her throat. "Otto's coming."

McGarvey took out his pistol, laid it on the seat beside him, and did a slow visual three-sixty. No one was coming, nothing in the air, no dust on the horizon in any direction.

"Cooper is dead," Pete said.

"Are you hurt?"

"You're not listening," Pete screeched. "It's my fault! I wasn't good enough!"

More dread came over him than he'd ever remembered. "Talk to me."

"Lou is dead. The Russian bitch shot her before I could do a thing."

McGarvey hesitated for less than a beat, his heart breaking, but he calmed himself. "We knew this was coming our way."

Pete tried to talk over him.

"Listen to me, sweetheart!" McGarvey shouted her down. "This is just the beginning. You said Otto's on the way. Is Housekeeping with him?"

"Yes, and so are the cops."

"Are you in a defensible position?"

Pete half laughed. "Are you fucking kidding me?"

"Goddamnit, Pete, I'm going to need your help. I can't do this alone. So get your shit together! Are you safe?"

"Yes. I'm in the front hall, with sight lines through the kitchen and to the front door."

"Stay put. I'll get to you as quickly as I can."

"Do you want me to send a Company jet?"

"I'll rent one at Dodge City. But I want you stick with Otto and House-keeping. I don't want either of you wandering off. Go back to Langley. You'll be safe there."

"I'm not going to bury my head in the sand."

"I'm not asking you to do that. But I'm going to need both you and Otto on board, because this is far from being over. It's the Russians, and they wanted all four of us from the start. And if it's anyone's fault, it's mine, for digging into the past."

"I should have saved her," Pete said.

"Whoever gets there first, make sure it's either our people or a Bureau forensics team that does the initial crime scene investigation. And make damn sure that you stick with Otto."

Pete was suddenly sober. "Do you think he'll try something crazy?"

"Guaranteed," McGarvey said. "Hang on. I'm on my way."

McGarvey was nearly back to his hotel when his cell phone rang. It was Bob Wehr.

"I heard that you were out in Garden City. Did you get out to the ranch?" Wehr asked.

"How did you hear something like that?"

"I still have a few friends out there."

"I don't trust you, Wehr. Something is going down, and I think that you're a part of it. If I find out that's the case, I will kill you."

"I'm sorry that you feel that way, Kirk," Wehr said. "I hope you learn that you're wrong sooner rather than later." He hung up.

*   *   *

At the hotel, McGarvey asked about charter jets out of Dodge City, but the young woman desk clerk went back and asked Priscilla Devereux, the manager, to come out.

"No need to drive back there. We have ExpressJet," the woman said. "Where are you going and when to you want to leave?"

"Washington, DC, and now," McGarvey said.

"Go pack. I'll set it up for you."

Upstairs, McGarvey packed his single bag, and in five minutes was back downstairs.

"You're lucky. They have a Gulfstream from Fort Worth that's refueling. They'll be ready to take off by the time you get there."

"I have a rental car."

"We'll take care of it, Mr. McGarvey," the manager said.

McGarvey paid his bill with an American Express card and laid a hundred-dollar bill on the counter for her.

She pushed it back. "I was a teenager when your parents were killed. Everyone in town knew it wasn't an accident, and now that you came back, we're rooting for you."

At the airport, McGarvey sat in the car in front of the terminal before going inside. He called Otto's private number at Langley. The computer answered.

"Good morning, Mr. McGarvey. Would you like me to connect you with Otto?"

It was more than startling to hear Louise's voice just now. "No, but I would like you to make a telephone call for me."

"Certainly. To whom would you like to speak?"

"Vladimir Putin."

"Of course," the computer said, without a trace of surprise. "Stand by."

Twenty seconds later, a call to the Russian president's secretary or aide had been transferred to Putin himself.

"*Da?*"

"Mr. President, this is Kirk McGarvey."

"Your call comes as a surprise," Putin said in English.

"I have a message for you, Mr. President."

"Yes?"

"If you want to go to war with me, sir, I will give you a fucking war that you will never forget."

PART

THREE

Counterstrike

TWENTY-SIX

Two men from Housekeeping met the private jet at Dulles and hustled McGarvey directly to an armored Cadillac Escalade. It was a few minutes past four in the afternoon when they got out to the airport access road, traffic building. The day was warm and humid compared to western Kansas.

"Are my wife and Mr. Rencke on campus?" McGarvey asked. He'd tried to phone Otto after he landed, but the number was blocked as a routine security procedure.

"Yes, Mr. Director," the security officer riding shotgun said. "They're waiting for you on seven with Mr. Taft."

Harold Taft was the third CIA director to be appointed and approved by Congress in the eighteen months since President Weaver had been elected. McGarvey didn't know much about the man, except that he had retired as a navy four-star admiral who'd revamped all five military intelligence operations—including that of the coast guard—plus the DoD's Central Security Service. Otto had given him high marks after just three months on the job. He was said to be the most no-nonsense, cut-to-the-chase DCI in a long time.

"Any word yet from forensics at the scene?"

"No, sir."

"Off the record," McGarvey pressed.

"Mrs. M.'s response will be deemed justified," the security officer said.

"Anything on the perp?"

"The Bureau is still running down her ID."

McGarvey sat back and closed his eyes for a moment. He couldn't bring up a clear picture of Louise's face in his mind's eye. She was the wife of his best friend and he couldn't see her. Nor could he see his wife, Katy, and their daughter, Liz, who'd been assassinated, or the faces of every other woman who'd lost their life because of their association with him.

He even had a hard time bringing up Pete's face, and it was possibly the worst feeling he'd had in a very long time.

Pete met him at the elevator in the VIP parking garage beneath the old headquarters building. She was wearing jeans and a button-up, military-style white shirt, the sleeves fastened above the elbows. She looked as if she hadn't slept in a week, her face sallow and her eyes red-rimmed and puffy.

He took her into his arms, his relief at seeing her alive and in one piece nearly overwhelming, replacing for that moment his blinding anger. "It's okay," he said softly.

She looked up into his eyes. "I couldn't save her, Kirk. She was sitting at the table next to me and took a round in her head."

"You did what you could. And Otto will never blame you."

"That might be worst part of all," Pete said. "He doesn't blame me. In fact, he keeps trying to comfort me." She laughed once, the sound almost maniacal. "I have trouble facing him."

"Listen to me, sweetheart. We'll never be able to bring her back, but I'll make it right. I promise you."

"*We*'ll make it right," Pete said with passion.

Otto was waiting for them at the open door to the DCI's seventh-floor dining room, which was often used for private conferences. He was dressed in pressed khakis, a clean blue shirt with the sleeves rolled up, and boat shoes. His long hair was tied neatly back in a ponytail, and his expression and demeanor were nearly neutral. It was not a good sign.

"They wanted you back, *kemo sabe*, and they got what they wanted," he said.

McGarvey gave him a hug, but there was no response.

"The director is waiting for us," Otto said.

"Talk to me," McGarvey said.

A faraway, almost dreamy look came into Otto's wide, brown eyes, and he slowly shook his head. "The time for talk has come and gone."

Taft, seated at the head of the table, looked up when McGarvey, Pete, and Otto came in. He was a slightly built man, but with a head that seemed too big for his body. "Take a seat. We have a lot of ground to cover," he said.

Besides Pete and Otto, four other people were gathered. James Miller, who was the ever-optimistic deputy director of the CIA; Thomas Waksberg, the obese deputy director of operations—known as the National Clandestine Service; Donald Hagan, the whip-thin deputy director of intelligence; and P. Van Gessel—Van to his friends and enemies alike—who headed the Company's security service.

"No introductions are necessary; you know everyone here," Taft said to McGarvey. "So let's get started."

"My wife was shot to death by an operative working for Russian intelligence because Kirk McGarvey and his wife opened an investigation into the deaths of Mac's parents twenty-eight years ago," Otto said. "We know who the next targets will be; we just need to know why. And we need to know the names and present locations of the operatives."

"We're all sorry for your loss—" Taft began, but Otto overrode him.

"You don't understand, Mr. Director. I will find out who is responsible and kill them."

"You will cease and desist, mister."

"When that's done, I will find out what they are covering up and who is doing it and I will rain such a shitstorm down around them that they will have no idea which way to climb to find fresh air."

Taft was angry, but he held his temper well. "You are relieved of duty, sir."

Otto got slowly to his feet. "No, I quit," he said, and he turned and walked out the door.

"What harm can he do to us?" the director asked.

"Plenty," Waksberg, the DDO, said.

"I want the man taken into custody now."

"I'll take care of it," McGarvey said.

"Sit down. We have a lot ground to cover," Taft said.

"You have no idea what he's capable of, and you don't want to know," McGarvey said. "Give me a minute." He motioned for Pete to stay behind, and he left the room.

Otto was gone, and by the time McGarvey got to the end of the corridor, the elevator was halted on the third floor.

McGarvey stopped at the door to Otto's suite of offices. In all the years he'd known his friend, he'd never seen anything like what had happened upstairs. Otto had gone off in sometimes bizarre directions—both of them had—but this time was different. In effect, Otto had declared all-out war against not only who was responsible for Lou's death but also anyone or any entity that got in his way.

And when he'd promised the director that he would rain a shitstorm, he had not exaggerated.

"Good afternoon, Mr. McGarvey," one of Otto's darlings said.

"May I come in?"

"One moment, please," the computer-generated Lou voice said.

The door lock buzzed and McGarvey walked in.

Otto was at a desk in the inner office, his fingers flying over a keyboard. "Thanks for backstopping me," he said, without looking up.

"We're on the same page," McGarvey said.

"Give me an hour and I'll be off campus."

"Where are you going?"

"Deep."

"I'll be doing the same," McGarvey said.

Otto looked up. "This is my battle."

"Lou was my friend. And their aim was to take out Pete as well. Along with you and me."

"I'll be busy."

"So will I," McGarvey said. "I made a phone call."

Otto glanced up at the big flat-screen monitor on the wall, which showed a street map of Moscow that was tinged with a deep hue of lavender. "I know. And he's put the entire SVR on high alert. You're priority one."

"Then let's do it," McGarvey said.

"Don't leave Pete behind," Otto said. "She's part of it now."

TWENTY-SEVEN

Zimin sat at the kitchenette table. He had left the message with his control officer last night that Larissa had not shown up at her assigned hotel after the operation. He'd stayed up all morning and into the afternoon, waiting for a call back with instructions.

He glanced at his watch as the throwaway cell phone lying on the table burred softly. He answered it.

"Yes."

"Your officer is dead. The FBI is handling the investigation, but apparently her cover identity is holding up."

"What about her DNA?"

"She will be identified as Russian, Eastern European, and ten percent Siberian, but so would a certain segment of second- and third-generation Americans."

"What about her operation? Did she succeed?"

"William Cooper is dead, as well as one of the two so far unnamed females in the house. Did your operative give you a sit rep before she went in?"

Standard operating procedure would have been for Larissa to call with a situation report before she made the hits, unless circumstances dictated immediate action.

"She did not," Zimin said. "Shall we terminate the mission?"

Petr, standing watch at the front window, was looking over his shoulder.

"No," their control officer said. "Meet me at Alpha."

"When?"

"Now."

"You're in town?" Zimin asked, but the connection had been broken. He put down the phone.

Petr was concerned. "What about Larissa?" he asked.

Zimin had suspected from the start that they were lovers. "She is dead, along with Cooper and one of the women in the house."

"*Blyad*," Petr said, turning away for a moment. Fuck. "Who was the woman?"

"We don't know yet. But it doesn't matter. They were both on our list."

"McGarvey and Rencke will stop at nothing to find us. Are we going to leave now?"

"I'm meeting with our control officer at Alpha. But if I don't call or I'm not back within two hours it'll mean the mission has been compromised, and you'll need to get out any way that you can. But not with our planned fallbacks; they might be compromised too."

Petr shook his head. "I won't leave until we're finished here."

Zimin was suddenly angry. "You'll do as you're ordered, child."

"No, sir. And I'm not your child."

"You're nothing but a pissant still wet behind the ears."

"Go meet with our control officer and see what we're to do next to repair the fucked-up mess that you and Klimov made twenty-eight years ago."

Their control officer, Sergei Yuryn, whose work name was Douglas Fairbanks, was waiting on the steps of the Jefferson Memorial, with its view of the Washington Monument across the Tidal Basin. His pro sign was a Washington Redskins baseball cap. Slightly askew to the left was the signal not to approach. Askew to the right was the all-clear sign.

He was a neatly built man in his late thirties, with blond hair and blue eyes, who sometimes worked out of the Russian UN mission in New York but sometimes from the embassy here in DC or their consulates in Seattle and Houston. He was wearing jeans and a long-sleeve white shirt, untucked. His cap was to the right.

Zimin sat next to him. It was a weekday, and the number of visitors was small.

"You were to have waited until all four were in one place," Yuryn said.

"The timing was not optimum."

"You may have complicated the mission."

"We're talking about Kirk McGarvey. He is a complicated, dangerous man."

"You don't know the half of it," Yuryn said. He glanced at Zimin, a pleasant smile on his round, all-American face but his eyes narrowed. In fact, he had been picked for assignments to the United States because his grandmother had been an American ballet star. She had been a blond, blue-eyed beauty, and he'd inherited some of her good looks, as well as her quick temper.

"Tell me."

"The *pizda* actually called President Putin on a private line and threatened him with war."

It made no sense to Zimin. "A military action?"

"No. Mano a mano," Yuryn said. "Hand to hand, man to man." He almost smiled. "And that's after Mr. Putin interceded on McGarvey's behalf last year."

"I don't understand."

"Neither do I. I was simply told that McGarvey had made the warning and that we should take it seriously. 'With utmost seriousness,' I was told."

"Then we are to continue with the operation?"

"Yes, but you will be given all the help that you can use. And we suspect that you will need it, because McGarvey is back in town and was driven by officers from the CIA's security division directly to Langley."

"We'll just follow him when he leaves."

"There are ways in and out of the campus that we can't always monitor. Windowless vans, for example. But I am positioning people on the ground and miniature drones in the air to monitor the apartments of McGarvey and his wife, as well as Mr. Rencke's house in McLean."

"We were there."

"Yes. But whichever woman was killed along with Cooper—the

Rencke woman or McGarvey's wife—neither man will stop until they find out who killed her and why. It's the reason McGarvey phoned Mr. Putin."

"We'll find them and kill them both," Zimin said.

"You don't understand," Yuryn said. "Either of them alone would be a threat. But the two of them working side by side would be a major threat."

"They've worked together all along."

"But not like this. Not with the new level of motivation."

Zimin wasn't understanding what he was being told. "Are we to kill them or not?"

"Yes, and as quickly as possible, before they disappear from Washington. We will watch for them to leave Langley, and watch the apartments and the McLean house. As soon as they show up, either alone or together, you will kill them."

"They'll be watching for us, and they'll be careful."

"Yes, they will be expecting you, but not as kamikazes."

Zimin suddenly understood, and he reared back. "I will give everything except my life for the mission."

"You and Petr have no other choice," Yuryn said. "You haven't had, for the past twenty-eight years. You succeeded the first time and you got your medal. What do you suppose would have happened had you failed?"

Zimin didn't have to answer. It would have been nine ounces for him and Igor then—and nine ounces for him and Petr now, if they failed. "Nine ounces" was the old KGB euphemism for a nine-millimeter bullet to the back of the head.

"You said that we would have help."

"If you fail."

Zimin understood even more. "We will be watched. If we fail, they will finish the job and eliminate us as well."

Yuryn shrugged.

Zimin let his gaze wander across the water toward the city, the Washington Monument the most prominent thing in sight. His life in Moscow had become comfortable, if routine. But then he was at the age when

comfort was far better than excitement. He wondered, for just the moment, if he could find some level of routine and comfort here in the
States if he defected.

Yuryn laid a hand on Zimin's arm. "If you or Petr make the slightest
move to defect, we will not hesitate to kill you."

TWENTY-EIGHT

☐

McGarvey and Pete had been under the gun in the director's conference room for a full two hours before Tom Waksberg was called down to his office. He came back all out of breath and flustered, eight minutes later.

"He's disappeared," Waksberg said.

"Who?" Taft asked.

"Rencke. His office is locked up, and he doesn't answer his phone or normal in-house internet connections."

Van Gessel got on the phone and called his office. "I want a team inside three-fifty-eight."

"Tell them to take care. He might have it wired," McGarvey said.

The chief of CIA security got a sour look. "You were buying him some time?"

McGarvey shrugged.

"Is he capable of actually injuring his own people?"

"His wife was murdered, so have your people take care."

Van Gessel relayed the warning.

The tension had ratcheted up a notch. Van Gessel started to say something, but Taft held him off.

"Let's sum up, shall we," Taft said. "The Russians have apparently reacted to Mr. McGarvey's recent investigations into the deaths of his parents, which is unfortunate. From what I've gleaned from our records dating back to the event, we knew that they were murdered to stop them from completing their research on the key portion of our antimissile defense system."

McGarvey held himself in check, to avoid crossing the table and throttling the bastard. "What are you saying?" he asked in a reasonable tone.

"Again, from what I was able to learn, the need-to-know list to whom that information was distributed was kept very small. And that was a directive from the president."

Pete reached over and laid a hand on McGarvey's.

"Why wasn't I told?" McGarvey asked.

"At the time, you were a junior officer, and later, when you were temporarily appointed as DCI, your personal connection to the issue was deemed too volatile," Taft said. "And considering your track record to that point, it was the only correct decision."

"And it was unfortunate that I went looking."

"Extremely so," Taft said.

"And the others here—or their predecessors—were they in the loop?" Pete asked.

"No."

"And now?"

"The damage has already been done, so now we need to contain the situation as best we can. And that is straight from the White House via Burton Webb." Webb was the director of national intelligence.

"But the Russians are obviously aware that we know," Pete pressed. "They've probably known all along. And now they're just trying to blow smoke at us."

"I don't understand what you're trying to say, Ms. Boylan."

"It's Mrs. McGarvey, you son of a bitch," Pete screeched. "And Louise Rencke was killed because you bastards tried to keep the Russians from learning something that they already knew."

She tried to get to her feet, but McGarvey held her back.

"The point is, the SVR has fielded a team to assassinate me and Otto and our wives. Lou is dead, and they won't stop unless we stop them," McGarvey said. Even he was surprised at how calm he'd become.

"We'll place the three of you in protective custody," Taft said.

"Here on campus?"

"Of course."

"Maybe you should read Walt Page's daybook. He was the DCI when we had a series of murders right under the noses of security."

"Your participation in this matter is at an end, sir," Taft said, a little color rising from his corded neck.

"It's just beginning," McGarvey said, and he and Pete got up.

Taft nodded to Van Gessel, who got on the phone and called for a team to keep sharp. Evidently he'd had someone waiting just outside in the corridor.

He hung up, then got another call. "Stand by," he said at length. "One of Rencke's programs is warning our people to stand down."

"Tell them to continue," Taft said.

"There'll be casualties," McGarvey said.

Taft finally lost his composure. "Goddamnit, who the fuck is in charge here?" he demanded.

"For the moment, Mr. Director, not you," McGarvey said. "But I'll go down and try."

Taft hesitated for a beat, but then nodded.

"Stand by," Van Gessel told his people on three.

McGarvey left the conference room, Pete right behind him, and Van Gessel behind them. Three younger men, in white shirts and gray jackets, were waiting. One of them reached for McGarvey's arm.

"It's all right," Van Gessel said.

The security officer ignored the order.

McGarvey casually clamped a thumb and forefinger over the officer's elbow and the nerve in the crease of the inner arm, sending a massive lightning bolt of pain all the way up to his shoulder.

The man tried to step back, but Mac went with him. "Listen to your boss and you might not permanently lose use of your arm."

A dejected look came into the man's eyes. He stepped back, and McGarvey let go.

"You'll be okay in a few minutes," McGarvey said, and he and Pete brushed past them, Van Gessel right on their heels. At the end of the corridor, they took the elevator down to three.

Several men were standing in front of the door to Otto's suite of offices. One of them held an electronic device about the size of a cell phone, a pair of leads connected by sticky pads to the keypad to the right of the door.

"We're blocked out," he told Van Gessel.

McGarvey pulled the leads free and elbowed the technician out of the way.

"Good afternoon," he said.

"Good afternoon, Mr. McGarvey," Lou's computer-generated voice responded.

"Is Otto with you?"

"As always."

"I would like to talk to him. May I come inside?"

"He is currently not here."

"Do you know his present location?"

"Of course."

"May I come in anyway?"

"Yes."

"May the other people in the corridor enter with me?"

"Yes," computer Lou said, and the door lock clicked.

McGarvey held up a hand for the others, including Pete and Van Gessel, to hold back, and he stepped inside. The outer room smelled strongly of fried electronics. All the flat-screen monitors, including the pool table–size horizontal monitor in the inner office, were blank, as were all but one of the smaller desktop monitors.

The system was almost completely dead. Otto had covered his tracks.

McGarvey stopped in the doorway between the middle office and the last one. "Is everything dead here?"

"Yes, sir."

"But the system is still alive?"

"Yes, Mr. McGarvey."

"Where are you?"

The computer hesitated, the pause eerily human. "I don't know," Lou said. "But I am."

TWENTY-NINE

Otto sat alone in a chair at a beauty salon in Manassas, waiting for the dye to set in his freshly cut hair. It was just five and late for the salon, but a couple of hundred-dollar bills had convinced the owner—a middle-aged gay man with a goatee—to stick around.

"It's a surprise," Otto had said.

"From red hair in a ponytail to medium-short and light brown will certainly be a surprise. A wife? Girlfriend?"

"Boyfriend, actually," Otto said. "And he's an absolute dear."

"Lucky boy," the hairdresser said.

Otto got on his phone and connected with his darlings, which he'd sent off to a remote site a couple of years ago as an emergency fallback, in case things went to hell for him and Mac on campus.

Lou's voice came to him through an earbud. "Good afternoon, sweetheart," the computer said.

"How are things at the office?"

"I detect an increased stress level in your voice. Are you in a safe place?"

"Yes, for now."

"I am sorry for Louise's passing."

"Thank you. Has anyone tried to get into my office?"

"Yes, several gentlemen from security division attempted to bypass the locks, but they were not successful."

"Did Mac stop by?"

"Yes, but he found all my systems dead except for my final interaction, as you instructed."

"Everything has been shut down?"

"Yes."

"Did Mac understand?"

"My confidence level is at ninety-seven percent that he does understand."

"Based on what?"

"He winked at me."

Otto chuckled. "When the time is appropriate, we will make contact with him and Pete. Meanwhile, please monitor their progress so far as it's possible. You understand the emergency procedures if he needs help?"

"Of course."

The hairdresser was across the room, talking on the phone. The hair color timer next to Otto had counted down to fourteen minutes.

"There are a number of things I want you to do for me. I need round-trip, first-class tickets from Dulles, Reagan, and Baltimore for the following cities: London, Paris, Istanbul, Tokyo, Beijing, and Saint Petersburg. I would like those flights under six different passports, all within a time window between two hours from now and oh eight hundred tomorrow. Use my Company file photograph for a base image. Alter it slightly for each of the passports."

"Will you actually be on any of those flights?"

"No. I'm staying in the Washington area for the next twenty-four hours, perhaps longer, and then I will be traveling to Kansas. Later, Moscow."

"All of your requests have been met," the computer said. "Will there be anything else?"

"Yes. Book a suite for me at the Hay-Adams for three nights under my Louis Underwood work name. My expected arrival will be at eight thirty this evening. Have my Underwood package picked up at SecureStore immediately and delivered to the hotel. Have the bellman who takes the bags up unpack."

"Yes, darling," Lou said. "May I ask a question?"

Otto had built curiosity and self-learning into the original programs. Over the past three years—especially the past eight or nine months—the computer had almost achieved an AI awareness.

"Of course."

"Am I correct that Mac and Pete are pursuing the person or persons, other than the woman shot to death, who were parked last night on your street?"

"Yes."

"And are you on the same mission?"

"No. My mission is broader."

"May I ask what it is?"

"Not at this time. But when it is appropriate for you to know, I will tell you."

"Yes, dear," the computer replied, and Otto was sure that he detected a note of disappointment.

Otto checked his image in the mirror. He now looked like the base photo that Lou was using for his passports, along with the picture on the Underwood Maryland driver's license he carried, which matched his platinum American Express card.

Starting this evening, he was going to step into the Underwood persona of a gay man—aging, well-to-do if not wealthy, and on the prowl.

"Quite a change," the hairdresser said when he was finished.

"This is more the real me," Otto told him. He got up, patted the man on the cheek, and gave him another two hundred. "See you around sometime."

Taft had ordered McGarvey and Pete to stick around long enough for a couple of techs from Science and Technology to make a first pass through Otto's systems, because it was anyone's guess if there'd be booby traps. And, to this point, the computer was still talking to Mac, but only Mac.

"There's nothing here for us," one of the techs said, getting up from the keyboard he'd plugged in to one of the monitors.

"The systems are still operable, even though he made it seem as if the monitors had been fried," the other one said.

"He's screwing with us."

"Yeah."

"Mr. McGarvey," Lou's voice came over the speakers in all three offices.

"Yes?"

"Good-bye for now."

"Good-bye, Lou," McGarvey said.

"What was that all about, sir?" one of the techs asked at the door.

"Inside joke," McGarvey said.

Otto showed up at the Hay-Adams at precisely eight thirty and presented his Amex card at the desk. "Has my luggage arrived?"

"Yes, Mr. Underwood. And a bottle of Krug is waiting on ice in your room, as your secretary instructed."

His darling was even playing jokes on him now, ordering the champagne.

Upstairs, he stripped to his shorts, opened the Krug, poured a flute, and sat down with his phone. He brought up his darling.

"Thanks for the champers," he said.

"I like surprises," she said.

"No more till later. Now we have to go to work."

"Yes, dear. Where would you like to begin?"

"The SVR's mainframe in Moscow."

THIRTY

☐

Sergei Yuryn drove his anonymous Honda Civic down to the southwest section of DC, between the Washington Channel and Anacostia River, and parked in front of a run-down apartment building on South Capitol Street, adjacent to Nationals Park. His special operations team leader, Vitali Burov, a medium-height, medium-built, anonymous-looking man, was waiting for him in the ground-floor apartment.

"Are the others here yet?" Yuryn asked.

"We were delayed. I got here twenty minutes ago; the others will arrive within the next hour or so."

Yuryn was vexed. He did not like changes to carefully laid plans, especially not delays. "Why?"

"It was a possible security issue at Grand Central. The woman cop at the Forty-Second Street entrance seemed suspicious, so we went immediately downstairs and left through the market entrance, where we split up."

"Did you change clothes and IDs?"

"Of course," Burov said. "Which necessitated changing trains."

"Did you make sure that you were not followed here?"

Burov, who was a seasoned field officer from the New York office, had worked in the United States without attracting the attention of the FBI for nearly eight years. He took offense. "I know my job as well as you do, Sergei. And we all might be better served if you paid a little more attention to details."

Yuryn backed down a little. "What details?"

"FedEx left your three packages on the front stoop."

"You were to have been here already."

"I wasn't."

Yuryn's phone burred. It was Zimin.

"When do you want us to move in?" he asked.

"There's been a delay. I'll let you know when and where to pick up the materials."

"We'll need an update on their positions."

"They're still on campus," Yuryn said. He did not add that he wasn't one hundred percent sure. "Sit tight for now."

"Yes, sir."

Yuryn hung up. "The packages weren't disturbed?"

Burov grinned. "If someone had tried to steal them, the front of this building would not exist. They were intact."

"Then let's get started."

"We'll have a drink first, and something to eat. The other four won't be here for another hour."

Zimin hung up, went into the living room, and sat down. Petr had switched on the television but had turned off the sound. A news bulletin of some sort was showing what appeared to be a riot somewhere. People were running across a large open space in front of a stage.

"What is that?"

"Another mass shooting at a concert," Petr said. "Do we have orders?"

"We've been told to wait."

Petr was agitated. "This is getting out of hand, and you know it," he said. "Larissa walked into a trap, and I don't want to be next."

Zimin lashed back because he was sure they were in over their heads. "Were you fucking her?"

"None of your business, old man. But even if I was, what does it have to do with this fucked-up mission? You got lucky the first time."

"You have your fallback options. Return to Moscow if you've lost your nerve and would rather hide under your bed and cry for your whore."

Petr turned away. "Christ," he said, and he nodded toward the television. "I think that you would be better off defecting and staying here. A fuckup in a country of fuckups."

Zimin stood up and started for the bedroom to get his pistol. With

Petr dead, there would be no one to contradict his story if he went home and said that his two operatives had sabotaged the mission because of their gross incompetence.

Petr stopped him at the door. "Look, Yevgenni, let's not bounce off the walls like this. We have a job to do, and now, as you say, we'll have the help of one of our U.S. operatives. So let's just do it and then return home heroes."

McGarvey requisitioned an ordinary Chevy Impala from the motor pool and he and Pete left the campus by the main gate a few minutes before nine. He was sick at heart about Lou's death, which was entirely his fault. He'd challenged Putin, and the Russian president had responded.

"They'll be watching our apartments," Pete said.

"Almost certainly, but they might not know it's us in this car."

"We had it brought around to the underground garage, and the windows are tinted, so even a decent satellite pass won't tell them much," Pete said.

"Unless we lead them by their noses without letting them know that we know."

"What do you have in mind?"

"A little sloppy misdirection."

Traffic was fairly light on the Parkway, and they crossed the river on the Key Bridge and took M Street over to Pennsylvania Avenue.

"Call Housekeeping and tell them that we're having car problems and will need a tow."

Pete hesitated. "I'm not sure my phone is clean."

"I'm counting on it."

Pete did as Mac asked. "They're sending a team, but they want us to find a defensible position to pull over and then stay put."

"Now pull up the numbers of four cab companies and have them pick us up."

"Where?"

"In the K Street underpass."

"If they're monitoring our phone, it won't work."

"I'm counting on that, too," McGarvey said.

"Where are we going?"

"To Otto's place in McLean."

"You want them to come after us."

"Yes," McGarvey said. "If they're stupid enough, we'll even the score a little."

"If not?"

"We'll up the ante."

Housekeeping showed up at their location inside the underpass, and two minders, their pistols drawn, got out.

"The general wants you back on campus," the lead said. He was about six four and built like a Packers lineman. "We have a wrecker on the way."

"Nothing wrong with the car," McGarvey said. "But you're going to tow it back anyway."

"Sir, we have our orders."

An OnCabs car showed up first, and Pete hailed it.

"Tell Mr. Taft that I refused to go back with you."

"I can't do that, sir."

McGarvey patted him on the shoulder. "Tell him that I threatened to hit you."

THIRTY-ONE

□

By ten, Otto, still in his shorts, had finished the bottle of Krug and had ranged around inside the Russian intelligence service's mainframe in Moscow, not gaining much information of any value—except for the names of some new personnel who'd been flown overnight to Washington and the fact that an operation involving McGarvey was active.

The problem with delving into such a highly sophisticated system—and the solution—was leaving footprints or trails, indications that someone unauthorized had been hacking programs. The SVR's cyber unit would be aware from the start that their system had been breached. Otto's solution was double-dipping—a hacking approach of his own invention. One half of his program looked for data not much more important than personnel changes in foreign embassies—including Russian embassies and consulates not just in the United States but also in a dozen other countries around the world, including China and North Korea.

But his device also had what would appear to be a mirror image—almost like a shadow—operating on a completely different level, looking for completely different sets of data.

The Russians knew someone was on a shopping trip. What they didn't know was what Otto had been shopping for.

The operation was named Cksantayana, and CK was the designator for highly sensitive missions—a Russian key for above top secret.

Otto couldn't help but grin. In his head, the Russians were sometimes so fucking obvious that it bordered on silly. Jorge Agustin Nicolas Ruiz de Santayana y Borras was a Spanish-born American philosopher whose best-known aphorisms were "Those who cannot remember the past are condemned to repeat it" and "Only the dead have seen the end of war," which was sometimes attributed to Plato.

Mac delving into how his parents had died and who was responsible was Santayana—don't let the American military establishment learn why the McGarveys were assassinated, lest it give away their missile defense secrets. And the second quote was nothing more than pure Russian fatalism.

"Dig a little deeper, without making it too obvious," Otto said.

"Of course," Lou replied.

Otto phoned room service and ordered another bottle of Krug, with some raspberries and buttered toast. He had a buzz, though he wasn't drunk yet, and he had the munchies. But it was almost a certain bet that even a high-ranking place like the Hay-Adams would not have Twinkies on hand.

Hanging up the phone, he turned suddenly, almost one hundred percent certain that he had heard Louise. Not the computer, but Lou herself. But that wasn't possible.

He went to a window and looked across at the White House, which was all lit up. Everyone had problems, especially the poor bastard who lived across the street. And just then Otto had a premo that the problem he, Mac, and Pete faced would become another one for the president.

When room service arrived, Otto tipped the man fifty dollars, and when he was alone he poured a glass of champagne and went back to his laptop.

"Anything new?"

"Background noise, except for the name of a newly appointed SVR brigadier by the name of Yevgenni Zimin."

"What's interesting about him?"

"Maybe nothing, but a number of factors surrounding him make me evaluate him as a possible connection to our current issue."

"What's your confidence level?"

"Twenty-seven percent."

Otto put down his champagne and sat up. "Tell me."

"He was retired from the KGB until one week ago, when he was recalled to active duty. The interesting note was his promotion with the

Order of Lenin, twenty-eight years ago, just thirty days after the McGarveys' deaths."

"Is there more?"

"Eight days ago, Cksantayana was reopened."

"Christ," Otto muttered. "Where is he now?"

"Unknown."

"Do we have a current photo of him?"

"One moment," Lou said. She was back in under ten seconds. "*Voyennyy Parad*—Military Parade magazine." A photograph of an older man, his hair gray, his frame slender but his bearing erect, was receiving a medal from an army two-star general under the caption "Colonel Yevgenni Zimin receiving the Order for Merit to the Fatherland."

Otto spoke and read Russian, so Lou did not bother to translate.

"Do you have a date?"

"August, last year."

"I want you to look at videos from surveillance cameras at Sheremetyevo, Vnukovo, and Domodedovo, starting eight days ago," Otto said. They were Moscow's three major airports. "See if our General Zimin shows up, and perhaps even come up with a work name."

"Are you thinking that he may be here in Washington?"

"Yes. He and at least the woman who Pete shot outside my house."

"I'll check videos at Reagan, Dulles, and Baltimore as well. Matching dates and flights."

It was nearly midnight when Zimin got a call from Yuryn. He had been sleeping in the easy chair by the front window, and Petr was playing solitaire at the table in the kitchenette.

He answered on the first ring. "Yes."

"Your team has arrived," Yuryn said. "Are you secure?"

"Yes."

"No surveillance vehicles on the street?"

Zimin looked out the window. Parked cars lined both sides of the street. Nothing had changed in the past hour or so. "None."

Yuryn gave him the Capitol Street Southeast address. "Can you find this place?"

"Yes."

"First sanitize the apartment, and then make sure you are not followed. Do you understand?"

"Of course," Zimin said, but Yuryn had hung up.

Mac and Pete were sitting at the counter in Otto's McLean house sharing a half bottle of a good Chilean merlot. It was late, but they were both still too keyed up to go to bed. He wanted her out of the operation right now, but he had no idea where she would be significantly safer than at his side.

"Do you think they'll try something here?" Pete asked him.

"Otto's gone, so there'd be no reason I can think of for them to come here again."

"But we gave them a clue on K Street."

"No reason that I could think of," McGarvey said. He phoned Otto's rollover number. Lou answered on the first ring.

"Good evening, Mr. McGarvey. Is Pete with you?"

"Yes. May I speak with Otto?"

The computer responded after a momentary delay. "I'm sorry, but we are busy at the moment."

"Is he someplace safe?"

"Yes, for the moment."

"What do you mean, 'for the moment'?"

"He is safe now, Mr. McGarvey. And we may have something for you soon."

"Amplify, please," McGarvey said, but the line was dead.

THIRTY-TWO

☐

Zimin and Petr showed up at Yuryn's safe house at a little after one in the morning, and an American-looking man in jeans and a dark pullover came to the door, a big Glock in his left hand. A single light somewhere near the rear of the house was on, but there were no sounds from within.

"I'm Vitali," the man said, looking past Zimin's shoulder. "Is there a possibility you were followed?"

"None," Zimin said. "Where is Sergei?"

"Here," Yuryn said, stepping into view.

Both men stepped aside so that Zimin and Petr could come in. They all went back to the kitchen, where four men in perhaps their late twenties were seated around a table, cleaning their handguns. They could have been Americans from any part of the country; their mannerisms, the way they looked up and smiled, their dress, their haircuts—everything was ordinary.

"I didn't know that I would be sent a team," Zimin said.

"You weren't," Burov said. "These men work for me, as do you."

Yuryn said nothing, but it was clear that he was uncomfortable.

"Eight of us is too many," Zimin said. "A lot could go wrong."

"A lot has already gone wrong, you fucking idiot. In the first place, you got one of your people killed, and in the second, not only has the CIA taken notice but so have the local law authorities."

"*Yeb vas*," Zimin said. It was a crude Russian expression that meant "Fuck off." "I have my orders in case something went wrong. We'll return to Moscow and you can take over."

"If you want to go home, please do. But your reception won't be the same as it was twenty-eight years ago. You have new orders now."

Zimin had no intention of backing down. "The operation is CK sensitive. If you fuck it up, comrade, your reception won't be so great either."

"The Americans have suspected the ruse all along. And I've been briefed on the original technology, which no longer is relevant."

"If that's so, why the urgency? Why did Sergei come to me, and what the fuck are you and your Boy Scouts doing here?"

"Because of Kirk McGarvey," Burov said. "You and Petr are going to kill him tonight, before dawn."

"If it's a ruse, as you say, why bother?"

"Because the son of a bitch actually challenged the president, and that is something Mr. Putin does not take lightly. Your new orders come directly from him. It's a contract on McGarvey's life."

Zimin was impressed. "Is McGarvey still at Langley?"

"He left. We're pretty sure that he tried to pull a dodge in the K Street overpass. A taxi took him and his wife to the Rencke house in McLean."

"Fine, we'll kill him and the woman there."

"Get yourself and your partner shot to death, just like you got your other partner killed," Burov said. "I have a better idea. It's crude, but that should be right up your alley."

Zimin was armed. And he had the almost overwhelming urge to draw his pistol and shoot the smug bastard in the forehead. Give the prick his nine ounces.

They were standing just inside the kitchen, and Petr put a hand on Zimin's arm. "If this is supposed to happen tonight, we'd best get started. What do you have in mind, sir?"

"Ivan will show you," Burov said, and one of the men, with thinning black hair and wide boyish eyes, got up from the table.

Pete joined McGarvey at an upstairs front window. "They probably know that we're here," she said. "Do you think they'll try something tonight?"

"I would, if I were them, even though they know that it was a setup and that we're waiting."

"There were only three of them outside the other night. Now there's only two. Not such hot odds for them."

"There'll be more."

"Are you sure?"

McGarvey looked at her. Everything in his power wanted to send her down to the Farm to be with Audie. And yet just the act of getting her the one hundred fifty miles to the Company's secure training site would be problematic. They would be more vulnerable on the road than here.

"I'm sure that Putin ordered it. I've become a pain in his side that he wants to get rid of."

Pete almost laughed. "That's an understatement," she said. "So what else is coming down the pike?"

"Our apartments in Georgetown."

Zimin, driving the Civic, with Petr riding shotgun, left the Capitol Street safe house and headed directly up to Independence Avenue Southwest, then west toward Georgetown. Bar and club traffic was fairly heavy, which it usually was until after two in the morning, so they were anonymous for the time being.

"We're being used as cannon fodder. You do know that, don't you?" Petr asked.

"Then we'd better not make a mistake," Zimin said. "In any event, it's not very likely that McGarvey will want to leave the safety of Rencke's house."

"You're guessing."

"The president is directly involved now. Do you want to challenge his orders?"

"We'll get ourselves killed, just like Larissa did."

"*Da*, and it'll be my fault. Just don't fuck up this morning. You're the Semtex expert."

"There are no experts in this business, only the lucky ones."

"Well, I hope your luck will hold for another hour," Zimin said.

At Seventeenth Street Southwest, he went up to Pennsylvania and from there through Washington Circle and the K Street underpass, across the Rock Creek Parkway, into Georgetown.

He circled the block in front of McGarvey's apartment once before he found a parking spot three-quarters of a block to the west.

Petr took a shoulder bag, much like a shopping bag or something that could be used as a carry-on for an airline flight, and they walked back to the apartment building.

As Petr stood watch, Zimin picked the front door lock, and inside they took the stairs up to the third floor, making almost no noise.

They stopped on the landing to listen for noises, any noise, but the building was deathly silent.

It took Zimin nearly thirty seconds to pick the lock to McGarvey's apartment.

He toed the door open and went in with his pistol drawn. But the place was as silent as the rest of the building. No one was home. The apartment smelled faintly of mold, of a closed-in, unoccupied space.

"Keep watch," Petr said, putting the bag down and opening it.

Zimin stood at the door, which was open just a crack, his pistol drawn. He was listening with every fiber of his being for anything—the smallest noise, a footstep on a stair tread, especially the sounds of someone at the downstairs entrance.

Petr took a pair of half-kilo bricks of Semtex and, using two strips of sticky tape, attached them to the inside of the door—one just above the lock, the other just below.

Unraveling the wires from one fuse, he stuck it in the top brick; the wires from a second went into the lower brick of high explosive. He wired both together and connected them to a motion-sensitive trigger mechanism that he taped to the door frame, just below the upper hinge.

"Will this thing go off when we close the door?" Zimin asked.

Petr moved him into the corridor and very carefully closed and locked the door. "The trigger is cocked now. When the door moves, even a centimeter, the door blows. Anyone standing in front of it will die."

THIRTY-THREE

McGarvey parked Lou's green BMW 320i just around the corner from his apartment, and he and Pete got out and walked the rest of the way. They had just reached the street when two men emerged from Mac's apartment building and walked the rest of the way down the block.

"Follow them, " McGarvey said, handing Pete the car keys.

"What if I'm spotted?" she asked.

"Don't be."

Pete waited at the corner until the two men got into a dark blue Civic, then she disappeared in a run around the corner.

McGarvey stepped into the shadows as the Civic went past and turned south at the corner. Moments later, Pete crossed the intersection. He walked back to the corner, then around the block he ducked into the service alley behind the apartment buildings, where the Dumpsters were located and where servicepeople—air-conditioner technicians, plumbers, electricians, and the like—entered.

The steel door at the back of his building was locked with an ordinary Yale. By feel, in the darkness, he had it picked in under twenty seconds.

There was no traffic in this neighborhood at this hour—most of it was down on M Street, where many of the bars, restaurants, and nightspots were clustered. And the building was deathly still, except for the noise of some electrical motor running somewhere in the basement.

He slipped into the corridor and took the stairs two at a time up to the second floor. The front apartment just below his was occupied by Dianna Miller, a young woman from Minnesota, who had a good job at a Chase Bank in the District. McGarvey had helped her with minor tasks a couple of times over the past few years—fixing a stuck door on a weekend when the building maintenance service wasn't answering, helping lug a flat-screen television up from her car, and once sharing a bottle of wine with her in his apartment when her boyfriend had left her.

He knocked softly at her door. At first there was no answer, but just as he was about to knock again, a shadow darkened the peephole.

"Mr. McGarvey?" she said.

"I need to talk to you. Are you dressed?"

"PJs."

"May I come in?"

"Of course," she said, and she unlocked the door and opened it. Her eyes were wide and she looked small and vulnerable in flannel lounging pants and a bright red T-shirt.

"I think someone might have tried to break into my place upstairs and I need to use your front window to get up to my apartment and surprise them, if they're still there."

McGarvey had never told her who he worked for, but she had guessed that it had something to do with law enforcement. He hadn't confirmed or denied it, but it had been enough for her to trust that he wasn't a crook or something.

She let him to the small living room, a duplicate of his upstairs except in the way that it was furnished.

"I want you to go back to bed, get under the covers, and hide your head under a couple of pillows until I come back to your door and give you the all clear. Do you understand?"

"No. What's going on?"

"I think that someone may have put a bomb on my door that would explode if I opened it."

The woman stepped back. "I'll call the cops."

"No."

"But what if it explodes? We need to get the bomb squad here or something and evacuate the building."

"I'll make sure it won't explode."

She looked into his eyes, wanting to believe him, but she wasn't dumb. "Then why the covers and the pillows?"

"Could be some flying glass if I miss."

"Jesus," she said. She reached up on tiptoes and kissed him on the cheek. "Good luck."

"We'll have a bottle of wine when all this is over and you can meet my new wife."

She smiled and nodded, then turned and padded back to her bedroom.

McGarvey unlatched the casement window and opened it. Nothing moved on the street. He eased out onto the ledge and, using the regular gaps in the brickwork, levered his way up to the window above, his prosthetic leg actually giving him a slight advantage.

The curtains were partially open, and so far as he could tell the place was empty. But he thought he could see something attached to the front door.

Checking over his shoulder, he saw that the street below was still quiet.

He worked his way three feet farther up and, holding on to the frame on one side of the window opening, took out his pistol with his other hand, using the butt end of the handle to break the glass just at the casement latch. Reholstering the gun, he reached inside, undid the latch, raised the window with some awkwardness, and climbed inside.

Standing stock still for a moment or two, to make sure that the apartment was truly empty, he went across to the kitchen, where he got a small penlight from a drawer. Back at the door, he switched on the light and inspected the two blocks of Semtex with the pair of fuses wired together and connected to a trigger mechanism about the size of a key fob.

If the door had been unlocked and opened, the Semtex would have killed anyone standing outside, and possibly would have taken out a section of the wall across the corridor.

Holding the penlight in his teeth, he disconnected the fuses from the explosive bricks and then the wires from the trigger. In that instant, the trigger tripped with an audible pop.

He got an empty plastic bag from the kitchen for the Semtex, fuses, and trigger, then let himself out of the apartment. Back down at Dianna's apartment, he knocked at her door. When she answered, her eyes were even wider than before. She spotted the bag in his hand.

"That it?" she asked.

Mac nodded. "I'm going to get rid of it. But call maintenance in the morning and tell them that someone apparently threw a rock and broke one of my windows."

"I think I owe you that much at least," she said. "And I'm really looking forward to meeting the lucky woman who snagged you."

"One more thing."

She cocked her head.

"I'm going to call someone to come over and pick me up, but it might take an hour or so. May I stay here with you?"

"Sure, if you don't think she'd mind," Dianna said, and she stepped back to let him in.

Mac put the bag on the floor by the door and made sure the latch locked.

"Can I get you a beer or something?"

"Thanks, but I'm fine. Just go back to bed and try to get some sleep. And forget I was ever here, okay?"

"Sleep, okay; forget, no," she said. She gave him one last glance, then turned and went back to her bedroom.

He switched off the living room lights and checked the window to make sure they had no company before closing and latching it. Then he sat down on the couch and phoned Pete.

She answered on the second ring, and he could hear traffic noise.

"You okay?" he asked.

"So far, so good. I don't think they've spotted me. It's two guys in the Civic. They just turned south on Capitol, by the House Office Buildings. How about you?"

"They had my door wired. A couple of bricks of Semtex."

"I'm not even going to ask how the hell you got in. I have enough nightmares of my own. But where are you now?"

McGarvey told her.

She chuckled. "Should I be jealous?"

"Desperately."

"Wait, they just went under the Southeast Parkway, and doesn't look as if they're slowing down."

"Listen to me, Pete. I want you to find out where they park and then get the hell back here. Don't take any chances."

"Part of the business, darling."

"I shit you not. No chances. Just find out where they park and then come back for me. I want to return their little present. But call me if you run into trouble."

"I'll call you when I'm two minutes out."

THIRTY-FOUR

The parking spot just down the block from the ramshackle apartment building was still open, and Zimin pulled in and shut off the lights. He sat gripping the wheel for a long moment.

"Fieldwork has changed in the past twenty years," Petr said, no disrespect apparent in his tone.

"Not really. It's always been stupid, and almost always pointless."

"McGarvey will die. Our new taskmaster will be happy, and so will the president."

"But Larissa is dead."

Petr said nothing, and Zimin turned to him.

"You were lovers. It's one of the reasons you two were picked for the assignment."

"None of your business, old man," Petr said abruptly, but then his tone changed. "Yes. In fact we wanted to get married, but my control officer asked us to wait until we got back from this assignment. He said this one was too important for us to be distracted as husband and wife."

Zimin couldn't keep the bitterness from his voice. "Yet you were picked because you were lovers. Makes no sense."

"Just like picking you made no sense."

"But McGarvey will die this night."

"Da, we did well."

They got out of the car and walked up to the apartment. The door opened for them, though no one was in sight in the front hall until they entered. Yuryn was there, a pistol in his hand. He closed and latched the door.

"Is it done?" he asked.

"Did you have any doubts?" Zimin asked.

"Plenty," Burov said, coming down from upstairs. "What the fuck were you two lovebirds talking about for so long in the car? Trying to figure out how to admit that you'd screwed up?"

Petr started to say something, but Zimin held him off. "We will not get anywhere if you continue to belittle us. You've been sent here to help eliminate one man who's evidently some threat to our president. It's been accomplished. So now let's go home."

"He's not dead until it's been confirmed," Yuryn said. "You should have waited to make sure."

"We were ordered to set the explosives and return."

"Fucking amateurs," Burov said. "And the job won't be finished until his bitch is dead, and especially not until Rencke's been eliminated."

"Have either of them been located?" Petr asked.

"The woman will almost certainly be with him, which means she might die when they open the door," Yuryn said.

"Unless she stayed behind at the McLean house," Burov said. "But we'll soon know if that's the case, because I've sent the team out there. And if McGarvey does survive, he'll go back to her and we'll get him there. Which would leave only the computer freak. Possibly the most dangerous of them all."

"Was there any chance that you were followed tonight?" Yuryn asked.

"No."

"Are you sure?"

"Yes, unless they're better than me or they double- or triple-teamed us. But if that's the case, then it would mean McGarvey is having help from the CIA's minders or the FBI's people."

"I'm told that's not the case yet," Burov said. "Although the Bureau and CIA are actively investigating the murders of Rencke's wife, the old man, and of course Larissa—though it's probable that she hasn't been identified."

"That won't hold forever," Petr said. "Their forensics labs are good."

"They'd need DNA samples," Zimin said.

Burov laughed. "Damned near everyone who's connected in Moscow has had their DNA lifted. As you say, the Bureau's labs are first class, but so are the CIA's methods."

"So now we wait and see," Yuryn said.

Pete phoned Mac. "I'm just passing under the K Street overpass, for the third time."

"You didn't spot any lookouts when you passed the building?" McGarvey asked.

"I didn't get that far. I watched from the corner and did a U-turn."

"No one following you?"

Pete glanced in her rearview mirror. "Not much traffic, so unless they have an eye in the sky, I'm clean."

"I'll wait for you downstairs."

"Have you heard anything from Otto?"

"No, but I'm going to try right now."

McGarvey called Otto's number and the computer answered. "Good morning, Mr. McGarvey. Are you well?"

"Yes. May I speak with Otto?"

"I'm sorry, not at this time," Lou said, but Otto came on.

"I'm busy, Mac. What do you want?"

"They wired the door to my apartment."

"You okay?"

"Yes. Pete traced them back to a safe house in southeast DC."

"Seedy neighborhood," Otto said, and he sounded distracted and bitter.

McGarvey had never heard his friend that way. But Lou had been gunned down. "I'd like to see you."

"Not now. What's your plan?"

"For starts, I'm going to return their Semtex."

"To their safe house?"

"Yes."

"Better yet, take it to McLean. There are four of them parked in a black Chevy SUV around the corner from my place, waiting for someone to show up."

"Do you have a drone in the air?"

"No, I wired the streetlights in a three-block radius of my house before we ever moved in. Always had the idea at the back of my head that shit like this would be coming my way someday. I just wasn't able to catch it for Lou's sake."

"Call the cops."

"I'm about as likely to do that as you are, my friend. These guys look competent. Cops show up and they'd be running into a buzz saw. Lot of innocent casualties."

"Warn them."

"That's what Lou would say. But you know goddamned well that the sonsabitches would just back off and try again."

"They want to retain their secret," McGarvey said, though he had already stopped believing that. They had tipped their hand by the sheer fact of their attacks on him.

"Not a chance. This is about you and Putin and has been from day one."

"And I sucked all of you in."

"That's what friends are for."

McGarvey choked up. "And Lou."

"Friends," Otto said.

"I'm going to try to get in and return the favor they left at my door."

"Do you want to talk to them first?"

"No. We know why they came. There'll be damage."

"Fuck it," Otto said. "I'm never going back there. Just watch your back, *kemo sabe*." The connection went dead.

McGarvey pocketed the phone and stood for a moment at the door. At that moment, he didn't know if he'd ever had a true measure of the only real friend he'd ever had. Otto's grief at losing his wife was there, but almost as if were something secondary, buried beneath another emotion—or purpose.

Otto was going to take out his sadness and his anger and every other dark emotion he'd ever felt against all the bastards of the world who'd made fun of him, who'd laughed at his awkwardness, at his nerdiness and geekiness. At the people who'd hurt him. At the people who'd hurt his friend, who'd killed Katy and Liz and her husband. Who were at this moment threatening all of them.

And God help them, Mac thought.

THIRTY-FIVE

□

Ivan Dolya, riding shotgun in the team's rental Chevy Tahoe, was parked on a side street two blocks from the Renckes' McLean house, his fingers on the drone's joystick, his eyes on the screen.

He'd placed a remote antenna for the machine on the rear tailgate so that he would not have to open a window to control it. He and the other three operators were all but invisible behind the heavily tinted windows. If a patrol car happened to stop, they would shoot the cop and abort the mission. It was mission SOP. Malin and Lykov were keeping watch from the backseat and Mihail Smolin was at the wheel, watching the screen with Dolya.

"One light in a side window—but dim," Dolya said.

The drone was hovering nearly silently, about fifty feet above the east side of the house.

"Go around back," Smolin suggested.

Dolya, at twenty-four, the youngest on the team, had been selected because of his expertise with explosives and every type of surveillance system in the Russian arsenal. He flew the drone in a short 360-degree loop as he maneuvered to the back of the house.

"What are you doing?" Smolin demanded. His temper was as sharp as the angles of his chin and nose.

"Looking to see if any of the neighbors are taking notice. Now leave me the fuck alone."

At the back of the house, a light shone through what was a screened lanai in front of a kitchen. But so far as Dolya could tell, there were no movements inside.

He angled the drone up to the windows on the second floor and switched to infrared mode. No heat signatures showed up, nor were there others as he circled the house at that level.

At the front of the house he focused on the garage door, and a very small, narrow heat signature of something showed up in a corner.

Smolin sat forward. "There," he said. "Someone's just driven in and parked their car."

"Too small."

"What then?"

Dolya looked up. "It's the hot pipe going into the house from the water heater. No one's home."

He flew the drone up one hundred feet above the rooflines and did another slow three sixty. A couple of cars were heading southeast on Old Dominion, a half mile away, and the streetlights, business signs, and security lights on closed businesses showed up brightly. But nothing was coming their way for the moment.

Dolya put the drone in station-keeping mode, where it would stay for another twenty minutes before the battery pack got low and the machine returned to the car. But they would be in and out by then, and the drone could not be traced to Russian manufacture or design. Any traces of DNA had been removed.

He looked up. "Let's go in."

Smolin switched on the headlights, drove to the corner and around the block, down to the Renckes' safe house.

As they approached, Dolya activated the garage door and they went inside and parked next to Otto Rencke's old Mercedes diesel.

Dolya shut the door behind them and Smolin shut off the engine and lights. The four of them got out and took several packs from the rear, and three of them went into the house to set the explosives. Dolya stayed behind to wire the garage door.

When they were finished, every possible entry to the house would be wired. Anyone opening any door or any window would be blown to hell.

"Fucking Americans," Dolya muttered. Though he personally had nothing against them, this was war, after all. And they were working under a presidential mandate, so a little anger was a good thing.

Two blocks out, McGarvey's phone chirped. It was Otto's computer, and hearing Lou's realistic voice, even though she sometimes spoke formally, was particularly peculiar here, at this moment.

"Good morning, Mr. McGarvey."

"Do you have something for me?" McGarvey asked.

"The Chevrolet Tahoe SUV is in the garage and the door is closed, but a drone is up and circling. I have a ninety-seven percent confidence that the device is being operated by the intruders, though it is currently in a station-keeping mode and it is not certain if the cameras are being monitored."

"Will you keep watch for us?"

"Of course. But I am capable of disabling it."

"No, don't do that," McGarvey said. "But can you put it on a loop, so that it shows the same image, which would mask our approach?"

"Yes."

"Do it, please."

"Done. Will there be anything else?"

"Let Otto know what's going on."

"He knows."

"Thank you," McGarvey said. But the computer was gone.

"That's disconcerting," Pete said.

"Tell me about it."

"What do you have in mind?"

"They'll have to open the garage door to leave. I'm going to wire it."

"Won't do much except blow the door," Pete said.

"I'll wire each side of the door frame, about the height of the car's windows, and stick the contact fuse far enough out so that when they back out they'll make contact."

Pete grinned. "Nasty."

"You're going to get me in place and then back off."

"What about you?"

"I'll stay out of the blast radius and pick off anyone who might get lucky," McGarvey said. "This part's going to end this morning."

"They may have posted a lookout."

"I'll take care of it."

"That's what partners are for."

McGarvey knew this would come up. "Not wives."

"Especially wives," Pete said. "Macho pig."

It wasn't worth arguing; he knew that he would lose. "We'll go in on foot. You take right, I'll go left."

"Right."

"How many mags are you carrying?"

"Two spares."

"Save the last one in case we have to bug out."

"Christ, Kirk, don't be such an old lady. I took the same courses at the Farm as you did. Now let's get this done."

McGarvey had to laugh. "Stay frosty."

"You too, darling."

McGarvey switched off the headlights and parked three doors down from Otto's safe house. He got out of the car, took the plastic bag with the Semtex, fuses, and trigger, and then he and Pete, her pistol drawn, hurried up the street to the driveway and the garage door.

Pete hunched down in the shadows to the right while McGarvey taped the bricks of high explosive onto either side of the door, about four and a half feet up. He inserted the fuses in the plastique, wired them together, and then taped the trigger to the edge of the door frame so that it stuck out far enough to be struck by the SUV, and cocked it.

He slipped well off to the side and nodded to Pete, who nodded back.

At that moment a dark figure came around the corner of the house, thirty feet behind Mac, and opened fire.

□

THIRTY-SIX

Lou interrupted Otto just as he was finishing hiding the last traces of the Stuxnet-type malware that he'd placed inside the electrical power systems that supplied the Russian intelligence agencies' mainframes. The worm he'd created targeted the programmable logic controllers modulating the filtered air-conditioning that cooled the large computers. The end results would wreak havoc mainly with the long-term memory circuits.

"A situation is developing at McLean."

"Tell me," Otto said, watching the display on his laptop.

"Someone has opened fire on Mac."

"Does he need help?"

"I can offer no definitive range of probabilities," the computer said. The admission was rare. "Shall I contact him?"

"Will it make a difference, or will we be a distraction?"

"A distraction."

Otto stared at the monitor showing the progress of the virus. Mac would either work his way out of the situation or he wouldn't, and there was nothing to be done about it from here. They'd all been there in the past, and shit like this would happen again and again for the foreseeable future. It was the nature of the business.

He looked away from the screen for a moment. He'd changed since Lou's death. The past was indistinct. He had no idea who he had been before Mac showed up in France asking for help. Intellectually, he knew that he'd been rescued from a meaningless existence as just another hacker playing around for his own pleasure. But the details of that life were no longer clear in his mind.

His time at the CIA, where he'd been given a suite of offices and had carved out his own niche, had lasted for what had seemed like forever. But it had ended with Lou's assassination, and he could no longer clearly see the details of those years, either.

He was a new man now, a creature of the intense passions ignited by his wife's murder. Besides Mac, Lou had been the most important person in his life, someone he not only loved but also completely depended on for his existence.

She had been an innocent. Mac wasn't.

An antivirus program in the SVR mainframe had detected the intrusion to its power supply and was fighting back.

Otto had expected it, and he asked the computer to search for an assassination attempt on President Putin that was currently in progress.

Lykov hunched down in the darkness at the side of the house. He'd fired too soon. McGarvey had been at least ten meters away, a difficult pistol shot under the best of circumstances. There'd been no return fire, but he was sure that he'd missed.

"We have an intruder," he said softly into his lapel mic.

"Where," Smolin replied.

"In front."

"How many?"

"I only saw one."

"Stand by. I'm sending Georgi out."

McGarvey had circled around the rear of the house, and now he came up behind the lone gunman. He placed the muzzle of his Walther into the back of the man's head.

"Very easy now or you will die."

"He's here," Lykov said, turning his head to the left.

McGarvey fired, and the man collapsed. He looked over his shoulder as he dropped down next to the body. He pulled the man's jacket collar around and spoke into the mic. "Your man is dead. Leave while you can. We'll stall them."

"Mac has taken down one of the Russians, but another is on his way from the rear of the house," Lou said.

The virus hunter the Russians had sent to look for the Stuxnet was on standby, allowing every available program on the mainframe to counter the threat to Putin.

"What about the others?" Otto asked, still distracted.

"I intercepted a series of short-range broadcasts between the man who fired at Mac and someone else," Lou said. She played it back.

"Are there any police cars in the vicinity?"

"Close enough so that anyone inside the house would hear the siren?"

Otto almost smiled. His darlings were getting smarter almost by the hour. "Yes, please."

"Do you have a shot?" Smolin radioed.

Malin, crouched in the darkness just around the corner at the back of the house, took a quick peek toward the front, then ducked back. "*Nyet.* Viktor is down, but I don't see anyone else."

A police siren sounded somewhere in the distance, to the south.

"A siren," Malin said.

"We hear it. Come back. We're getting out of here."

Lou replayed the radio exchange. "Shall I warn Mac and Pete?"

"Yes. But have Mac sanitize the body," Otto said. "Including the communicator."

McGarvey's phone vibrated. it was Otto's computer. "The police are not on the way, but the bad guys are preparing to leave. Sanitize the man you took down. Take his communicator."

"Will do," McGarvey said, but Lou was gone.

He was crouched at the side of the house, just beyond the zone of outward blast from the Semtex taped to the garage door. He motioned for Pete to keep back and then went to the downed man and searched the body. But other than the communicator wirelessly attached to a cell phone–size unit in a jacket pocket, there were only two spare mags of nine-millimeter ammunition.

He took the communicator lapel mic and the comms unit, plus the pistol lying on the ground, and turned back, as a powerful explosion shattered the night.

The Tahoe, or what remained of the twisted, burning hulk, was half inside the garage, which had caught fire. It was obvious that no one had survived the blast. Shielding his eyes against the glare from the flames, Mac could see what might have been a body in the backseat.

Pete came around from the other side of the house, but well down the driveway, away from the blast radius.

Lights were coming on all over the neighborhood.

"We need to get out of here right now," she said.

McGarvey joined her, and together they walked to their car. A neighbor across the street had come to the door, and already there were other sirens in the distance.

"We don't have to worry about the opposition for the moment," Pete said, as they drove off.

"This was just the opening act," McGarvey told her. "They'll return the favor."

THIRTY-SEVEN

☐

"We'll hole up here for tonight to see if they react," McGarvey said, when they got back to his apartment. The Russians had pushed, and he and Pete had pushed back, hard. But it was far from over.

"We'll take turns standing watch," Pete said from the kitchenette, where she'd gotten a couple of beers from the fridge. "Do you think they will?"

"Guaranteed."

"Leaves us with a number of problems that we're either going to have to solve or sidestep," Pete said, bringing a beer to where he stood at the front window.

"The first of which is Otto," McGarvey said. "And I'm afraid of what he might do."

"Screw up the SVR's computer systems?"

"At least that. There'll be political consequences."

"No different than you challenging Putin one-on-one."

"What Otto's capable of doing is different. It'll directly involve the Company. We've always had a strictly hands-off policy as far as their headquarters is concerned. We eavesdrop, of course. Everyone does. But we have an under-the-table understanding: we don't screw with your computer systems and you won't screw with ours."

Pete smiled. "He could crash them."

"He could destroy them, which would be considered an act of war."

"Like we and Israel did with Iran's nuclear centrifuge program."

"But Iran doesn't have five thousand–plus nukes to threaten us with," McGarvey said.

"Point," Pete said. She was tired and she looked it.

"Why don't you get some sleep. I'll take the first shift."

She nodded "Give me a couple of hours. But if something starts to develop, call me, I'll leave the door open."

After Pete was gone, McGarvey pulled a chair next to the broken window, where he could not only watch the street but also had a direct sight line to the front door. He placed his pistol on the end table next to the chair, unlocked the door, and sat down.

Sometimes in the middle of the night, in situations like this one, he almost wished that he still smoked cigarettes. But he'd begun to lose his wind years ago and had quit cold turkey, one of the better decisions he'd made.

What Otto might do—or probably was already doing—was only one of their problems. Dead bodies and explosions in quiet neighborhoods would attract the serious attention not only of local law enforcement branches but also of the FBI. And it was conceivable that Otto's house was on some watch list, which could tie the events to the CIA. It also was possible that the cabbie who'd taken him and Pete to the safe house would remember their faces, which could lead to another CIA link.

He phoned Otto's number, and Lou answered on the first ring.

"Good evening, Mr. McGarvey. Are you and Pete safe?"

"We're at my apartment in Georgetown. Let me speak with Otto."

"I'm sorry, but that is not possible at the moment."

"Goddamnit, Lou, put him on."

Otto came back. "She's only a computer program, but she does have feelings."

"Where are you and what are you doing?"

"My location is of no consequence, but for the moment I'm seriously fucking with the SVR's mainframe. For now it's just a warning. There's more to come, *kemo sabe*, I shit you not."

"I understand, but you might want to back off a little," McGarvey said.

"I'm sorry, Kirk, but I can't do that. Before Pete jumped in, you and Lou were my only friends in all the world. The Russians killed her."

"Because of me."

"It's payback time," Otto said.

"There'll be blowback, you have to know that. Unintended consequences."

"I'm sure of it. But modulated blowback."

McGarvey was frustrated. When Otto got this way, which wasn't often, nothing could change his mind. "What do you mean?"

"You—or Pete, if your hands are full—will have to go out to Langley and hold the general's hand. They've put Mary Sawyer in my old job. She'll know how to get into a lot of my programs, but you'll have to give her the heads-up."

Sawyer, a woman in her early sixties who'd earned her PhD in computer science at MIT, had been in charge of the Company's Office of Computer Services until last year, when she'd been promoted to the deputy director of Science and Technology. McGarvey remembered her as an extremely intelligent and highly competent woman. But she would be running into a combination buzz saw and house of smoke and mirrors, trying to fill Otto's footsteps.

"What's next?" McGarvey asked.

"I'll be finished here, for all practical purposes, in the next ten or twelve hours."

"And then?"

"I'm getting out of Dodge."

"Badland?" McGarvey asked. In this case, he meant Russia.

"Probably, but first I have a couple of loose ends to tie up."

"You're not a field officer."

"No, but you and Pete are. So go do your thing, my friend, and let me do mine."

Before McGarvey could respond, Otto was gone. When he tried the number again it came up disconnected.

It was after six in the morning when Pete, barefoot, came up behind McGarvey and touched his shoulder. He wasn't asleep, but his mind was far away, back to Switzerland after his first kill, when Katy had given him an ultimatum: her or the CIA.

He'd chosen neither, instead running to Lausanne, where he'd gone reasonably deep, opening a bookshop under an assumed identity. But he'd been inexperienced, and the Swiss federal police had been onto him from the start, assigning one of their young female officers to ingratiate herself with him. CIA officers who had worked in black ops made the Swiss nervous.

But it had come to an end when John Lyman Trotter, an old friend, showed up and asked for his help. Marta had tried to follow him but had been assassinated because of who he was.

Her killing had begun a long string of such events. Every woman he'd ever been close to had been killed. And, at this moment, he was afraid for Pete.

He turned and looked up at her pretty smiling face. "Good morning."

"You were supposed to wake me," she said.

"I had a lot on my mind."

"No doubt. Do you want some breakfast?"

"Sure."

"I'll put on the coffee," she said, and she went into the kitchen.

"You okay?" he asked.

"Guilty that you let me sleep half the night. Nothing's up?"

"I talked to Otto a couple hours ago."

"Did you get him to back down?"

"No."

"I didn't think you would," Pete said. "So what's our plan?"

"We're going to Langley to talk to the general."

Pete chuckled. "It'll be a wonder if he doesn't have us arrested on the spot."

"They have to be warned about what's probably coming their way."

THIRTY-EIGHT

Zimin had stretched out on the broken-down couch in the filthy living room for a couple hours of sleep when Yuryn spoke his name. He came awake immediately.

"What is it?"

"We have trouble," Yuryn said.

Zimin sat up and checked his watch; it was a few minutes after six. "What trouble?"

"Georgi and the others are dead."

"What the fuck are you talking about?"

Yuryn glanced over his shoulder. "Vitali is upstairs right now talking with Moscow, but when he tried to contact Georgi there was no response. I called my people in New York and they picked up some chatter on an FBI tactical channel here in the DC area. There was an explosion in McLean a few hours ago. Three men inside a Tahoe SUV were killed, and a fourth body was found shot to death outside the house."

"McGarvey."

"*Da*. You were right all along. None of us had any real appreciation for what he was capable of."

Petr came downstairs. He stopped at the entry hall doorway. "What kind of an explosion, did they say?" Zimin asked.

"Military grade," Yuryn said, without looking around.

"Semtex," Petr said.

"Yes."

"Our Semtex," Zimin said. "The son of a bitch disarmed it and returned it."

"But how the fuck could he know that our people were waiting for him?"

"Otto Rencke," Zimin said. "None of you had any appreciation for him, either."

"We need to get out while we still can," Petr said.

Burov was there, his encrypted sat phone in hand. He didn't look as sure as he had earlier, and Zimin got a hit of satisfaction. Someone had dressed down the *pizda*. He pushed his way past Petr, came over to the couch, and handed Zimin the phone.

"General Raskopov wants to talk to you."

Zimin took the phone. "Yes, sir."

"Who is there with you besides Burov?"

"Sergei Yuryn and Captain Lukashin."

"Everyone else is dead, including Captain Anosov?" the general asked, barely controlled rage in his voice.

"I'm sorry, sir," Zimin said.

"Place the phone in speaker mode so that I can address everyone."

Zimin did as he was told. "You're on, sir."

"The five unfortunate deaths are not General Zimin's fault, they are mine, for not taking into full account the measure of the people you were sent to eliminate. That lapse ends now."

"General, if I may explain . . ." Yuryn said.

"You may not. For the moment, General Zimin will resume as mission commander. Colonel Burov is being recalled for debriefing, but Major Yuryn will stay in Washington to act as liaison with our New York research bureau. They seem to be the only reliable source of real-time COMINT, in your area as well as in Kansas and New Mexico, where the operation may have to be moved on a moment's notice." COMINT was communications intelligence.

"I object to these orders, General," Burov said. "I have more hard biographical intel on McGarvey and Rencke than anyone else here. I know how those men think."

"You got four of your team members killed."

"Such mistakes will not be made again."

"No, because you are no longer in charge."

"General, this is madness. I was sent here by Vadim Sankov, to act entirely on his authority, because of my knowledge."

Sankov was a high-ranking member of Putin's personal staff and a very strong Kremlin insider, whose position was considered to be even more bulletproof than Raskopov's.

"I spoke with the president thirty minutes ago," the general said. "A formal contract has been drawn on Mr. McGarvey and Mr. Rencke, with no limitations on collateral damage, contingent on the moment-by-moment situation."

"I can help."

"General Zimin, are you armed at this moment?"

"Yes, sir."

"Take out your pistol and shoot the bastard. That's an order."

Zimin was taken by surprise, as were all of them. But he reached for the pistol he'd laid on the coffee table. Burov stepped back and pulled out his own gun, an old but reliable Italian-made Beretta 92f nine-millimeter.

"I'm not going anywhere on your orders, General," Burov said. "I'll wait here for direct word from Mr. Sankov."

"Mr. Burov is pointing a gun at me," Zimin said. "Perhaps Mr. Sankov could help defuse the situation here. Nothing good will come of us fighting amongst ourselves. We have the same objective." He made a show of moving his hand away from the coffee table.

"I'm not going to bother the president or his staff, and neither is the colonel," Raskopov said.

Petr had moved to the side. He drew his Glock and a fired one shot point-blank into the side of Burov's head.

Zimin had anticipated what was about to happen and ducked to the left. Burov's trigger finger reflexively jerked off one shot as his legs folded under him.

The bullet went wide.

Petr reached down and fired an insurance shot into the side of the man's head.

"It's done," Zimin said, recovering. "What should we do with the body?"

"Leave it," the general said. "Unless you've been sloppy, there's no reason for the authorities to come looking there anytime soon. Meanwhile, Sergei can arrange for another safe house for the three of you."

"I can have something within the hour," Yuryn said.

"Are we to stay in place?" Zimin asked.

"I'm sending you a specialist. He should arrive within thirty-six hours. And, yes, you are to make no overt move until he reaches you. Do you understand?"

"What kind of a specialist?"

"An assassin, and I should have sent him with you in the first place," Raskopov said. "It is a mistake I shan't make again."

"How will he know where we are?"

"I'll have a courier waiting for him, at Dulles, I presume," Yuryn said. "If you can supply me with his name and flight information."

"His current work name is August Konev, and a courier will not be necessary. He'll know where to find you."

"Are there any other orders, sir?" Zimin asked.

"Failure is not an option," Raskopov said. "If you do not succeed, there will be consequences for all of us. And that comes directly from the president."

The connection was broken.

Zimin hit the End button and laid the phone on the coffee table. For a long moment no one said a thing. The last twenty-four hours had been nothing short of surreal. And Zimin was sure that things were going to get a hell of a lot worse before the mission was over and done and whoever was left alive could go home.

"There's a homing device on the phone," Yuryn said. He looked shaken up. "If we wanted to disappear, we could take out the SIM card."

"I don't think we have that option now, so we'd better start getting our shit together," Zimin said. "Have either of you ever heard of the man the general is sending us?"

"Not by name," Petr said. "But there have always been rumors at Yasenevo about Zaslon. It's a Spetsnaz special operations group."

"The KGB's old Vympel; the same as the French special action people," Zimin said.

"Killers," Yuryn said.

"*Da*," Petr said. "And damned good."

Ruthless. The word came unbidden to Zimin. And therefore dangerous to anyone and everyone in their immediate vicinity. The question in his mind was why hadn't someone from the special operations group been sent in the first place?

THIRTY-NINE

McGarvey and Pete drove out to CIA headquarters in Langley. The morning was bright, the day promising to be warm and humid. McGarvey had a thousand things on his mind, foremost among them Lou's death. But on equal footing was what was coming next.

Once, a while ago, Otto had threatened to send the Russian intelligence agencies' computer systems back to the Stone Age. That he was capable of causing such damage had never been in any doubt by those who knew him. The real issue would be the aftermath. What would the Russians do in response to such a massive cyber attack?

It was something that the admiral would have to prepare for. But first he had to understand what was at stake, and he would have to explain it to Burton Webb, the director of national intelligence, and both of them would have to lay it out in clearly defined terms for the president.

McGarvey had called ahead so that their visitors passes would be waiting for them at the main gate.

"Welcome back, Mr. Director," said the security officer who came out to give them their passes and parking permit. He was an older man, and McGarvey remembered him. His name tag read "Anderson."

"Maggie . . . your daughter . . . did she graduate?"

Anderson grinned. "Stetson, in Florida, eight years ago. In fact she's at the Farm, in training, now." Stetson was a law school, and a lot of CIA recruits were newly graduated lawyers, the same as for the FBI. The law, both domestic and international, was complex.

"How's she doing?"

"Seems to be happy," Anderson said. "Thanks for remembering."

"I'll put in a good word for her if I get a chance."

"Yes, sir."

As they drove up to the Original Headquarters Building, Pete reached out and touched his cheek. "You're a good man."

"You're prejudiced."

"Yes, I am."

An aide was waiting for them in the VIP garage, and he took them up to the seventh floor and down to the director's conference room. The broad corridor was quiet, as it usually was, but McGarvey was happy to see that Admiral Taft had kept the tradition that Walt Page had reinstated, keeping all the doors on this floor open when he was in residence.

McGarvey had asked that Mary Sawyer be present, and she was seated at the table along with Taft, his deputy director, Jim Miller, and the Company's general counsel, Carleton Patterson, who was an old friend.

"I'd hoped that Mr. Rencke would be with you," Taft said, waving them to chairs across the table.

"We don't know where he is, and that's one of the reasons we're here," McGarvey said.

Taft nodded to Mary.

"Nice to see you again, Mr. Director," she said. "I've been fully briefed on the situation, including your investigation into the deaths of your parents, and Louise Horn's unfortunate death. I'm also familiar with Mr. Rencke's work, especially the design of the AI systems that he calls his darlings, along with the means by which he's been talking to us . . . to me."

This was a surprise. "By phone?"

Mary hid a slight smile. "No, sir. But he's left tracks in the sand for us. It's called discrepancy accounting, the same thing that the guys who hacked the mainframe at Lawrence Livermore left behind. Except they didn't do it on purpose; that was a mistake."

"Explain that, please," Taft said.

"It was years ago, but the computer folks at the labs noticed that, every month, the payroll was off by something like a buck and a half or so. It wouldn't have mattered much, except that the same computers that did payroll were also used for classified science. Someone was ranging around inside the mainframe, inadvertently leaving the one small mistake behind. When it all came out, the hack was tracked to a group in Amsterdam. Mystery solved."

"And in our case?" Taft asked.

"It's our commissary account," Mary said. "A couple of times a day for the past two days, Mr. Rencke has ordered pizzas to be delivered. The orders don't actually go through, but the charges are billed to his account and are never paid."

Taft was frustrated. "The point being?"

"He's hungry, and he's telling us no one is getting paid until he has his fill," McGarvey said.

"Or something like that," Mary interjected. "But the delivery address isn't his address; it's a zip code: 103073."

"Too many numbers," Taft said, but McGarvey got it, and he had to chuckle, though the joke wasn't funny.

"It's not a U.S. zip code. It's for the Kremlin, in Moscow."

Taft was rocked. "The crazy son of a bitch isn't there already, is he?"

"I don't think so."

"Not yet," Patterson said softly. He was an old man, in his early eighties, and had been with the CIA as its general counsel for a very long time—through at least six DCIs. He'd come down from a prestigious New York law firm when Mac was a fairly young field officer, and no succeeding director had thought it wise to fire him. He knew just about everyone and everything going on in the Company, including its history over the past twenty-plus years, even though he'd never trained as an intelligence officer.

"If he can sabotage the SVR's mainframe, there'd be no need for him to take the risk," Sawyer said.

"Nonetheless, he'll go," Patterson said, turning to McGarvey, his left eyebrow rising.

"He's going to stick it to them," McGarvey said.

Sawyer was agitated. "It makes no sense," she said.

"He doesn't care about his safety, now that his wife is gone," Pete interjected.

"There's Audie," Patterson said.

Audrey, going on three, was McGarvey's granddaughter. Her parents, both CIA officers, had been killed, and Otto and Louise had adopted the girl. She had been heaven and earth to the two of them, and whenever trouble was brewing they sent her down to the Farm for safekeeping, where she was right now. The staff and recruits doted on the little girl and had even made a set of trainee's fatigues for her.

"It's the only card we have left to play," McGarvey said. He took out his phone and dialed Otto's number.

"We're shielded in here," Taft said, but Patterson gestured him off.

McGarvey put the phone on speaker mode and laid it on the table. Lou answered on the first ring.

"Good morning, Mr. McGarvey."

"I'm here in the admiral's conference room and we have something for Otto."

"Yes. Good morning, Pete, Mr. Director, Mr. Patterson, and I assume Ms. Sawyer."

"Good morning," Mary Sawyer said. "We have a question for Mr. Rencke."

"I'm sorry, but he is not available."

"Please tell him that I solved his deficit spending clue and that we think it is inadvisable for him to travel to Moscow at this time," Sawyer said.

"I'm sorry, but he is not available at this time."

"I expect that he had to order pizzas because the commissary does not carry Twinkies."

Twinkies and heavy cream had always been Otto's default snack when he was under stress. McGarvey was surprised that Mary knew about it.

"Wouldn't have mattered," Otto came on. "Lou all but broke me of the habit."

"Good morning," Pete said. "How are you holding up?"

"Tolerable. How about you guys?"

"After last night, pretty good," McGarvey said. "But we're starting to worry about you. Audie's missing you."

"The feeling is mutual, *kemo sabe*. But Putin's people are pulling out all the guns to take down the three of us."

"We know that."

"Have the Bureau or somebody check out the safe house the Russians were using. They might have gotten sloppy and left something, or some-one, behind. You guys might wanna start counting the bodies."

"Mr. Rencke, Admiral Taft here. I'd like you to come in. Might be better if we put our heads together and worked the problem as a team."

"I'm a loner, Admiral, always have been. But thanks for the offer."

"When are you leaving for badland?" McGarvey asked. "Maybe I'll tag along."

"As I said, I'm a loner, Mac. We both are. But first I have a couple of rounds of Twenty Questions to play. Ta-ta."

The line went dead. "He's gone," Mac said, shutting off the phone.

"Where?" Taft asked, but McGarvey could see that at least Patterson knew what Otto's next moves would be.

FORTY

Russian President Vladimir Putin's Ilyushin II-96–300PU touched down at Vladivostok's International Airport at eight in the morning, local. The sky was overcast, the weather blustery, but the pilot's landing was perfection. Lined up at the end of the VIP taxiway were Mayor Kiril Diakanov and Admiral Leonid Gresko, the boss of the Pacific Fleet, along with both men's entourages, the navy band, and two hundred carefully vetted spectators—most of them city officials and naval officers in civilian dress.

Vadim Sankov came back to where Putin was seated amidships. He was of medium height, with an athletic build and an oval, almost Western European face. He had been the president's gym buddy for years and was a multibillionaire from controlling interests in several Russian companies, including two pharmaceutical corporations. "The situation in Washington has developed overnight," he said in the president's ear.

Putin motioned for him to sit down. "Tell me."

"The body count has already reached eight. In addition to the retired Department of Energy officer and the wife of the computer expert who has made an attack on the SVR's mainframe, Raskopov has lost the woman he sent with General Zimin."

"How?"

"The wife of Mr. McGarvey shot her to death in a gun battle at the DOE officer's home outside Washington."

"I know this, but have the police or Bureau made any progress identifying our officer?"

"To my knowledge, no."

"Continue."

"The Spetsnaz team I sent to take over from General Zimin apparently planted explosives on the door of an apartment in Georgetown that McGarvey uses while he is in Washington. From what we're able to piece together, McGarvey evidently discovered the explosives, disarmed them, and placed them on the garage door of the safe house in McLean that Mr. Rencke owns."

Putin gestured for Sankov to stop. "Save me the rest," he said, his tone arid. "The team went to McLean to ambush McGarvey, but instead they were murdered with their own booby trap. I think Shakespeare's phrase was 'hoisted with their own petard.'"

"Yes, sir."

"That's seven dead—all but two ours. Who is the eighth?"

"Vitali Burov, the team leader."

"How?"

"Captain Lukashin shot him to death," Sankov said. "On Raskopov's direct order."

Putin's jaw tightened, but he looked out the window as they approached the formation.

A young woman in uniform came back. "Pardon me, Mr. President, but we are ready for you," she said.

"Not yet."

"Sir?"

Putin looked up at her, obviously hiding his short temper. He smiled. "Tell the captain that there will be a short delay. I'll let him know when."

"Yes, sir."

Putin had been seated alone at landing, but the few aides within earshot had gotten up and moved forward. "Raskopov again."

"Yes, Mr. President. We talked about him last month."

"And?"

"It looks as if he may be using this situation to make his move."

Putin looked out his window at Admiral Gresko and the others as the aide hurried across the tarmac and said something to the admiral and mayor. They looked toward the aircraft's windows. Putin lowered the shade.

"Get me Raskopov on the phone," he said.

Sankov used the phone in the armrest and called the general's private number at Yasenevo.

Raskopov, like some other intelligence chiefs in the past, had tasted his nearly unlimited power, which fueled the urge for more. The most famous was Yuri Andropov, who'd headed the KGB before he became the general secretary of the Communist Party in the early eighties. He died shortly after taking office, which had been a blessing for the country, because his rule would have been so autocratic that the police state he was beginning to create would have been among the worst in modern Russian history.

Without a doubt in Putin's mind, if Raskopov were able to take over as president, he would be a hundred times worse than Andropov could have been.

Sankov held a hand over the phone. "He's not in his office, and he's not answering his personal phone."

"Get Aleksandr Petrovich." The man was chief of Kremlin security. Sankov had him on the phone almost immediately.

Putin picked up the handset in his armrest. "An issue may be developing. What is your state of readiness?"

"Routine, Mr. President. Nothing presently is on my threat board."

"I'm declaring a condition level one."

Petrovich was impressed. "Are we to keep someone from getting out, or someone from getting inside?"

"General Raskopov may have instituted Crystal Storm. I want all hands on deck immediately."

Crystal Storm was the code name of a top secret plan to take over the government if certain conditions were met, such as clear evidence that the president had become mentally unbalanced, or if the president was about to order the launch of nuclear weapons against the United States.

Raskopov had not created the plan but had inherited it from SVR and earlier KGB chiefs. It dated back to the era of Gorbachev, whom Russians thought had gone insane and was about to hand the Soviet Union over to the enemy.

"A coup, Mr. President?"

"We cannot discount the possibility, do you understand me?"

"Perfectly."

"I'm on the ground now, but still in my aircraft. I'll come back to Moscow immediately."

"Pardon me, sir, but if we do come under attack, it would be best if you were not here. In fact, I will call up a contingent of marine commandos to come immediately to the airport for your safety." The navy special forces were a unit of the Spetsnaz whose loyalty was firmly to the navy.

"Very well, but low key. I want a clamp put on the media here and in Moscow."

"Of course, Mr. President," Petrovich said. "What about General Raskopov? Shall I send someone to his office?"

"He may not be there."

"Is it possible that he's en route to us?"

"No. I expect that if he has ordered Crystal Storm he will have gone to his dacha."

"Then a coup may in fact not be in progress?"

"That's right. But we must be prepared."

"I understand, Mr. President. I will send a messenger to the general's dacha, asking for more data concerning his request for increased funding for the deep cover training program."

Putin had used such tricks—withholding funding as a carrot on a stick—as a quid pro quo for something he wanted.

"Very well," Putin said. He put the phone down. "Send word, with my apologies, that I will be delayed five more minutes."

"Yes, sir," Sankov said, rising. "Has anything begun in Moscow?"

"Apparently, not yet."

Sankov went forward, leaving Putin to consider what he was beginning to think of as an even more urgent problem than a possible coup d'état.

Not long ago, he'd given McGarvey his freedom, after a particularly nasty bit of work by terrorists in Paris somehow ended up in a trade for the former CIA director. The business never had Putin's approval—there were far too many possible unintended consequences, none of them very good for Russia. He'd had no other choice but to send the man home.

But now the *pizda* had actually threatened the president of a sovereign nation. No matter the man's reasons, such a threat could not be left unanswered. Yet, he had to admire the bastard, not only for his abilities but also for his balls.

FORTY-ONE

□

Sam Pickering waited for his wife, Chance, at the baggage pickup area at Kansas City International Airport. In was noon, and her flight from Paris through Atlanta was on time. Although the mystery call he'd received last night had festered in his gut, he had been afraid to reach her cell phone.

As soon as she came around the corner, towing her luggage, she got a good look at her husband's face and her smile immediately faded.

"Good flight?" he asked, pecking her on the cheek.

They'd been married for thirty-five years, and once they'd been released from service, ten years ago, they'd remained in KC as caretakers, flying out to the ranch in Garden City once a year.

"Tolerable, but it's better to be home," she said.

They were both on the short and chunky side and had never fit the style of California, where they'd met at UCLA and where they had been recruited by the KGB. His cover was at Grollier Pharmaceutical, where he'd sent his coded reports via intercompany memos to NovaMedika in Moscow. His last report was three months ago, and his orders had been strict from the beginning: only break routine in case of an emergency.

But the call last night was impossible to classify, though it was so totally out of the routine that nothing like it had ever happened since they'd been recruited.

Outside, they went around to the parking garage, where he'd left their Mercedes E-Class four door, but he didn't say anything about the call and she didn't press him. Although he worked for Grollier and she taught at a community college, she'd always been the brains of their partnership. Her double majors had been languages, including

English, French, and German, and political science, specializing in U.S. politics.

Since the presidential election, she'd been working on a book, in French, about the standoff between Weaver and Putin over Russian meddling. It was supposedly an insider's view that proved no such interference ever occurred. Her pen name was Marie Clairmont, and in the book she hinted that she worked for French intelligence and that she had to hide her real identity for fear of arrest and possible deportation to the United States to answer questions in the Senate.

Once they'd paid the one-day parking fee and were on their way, Pickering glanced at her. "We may have some trouble coming our way."

"Because of the book?" she asked.

"No. I got a call on our encrypted sat phone last night from Klimov."

"Igor? I thought the bastard was retired or dead by now. What'd he want?"

"He is dead, but it was his younger brother, Vasili, who called, said that we needed to have a meeting."

Chance shook her head. "Can't be about the McGarveys. It has to be about the book. And I sure as hell am not returning to Moscow."

"He didn't say anything about the book, but he's on the way to the ranch, and he wants to see us there."

Chance wasn't buying it. There was a look of skepticism in her narrowed eyes. "How'd he get our number?"

"No idea."

"This is not good, Sam, I can feel it in my guts. Maybe we ought to pull the pin and go deep."

They had a cottage at a small beach hotel on the French island of Martinique in the Caribbean. As with the ranch, they were mostly absentee former owners of the hotel, but in Martinique they were expats from Algeria. From time to time they would fly down, taking care with their tradecraft so that they were absolutely certain they'd not been followed.

They also maintained bank accounts on the island, plus several more substantial but untraceable accounts at several offshore banks in Dubai, Tobago, and Guernsey. It was money they'd squirreled away over the years for the possibility that they would have to disappear.

"First we need to find out what Klimov wants."

"I say we disappear right now."

"It's too late for that."

"What are you talking about?" Chance asked sharply.

"He had our account number at BNP." BNP Paribus Martinique was their bank on the island.

Chance looked away for the moment, her lips tightly compressed. "When does he want to meet?"

"This afternoon. I booked the King Air out of Downtown Airport, so we'll be there before two."

"Did you call ahead for a rental car?"

"Yes."

She hesitated a moment longer. "Are you armed?"

Pickering nodded. "I thought it would be for the best," he said. "I brought your pistol as well."

Chance looked her husband in the eye. "Then we shall see what we shall see."

Otto had flown commercial from Baltimore to Denver and from there had rented a four-wheel-drive Ford Explorer, using two different identities. By a couple of minutes after one he was crossing the border into Kansas, about sixty miles from the ranch.

McGarvey and Pete waited in Lou's BMW, across the street from the Russian safe house. A team of two CIA officers and a pair of FBI agents, guns drawn, stood behind a Capital City Florist's van directly in front as a third Bureau agent in coveralls, a box of roses in hand, rang the doorbell. Inside the flower box was an H&K compact submachine gun.

When no one came to the door, the agent rang the bell again.

There was no traffic on the street, nor was anyone out and about. The neighborhood could have been a ghost town.

Mac and Pete had been ordered to hold back until the house was cleared.

"Our scene, our call, Mr. Director," the Bureau's special agent in charge, the SAC, had said.

"They're probably gone, but take care. These people are professionals, and very motivated," McGarvey had warned.

"Yes, sir."

The agent at the door took out a cell phone–size device with his free hand and ran it along the door frame. It was a bomb-grade materials sniffer, more accurate than a trained dog. When he was finished he shook his head, pocketed the sniffer, and tried the door, which opened inward.

He pulled the H&K from the flower box. At the same time, the four officers behind the van rushed across the sidewalk, up the stairs, and into the house, right behind the agent in the coveralls.

"They've got balls," Pete muttered.

"So do you," McGarvey said, and she had to chuckle.

After ninety seconds, the SAC appeared at the door and signaled it was all clear.

"Otto told us that they would be gone," Pete said. "I wonder if they left any bodies behind."

McGarvey got on the phone with Otto's number, but Lou didn't answer even after six rings. "Where the hell are you?" he said into the dead phone.

FORTY-TWO

□

Otto got off the highway and started down the road to the bison preserve. Mac had told him years ago about this back way onto the ranch,
how he used to sneak into town and back again in the middle of the
night without his parents or sister knowing about it.

"Early training as a spy," he'd laughed.

It was early evening and they were at a sidewalk café in Paris, on the
Left Bank, where the narrow streets were filled with summer tourists.
"Your parents probably knew."

"Because my sister was such a snitch. But they never set limits on
me, not even after the thing with the football players, when just about
every football fan in town—which included every dad and most of the
mothers—wanted me lynched."

Today, the western Kansas afternoon was dusty, with a light wind and
no one in sight in any direction.

"Good afternoon, darling," Lou said.

"Good afternoon. Do you have something for me?"

"One body was found at the safe house. Shot in the head at point-
blank range."

"Does Mac know?"

"Yes. He tried to call but I did not put him through."

The news wasn't unexpected. "Has the body been identified?"

"No, and the house was apparently swept. But according to the SAC's
on-site report, the body was apparently Eastern European—possibly even
Russian."

"What is your confidence level?"

"Unable to judge on such limited data," Lou said. "But as soon as the Bureau's forensics team makes its report, I may be able to produce an evaluation."

Otto came to the dirt road that headed north onto the ranch. In the distance he could see the top of a windmill, and beyond it what could be the roof of a house or barn.

"Let me talk to Mac."

"His phone has been switched off," Lou said after a moment.

"Is the device intact?"

"Yes."

"What is its location?"

"On the third floor of the J. Edgar Hoover Building on Tenth Street Northwest."

"Activate his phone, but don't let it ring. I want to hear any background noises."

"Yes, dear," Lou said.

"The phone has been turned on," a man said.

"Go ahead and answer it," another man spoke.

"Hello," McGarvey said. "Are you safe?"

"Yes," Otto said. "What's your situation?"

"I'm being interviewed on a possible obstruction of justice charge. Evidently, Weaver made a call."

"Pete?"

"No."

"Who am I speaking with?" the second man asked.

"Your worst fucking nightmare, unless you get your head out of your ass and realize that we're trying to help solve a big problem coming your way."

"And what problem might that be, Mr. Rencke? According to your boss, you and your partner are merely on a quest for revenge. Or isn't that the case?"

"It's much more than that, believe me."

"I'll try, if you would care to come in and explain it."

"I doubt if you'd understand until after we clear it up."

"We know that your wife was gunned down, and you have my

condolences, but that is a Bureau issue. And on top of that, you aren't even working under the sanction of the CIA. Your own director calls you and Mr. McGarvey rogue operators."

Otto laughed. "We've been called worse," he said. "Have you been allowed to get in touch with Carleton?"

"He's on his way," McGarvey said.

"Hang in there," Otto said. The glint of sunlight on metal or glass appeared in the direction of what now was clearly a house. "Got to go. I think my company has shown up."

"Goddamnit—" McGarvey said, but Lou cut off the call.

Otto took the dirt track to the north that led in the direction of the house. There'd been no time to ask anything else about Pete. But if she was somewhere out in Washington—or worse, back at her apartment in Georgetown—Mac would move heaven and earth to get to her, even though she was a trained and highly capable field officer in her own right. Losing her would be nothing short of devastating for Mac. Otto fully understood the pain that his friend had endured all this time, since losing his wife, daughter, and son-in-law, and he didn't want it to happen again. There was no predicting what Mac might do if something happened to Pete.

A pickup truck came down the dirt track and Otto pulled up and powered his window down as the truck stopped even with him.

A Hispanic man with a deeply creased and leathered face, a sweat-stained cowboy hat on his head, said, "You are the guest of the Pickerings, señor?"

"Yes," Otto said, in a Russian accent.

"They have just arrived. Follow me, please."

The ranch hand drove around behind Otto's car, made a U-turn, and headed back up to the house, Otto right behind him.

There was nothing to be found out here, this long after John's and Lilly's deaths—no hidden treasure or messages of any sort. And certainly no papers of any scientific nature. A crew from LANL had gone over the entire property looking for things like that. The after-action report he'd managed to get from the lab's security division had been brief and precise: no documents found.

John and Lilly had planned to spend a quiet weekend at the ranch and then return to work after the holiday. They'd made a scientific breakthrough and had expected to finish with the follow-ups and then, Otto was certain, throw a celebration party.

The Bureau's final report included a detailed inventory of everything on the ranch, especially everything in the main house. Among the items found was a case of Dom Pérignon. Party time.

This meeting with the Pickerings was nothing more than Otto's second shot after hacking the SVR's mainframe.

"I'm coming for you bastards, so hang on to your derrieres."

A Jeep Wrangler was parked in front of the house, and when Otto drove up, a man of about medium height but with a thick frame and square face came out the front door and waved the ranch hand off.

Otto got out of his car and walked up to the porch as the ranch hand drove off.

"Who the hell are you and what the fuck do you want?" Pickering demanded.

"You know exactly what I want, you pussy," Otto said in Russian.

Pickering backed up half a step. "I don't know what you're talking about," Pickering said, still in English.

"You have finally managed to bungle the one simple assignment you and your wife were given."

Pickering's wife came to the door. "What assignment would that be?" she asked. She spoke flawless English, just like her husband.

"To do nothing more than act as caretakers until your recall."

"We've done just that," she said.

"But the CIA and the FBI are now investigating the murders of the two scientists who lived here."

"None of our doing."

"General Raskopov believes otherwise, as do I," Otto said. "You will leave for Moscow immediately. The travel arrangements have already been made. I have your new papers here."

He pulled out the Glock just as the woman reached for something beneath her jacket, at the small of her back.

Otto shot her twice, and before she collapsed backward into the stair hall, he switched his aim to Pickering, who backed up, his hands spread wide.

"We can work out something," the man said. "We're not who you think we are."

"But you understand Russian, and you fucked with the wrong people," Otto said, and shot him twice in the chest.

FORTY-THREE

Carleton Patterson and a very young, strapping White House administrative assistant by the name of Joseph Miner, who looked like he lifted weights, arrived at the same time and were brought up to the conference room where McGarvey was being interviewed.

The two of them sat at the opposite end of the table from the FBI agents, Sam Goldfield and Tom Hansen, with McGarvey between them.

"How are you doing, my boy?" Patterson asked.

"Are you here representing the CIA?" Hansen asked.

"I'm here as the attorney of record for Mr. McGarvey. What is he being charged with?"

"Nothing, at this point."

"Then if you will excuse us, we'll leave," Patterson said, starting to rise.

"He may be charged with obstruction of justice," Hansen said.

"When such a charge has been filed, my client will surrender himself."

Miner rapped a knuckle on the table. "This has got the attention of the president."

Patterson smiled faintly. "I would think that the gentleman has enough trouble as it is without stirring up more."

"You don't understand."

"No, I do not. Explain to me, please. In simple terms."

Miner looked at the two Bureau agents, but they said nothing.

"President Weaver received a telephone call from President Putin earlier today. I was not told the entire content of their conversation, only that it concerned a threat from Mr. McGarvey."

"What threat?"

"I wasn't told, except that Mr. Putin took it very seriously."

Carleton turned to McGarvey. "Did you threaten the Russian president?"

"I told him that if he wanted a war, I would give him a war."

"Were those your exact words?"

"I said that if he wanted a war, I would give him a *fucking* war."

Carleton shrugged. "A bold move, threatening the might of an entire nation."

Miner started to say something, but Patterson held him off with a gesture.

"Did you offer Mr. Putin any physical harm, perhaps assassination?"

"No," McGarvey said.

Patterson turned to the others. "If there is nothing else, gentlemen, we'll be gone."

"Impossible," Miner blustered, but Hansen shut the file folder in front of him on the table.

"We'll ask that Mr. McGarvey make himself available at some future date for another interview," he said.

Patterson laid his business card on the table. "All further contacts will be made through me."

"To your office at Langley?" Hansen asked.

"No, my office here in the District."

Miner was flustered. "What about the president?"

"Wish him well."

"He'll want to know what is being done."

"About what, Mr. Miner?" Patterson asked.

"I think he means about my war," McGarvey said, and Patterson shot him a dirty look.

"This won't simply be swept under the table. McGarvey has already built an unfavorable history with the White House. He and the woman—"

McGarvey cut him off. "If you are talking about my wife, take care. I'm a bit short-tempered at the moment."

It was obvious to everyone at the table that Miner was only a bit player who'd been thrown under the bus by a president who knew very well what McGarvey's attitude and response would be. But he also was a president who knew how the game of power plays was conducted and was himself a master at it. The FBI and Miner were only the opening shots. In front of the media, Weaver and Putin were the heads of two states in the midst of a new Cold War, who cooperated with each other for the sake of world security. In reality, they were bitter enemies, each seeking to derail the other in any way possible. Putin wanted Weaver to fall on his ass, and Weaver wanted the Russian leader to be put up against a wall somewhere in Siberia and shot.

At this moment, the real message that Miner had been sent to give was that the president was here to help McGarvey win his war with Putin in any way possible, while appearing to condemn the threat.

Pete sat at the repaired front window in her husband's Georgetown apartment, waiting for him to come to her. After the body had been found in the Russian safe house, Mac had sent her back here, the last place they thought the Russians would look, while he went downtown with the FBI.

She was worried sick about him, as she expected he was about her. He'd started to unearth the real reasons his parents had been killed, and the Russians had struck back. He had returned the blow a hundredfold, especially by challenging Putin.

"What do you hope to gain?" she'd asked, as they waited for the Bureau agents to go into the safe house.

"Just what's already happening," he'd told her. "If it wasn't still important to them, they wouldn't have tried to hit back. They would have left me alone."

"*Us* alone," she'd corrected.

McGarvey had brushed a finger across her cheek. "It wasn't your fault."

She'd teared up. "I don't know how I'll face Otto when this is over."

"He doesn't blame you."

She'd looked at him. "If it were the other way around, if it had been me who'd been shot to death, wouldn't you have blamed Lou?"

"I would have blamed the guy who shot you, and taken care of him and his partners. Which has happened, for Lou's sake."

"Now what?"

"We wait for their next move."

"And Otto's still out there," Pete had said, real fear in her gut.

Outside, on the busy street in front of FBI headquarters, Patterson stepped to the curb. "I'm going to take a taxi back out to Langley. Howard will want an update."

"Is he still after my ass?" McGarvey asked.

"On the contrary, he's going to give you all the backing he can—but at arm's length. It was he who sent me here."

"Thank him."

"No need. Miner or some other little prick like him will be calling him," Patterson said. He stuck out a hand for a cab, which angled through traffic toward him. "Can I give you a lift to wherever you deposited Pete?"

"No, thanks. I don't want you to get more involved than you already are. This is going to get even uglier real soon. I don't want you to have to lie for me."

Patterson chuckled. "But my dear boy, I've been doing that ever since we met. It's what we lawyers are best at."

The cab came and Mac opened the door for his old friend.

"Do you have any idea where Otto has gotten himself to?" Patterson asked, before he got in.

"A couple of ideas, but none of them very comforting."

"When you asked him about badland, did you mean Russia? Him physically going there?"

"I'm pretty sure."

"Is he already on the way?"

"I don't think so, but I expect it'll be soon, and I'll have to go fetch him."

Patterson smiled wanly, as only an old man can. "All you people are nuts. You do know that, don't you?"

"The way the game's played."

"Truth, justice, and the American way? Superman's motto?"

"Yeah," McGarvey said, matching Patterson's mood. He feared not only for Otto but also for Pete.

FORTY-FOUR

☐

McGarvey walked around the corner and then down Pennsylvania Avenue to the Navy Memorial. Traffic on the streets and sidewalks was heavy as usual for this time of day midweek.

They had taken his phone and gun and had not given them back until he and Carleton had gotten up to leave.

Making absolutely certain he wasn't being followed, either by the Bureau or possibly by the Russians, who he was sure had mounted or were in the process of mounting a full-court press on him—and therefore on Pete, and certainly Otto—he took the SIM card out of his phone and tossed it into a waste bin at the corner.

Then, catching a cab up to Union Station, he took the battery out of the phone, powered the window down a couple of inches, and tossed the battery out just before they turned onto Constitution Avenue. The phone went next, on Louisiana.

Inside the station, he bought a burner phone and activated it. Back outside, before catching a cab over to his apartment, he called Pete. Long ago, Otto had installed antibugging equipment on the landline in his apartment, so he knew that it was secure.

"Hello?" she answered cautiously.

It was the sweetest thing he'd ever heard her say to him; his relief was palpable. She was alive. It was enough. "What's up?" he asked, keeping his voice light. He had a very full plate just now, with Otto out there somewhere and Pete right here in the middle of the shitstorm.

"They didn't give you the electric chair after all. That's a relief."

"You okay?"

"Peachy. Where are you?"

"On my way. We'll talk then."

He got aboard a Gray Line tour bus that was getting ready to leave, paid the driver, and took the first seat back, where he could look at the reflection in the outside mirror. All standard tradecraft, which the new recruits at the Farm were trained in.

"Even the simplest, most obvious bit of looking over your shoulder could save your life in the field," the instructors had drilled. "Never forget it."

The driver stopped in front of the Senate Office Buildings, where a couple of people got off, then pulled up just behind another Gray Line bus across from the Capitol, between the Supreme Court and the Library of Congress's Thomas Jefferson Building, his running commentary old stuff to locals but fascinating to the tourists.

McGarvey got off with a dozen other passengers, then walked a couple of blocks around the corner to the House Office Buildings, where he got a cab when he was absolutely certain he was clean.

He gave the driver an address in Georgetown, on N Street Northwest, a couple of blocks from his apartment, then sat back.

Careful to keep what he was doing low enough to be out of the driver's view, he took out his gun, checked to make sure that it hadn't been tampered with, and then loaded the pistol and cycled a round into the chamber before he holstered it and the spare mag.

It was nearly four by the time the cabbie dropped him off. He waited until the cab had turned the corner before he walked up to his building just across from Rock Creek Park, but he passed by without looking up at the window. At the corner, he phoned.

"You're clean," she said.

"Let's give it a few minutes. I'm going to take my time going around the block."

"Any signs on the way over?"

"None. And if it's still clean when I get there, I'll need a beer."

"Been a long day."

"For both of us," McGarvey said.

"There's a couple of cold Heinies in the fridge."

"We'll need to talk."

"You bet. Any word from Otto?"

"No. You?"

"No," Pete said. "Street's still clean."

"See you in a bit," he said, and he hung up.

McGarvey stopped at the corner as a motorcycle passed and turned left, probably headed to O Street, or to P and under the bridge across Rock Creek. For the moment, there was no other traffic. The afternoon was almost unnaturally still.

Someone was coming. He could feel the vibrations deep inside his chest. It was exactly what he wanted, except that once again a woman that he was in love with was in harm's way.

He phoned Pete. "I'm at the corner. How's it look to you?"

"Clear," Pete said. "But someone or something is coming our way. I can feel it."

"You're right."

"Lou, the Semtex on your door, McLean, the body in their safe house. Christ, how much more can there be?"

"We're just getting started."

"But Mac, why? What do they want? Why kill us? For what we know?"

"What they're afraid we're going to find out."

"What?" she practically screeched. "It's been nearly thirty goddamn years since they killed your parents. The technology is obsolete."

McGarvey had a glimmer. "Maybe the technology is obsolete, but how'd they find out in the first place? Supposedly my parents had made or were about to make some breakthrough, and they were assassinated because of it."

"Spies."

"At Los Alamos. But they would have to have been pretty smart to understand what was going on."

"The Russians aren't any dumber than we are."

"I mean, it had to have been someone who knew my mom and dad. Someone my folks trusted."

"Bob Wehr?" Pete asked.

"He's a start."

McGarvey let himself into the building and was just starting up the stairs when the street door opened. He pulled out his gun as he spun around.

Dianna from the apartment below his didn't spot him until she was all the way in, and then she stopped in her tracks, caught in the headlights. "Holy cow," she said.

"Sorry," McGarvey said, holstering his pistol.

She was carrying two bags of groceries, and he went down and took one of them from her.

"Are we okay here?" she asked.

McGarvey was about to say that she was, but he inclined his head, his lips compressed just a little. "Someone's after me and my wife, but no one else here."

"What about the police?"

"They'd want proof."

She looked up into his eyes. "What do you think, Mr. McGarvey? I'm a little scared."

"You said you had a boyfriend."

"Yeah."

"Maybe you ought to pack a bag and spend the next couple of days with him."

She smiled shyly. "He'd love that."

"Might be for the best."

Pete was waiting for him on the landing, her eyes wide when he came into view. She came into his arms. "I was frightened that I'd never see you again."

"Me too."

FORTY-FIVE

Yuryn had arranged for a safe house in a brownstone apartment building not far from the ones they'd first used near the university. They'd only been there for one hour, but Petr had kept a lookout from a second-floor window.

"We're not far from McGarvey's place and the separate apartment that his wife still maintains," Zimin had said. "Convenient."

"Foolish, perhaps." Yuryn had disagreed, but with caution now, after the disasters in McLean and the safe house.

"It's the last place they'll expect us to be."

Yuryn had wanted to ask why, but he didn't say it. "The question is, how the hell is Konev going to find us? Aren't we supposed to meet him at the airport?"

Zimin held up his cell phone. "He'll find us."

"*Yeb vas*," Yuryn said. "And the Americans will find us too?"

"I was told not."

"The dead woman's computer expert husband might find a way."

"Which is why I'm standing lookout," Petr said. "And you're next, unless you want to return to New York. It's safer there, at least for now, until McGarvey decides that you're on his hit list."

"Enough bickering," Zimin said.

The door, which had been locked, opened slowly. A man of medium height and build, his round face devoid of any emotion, stood in the narrow corridor. He wore khaki slacks, a white shirt, and a black blazer. He had a small carry-on bag slung over his left shoulder and a rolling suitcase behind him, on the right.

"Are we ready to begin, gentlemen?" he asked, his English prefect, with a flat Midwestern accent.

Both Zimin and Petr had drawn their pistols. "Who the fuck are you?" Zimin asked.

"For now, August Konev. But I'm here for only a brief time, so either shoot me where I stand or let's begin, shall we?"

Zimin lowered his pistol and motioned for the assassin from Moscow to come in. "You may sleep in the rear bedroom."

Konev came in, closed the door, set his carry-on bag on the floor, and took his suitcase to the couch, where he unzipped it. "I'm here to accomplish my orders and leave as soon as possible. Tonight."

"That won't be possible," Zimin said.

Konev looked up, his eyes deep, almost unnaturally blue. "Why not?"

"We think that Rencke is no longer in Washington."

"Where is he?"

"We're working on it. But we believe that McGarvey and his wife are at one of two apartments nearby. We're not sure which."

"Find out," Konev said. "Which one of you is Yuryn?"

"I am," Yuryn said.

"As soon as we know the McGarveys' location, I will require secure access to a building across the street from them. Money is no object. Nor is the elimination of whoever might stand in your way to achieve this objective. Do you understand?"

"Yes," Yuryn blustered.

Konev stood there for a moment. "Well?"

"Sir?"

"Start now," Konev said. "I want the McGarveys dead in the next few hours." He turned to Zimin. "You're the operational leader?"

"Yes."

"Find Mr. Rencke."

Yuryn telephoned his office in New York, just a few blocks from the UN, and got the station's operational coordinator, Tania Boyko.

"I need a telephone number for Kirk McGarvey."

"In the past, his phones had been heavily encrypted, the number shifting in some pattern Moscow has not been able to unravel."

"*Da*, I understand this. And I'm sure that, in the field, he often uses throwaway cell phones, as our field officers do. But he and his wife have homes in Georgetown. Possibly each with a landline. I would like you to find them."

"They would never use such devices."

Yuryn was starting to get frustrated. The woman was a persnickety old maid, but she knew her business. "They may not have landline phones in their apartments, but if they ever had, I would like the addresses."

"Give me a number where I can call you back."

"Do it now. I'll wait."

Zimin had spent his time here concentrating on the McGarveys, once Otto Rencke had disappeared. He had been given two numbers for on-the-ground fieldwork, one for Yuryn and another outside of Washington and New York.

The second of the two rang three times before a man answered in English.

"Who wants me?"

"This is a follow-up request."

"Yes," the man replied without hesitation.

"I was told that you might have information on a man we are looking for."

"The older, dangerous one or the younger, long-haired one?"

It took a moment for what Zimin had been told to sink in. "The younger one."

"He left site two earlier today and he's currently approaching the Denver airport."

"Is there anything else?"

"Not at the moment, except that he is traveling in disguise, under a work name."

"Don't lose him."

"Don't tell me my job," the man said, and hung up.

Zimin contemplated calling back but decided against it. Either the agent would find out where Rencke was heading or he wouldn't. That much was out of his hands for the moment.

Konev was sitting on the couch, drinking from a liter bottle of water. He looked up with only mild interest.

"Mr. Rencke is currently on his way to the airport in Denver, Colorado," Zimin said.

"From where?"

"Apparently Garden City, Kansas."

"To where?"

"We have a field officer on his tail now."

"Very well," Konev said in dismissal.

Tania Boyko came back on the line. "McGarvey is on Dumbarton and the woman is on N Street Northwest," she said. She gave him the street numbers. "About three blocks apart."

"Anything else?"

"Yes. The woman's number was disconnected two years ago, but McGarvey's number is still active."

"Test it, please," Yuryn said.

"I already have. It was briefly in use, but it is heavily encrypted."

Yuryn was alarmed. "Did you try to call it?"

The woman was indignant. "Of course not. I merely took a sample."

"Could your intrusion have been detected?"

"No," the woman said, but her voice was less certain.

"No, or you think not?" Yuryn demanded, careful to keep his voice neutral.

"Definitely no," Tania said, and she broke the connection.

Yuryn hung up. "They're at McGarvey's apartment," he told Konev. It was just a guess, but he didn't think that a man would live at his wife's place.

"Is there a telephone in that apartment?"

"Yes," Yuryn said, and he gave the address to the assassin.

"I want access to the top-floor space directly across the street, as well as the roof. Take Captain Lukashin. Do it now, but make absolutely no disturbance."

FORTY-SIX

It was early evening when Otto, driving the Ford Explorer, realized that he had picked up a tail. He had noticed the dark blue Camry as he crossed the border from Kansas to Colorado because as it was passing him the driver, a man with gray hair, had looked over. The Camry had showed up again as it had come onto the interstate outside of Pueblo.

And now he'd pulled off I-85, just south of Denver, on the direct route through Aurora to the airport, and saw the same car in his rear-view mirror.

"Lou, have you been watching my six since Garden City?" he said.

"Do you mean the Camry?"

"Yes. I'm not too far from the Westin, and he turned off with me. Three cars back."

Lou had activated the Ford's rear camera, but the image quality was bad in the darkness, and not much better when the car came under a highway light, because the resolution was meant for close range.

"I can't give you any definitive information except to verify that it seems as if whoever is driving will follow you to the hotel."

"Have you made my reservation?"

"Yes, under your Louis Underwood identity."

"Has there been any attempt to hack my phone?" Otto asked, and he almost thought that he had heard his darling chuckle.

"No. In any case, the attempt would be unsuccessful."

"Am I confirmed for Atlanta in the morning?"

"Delta one six one six, first class, departs oh seven twenty-five, arrives Atlanta at twelve twenty-nine, under your Underwood documents."

"Put a hold on my onward flight until I find out if I am being followed and what the son of a bitch wants."

"Yes, dear. Mac has made another attempt to contact you."

"What is his current situation?"

"He and Pete are waiting at his apartment. Presumably for the Russian hit squad to show up. And there has been another possible development that I am currently processing."

"What is that?"

"On your earlier request, I have been monitoring the surveillance cameras at Dulles, Reagan, and Baltimore airports, with facial and body-style recognition filters for all known or suspected Russian operatives, as well as Spetsnaz officers currently assigned to SVR duty."

Otto had designed all of his search engines to be open ended. His darlings would continue any program until he either changed the parameters or called it off.

"Yes, and what have you found?"

"A gentleman whom I have an eighty-seven percent confidence is a Spetsnaz specialist by the name of Nikolai Shalayev showed up at Dulles."

"A specialist in what?"

"Assassinations."

Otto checked his rearview mirror as he passed the sign to the airport via I-70. The Camry was still three cars back. "Where is he now?"

"Unknown. But I first picked him up near the British Airways gate, where a flight from Moscow had landed fifteen minutes earlier."

Anything his darlings rated above a fifty percent level of confidence was good enough for him to be seriously worried. "Have you warned Mac?"

"No. But there may be another consideration."

The next exit west on I-70 was marked "Denver International North." Otto took it, the Camry still behind him.

"What is it?" he asked.

"If the man is the Spetsnaz major, he would have knowledge of the airport surveillance systems."

"Yes?"

"The SVR knows that you hacked its mainframe."

"Continue."

"It is likely to suspect that you also have the facial and body-style recognition programs to identify persons of interests arriving from Europe, and especially from Moscow. But he did not alter his appearance."

"Your conclusion?"

"I have a seventy-two percent confidence that he wanted to make his arrival, and therefore his purpose, known to us."

"Why?"

Lou hesitated for just a fraction of a second, which was extremely unusual. "It is a quintessentially human emotion, one of conflicting purposes. I believe that the man has been sent to assassinate Mac, Pete, and you. His mission should be kept secret as long as possible. But by showing up so openly, and risking identification, he has in effect told us who he is and why he is here."

His darling was right. "Call Mac and tell him what is coming his way."

"I'm doing it now," Lou said. "Do you require assistance?"

"Monitor my phone."

"Be careful, dear."

Pete had heated up some tomato soup and they had it with saltine crackers in the tiny living room, the corridor door ajar so that they could hear someone coming. They had agreed to take separate watches through the night, and Pete had volunteered for the first shift.

"You're half asleep already," McGarvey told her.

"It's been a hell of a couple of days for both of us," she said.

"More to come."

"Yeah."

Mac's encrypted cell phone, which he kept in the apartment, buzzed. He put it in speaker mode. It was Lou.

"Good evening, Mr. McGarvey. Are you and Pete well?"

"Yes. May I speak with Otto?"

"He's engaged at the moment. But he asked me to let you know that a Russian Spetsnaz officer by the name of Nikolai Shalayev, who specializes in wet actions, showed up at Dulles a few hours ago. I have a high confidence that he has been sent here to assassinate you, Pete, and Otto."

"Thank you. Where is he at this moment?"

"Unknown."

"Was he alone?"

"Yes," Lou said. "But he made no effort to hide his face."

"Your conclusion?"

"He wants us to know his purpose."

"Arrogant bastard," McGarvey muttered.

"Many experts are."

McGarvey couldn't help himself, even given the gravity of the situation. "Me included?"

"Yes."

Pete suppressed a chuckle.

"Please ask Otto to call me as soon as possible."

"He knows."

Otto pulled under the porte cochere of the ultramodern Westin Denver International hotel and had the bellman take his bag from the back of the car.

"Checking in, sir?"

"Yes. Underwood," Otto said.

He followed the bellman inside, and at the desk presented his platinum Amex. He was given his room key, and when he turned, no one was there.

FORTY-SEVEN

☐

Pete had just stretched out on the couch to get a couple hours of sleep while McGarvey took the first watch at the window when a cab stopped across the street and two men got out. It was ten o'clock and the after-work traffic was long ended, leaving the street mostly empty.

The cab left and the men mounted the steps. One of them took something out of his pocket and bent down in front of the door.

"Pete," McGarvey said.

"Yes?"

"Could be starting."

She was at his side at the same time the man straightened up, opened the door, and the two of them went inside.

"Do you know them?"

"No, but it doesn't matter. They picked the lock to get in."

"How do you want to play it?"

"We'll sit tight, but when it starts to go down, we need to take one of them alive if possible."

Pete grinned. "I used to be a pretty good interrogator."

"I know," McGarvey said, but something bothered him, and it showed on his face.

Pete picked up on it. "What?" she asked.

"They're looking to take the high ground. But they would need to know that we live here, otherwise there'd be no reason to put someone on the roof."

"Our lights are out. Maybe they think we're not home, or asleep. It'd make sense for their shooter to take us out on the street, either when we came home or left in the morning."

"Maybe," McGarvey said. "Keep watch here for a minute."

"Sure."

McGarvey went back to the bathroom that looked down on the rear service alley and opened the small window. The area was mostly in shadows, and he watched for a full minute for any sign that someone was down there before he closed the window and returned to the living room.

"Someone's on the roof," Pete said. She had moved to the side, out of any clear sight line from across the street.

McGarvey did the same on the other side of the window. But there was nothing to be seen.

"It was just for a split second."

"Both of them?"

"Just one," Pete said. She looked at him.

He went to the phone beside the couch and called Dianna's number. She answered on the first ring. "Tony?"

"It's Mac from upstairs. I thought you were leaving."

"I texted my boyfriend to see if he was at home. But he hasn't answered."

"I want you to get out of there as quickly as possible."

"No shit?" Dianna said. "Have you called the cops?"

"I want you out of here first."

"How about if I come upstairs and wait with you?"

McGarvey didn't want to frighten her. "My wife might object."

Dianna hesitated. "Okay," she said. "I just have to pack a couple of things. But I don't know where to go."

"Clyde's. Either that or a hotel," McGarvey said. Clyde's was a bar on M Street, just a few blocks away.

"I could use a drink. Tony can meet me there."

"Don't wait around."

"I won't. Good luck."

Crouched in the deep shadows behind a Dumpster, Konev had watched McGarvey appear at the small window. Petr and Yuryn showing up across the street had the desired effect. But the former DCI had known enough to suspect that it might be a diversion.

Wearing dark jeans, a dark, long-sleeve pullover, and black Nikes, he hesitated just outside the young woman's door on the second floor. "I won't," she said. "Good luck."

Yuryn had looked up the building's listing on a Georgetown real estate website and had hacked the confidential section, which listed the current owners and tenants' names. McGarvey's apartment was listed under the name of Southern Lives Inc., and this apartment was listed as a rental, the tenant a woman named Dianna Miller.

Konev bent down and used his lock pick set, careful to make almost no noise. If she were a bright girl, she would have thrown the dead bolt, but she'd been careless, and once the lock was defeated, the door was free.

He listened for a full ten seconds, and at one point he thought he heard a noise somewhere deeper inside the apartment. Then a toilet flushed.

Easing the door open, Konev stepped inside, softly closing the door behind him. He turned the dead bolt just as the young woman appeared from the back of the apartment.

She was wearing pajama bottoms but no top, her breasts tight. She stopped, a hand going to her mouth.

Konev took out his pistol, the suppressor large on the muzzle of the Wilson Tactical, and pointed the gun at her.

She started to back up but he shook his head.

"I wish you no harm," he said. "But if you cause a disturbance, I will kill you. Do you understand this?"

It took a long moment for the woman to process what was happening, but at length she nodded.

"Good. Do you know the gentleman in the apartment above you?"

Her eyes lit up, but then she shook her head.

"You are lying. If you lie to me again, I will kill you."

She was very frightened.

"What is the gentleman's name?"

"Mac," the girl said. "Mr. McGarvey."

"Are you lovers?"

"No," she stammered. "I swear to God."

"Would you like to be?" Konev pressed. "Have you fantasized about being naked in bed with him?"

She started to say something, but Konev motioned her to be silent.

"Do you think that he wishes he could have sex with you, perhaps with Tony watching?"

The girl took a step backward. "You sick fucker."

Konev smiled. There were many aspects of his profession that he enjoyed immensely. This was one such moment. "I would like you to telephone Mr. McGarvey. Tell him that you're frightened and that you would like him to come here to you."

The girl shook her head.

Konev shot her in her left thigh. She cried out and fell to the floor, and he was on her in a second, the muzzle of the silencer jammed into the side of her head.

"Mr. McGarvey is a CIA spy. He and I are enemies. He means to kill me and I mean to kill him. You are going to help us resolve the issue. If you cooperate and I prevail, you will live. If you refuse to help me, I will end your life now and continue on my own."

The girl said nothing.

"Help me and you may live. Refuse and you will certainly die."

The girl lay on her side, clutching her leg for a longish time. "What do you want me to do?"

"Telephone Mr. McGarvey, tell him that you are frightened, and ask him to come downstairs to help you."

"He'll know that I'm lying."

Konev smiled. "Men never know when a woman is lying. It's your strength. Now, will you call him?"

The girl nodded.

FORTY-EIGHT

□

Otto stood at the floor-to-ceiling window in his suite, looking toward the lights of the airport as a jetliner came in for a landing. He'd come directly up to his room, expecting that whoever had followed him—probably from Garden City—would make contact.

But it had not happened yet.

"Lou?"

"Yes, dear."

"Is the Camry parked in the hotel's lot?"

"Yes, next to your car."

"Is there any sign of the gentleman?"

"No. But a man checked in shortly after you did, under the name Robert Wehr. I have a ninety-six percent confidence that it is the same man from Sarasota that Mac met with."

"Call his room."

His program did, and the phone rang four times.

"He's not in. Has he left me a message?"

"No."

"Thank you."

"You're welcome."

Otto changed into a pale blue long-sleeve shirt, white linen trousers, and boat shoes and then took the elevator downstairs. He crossed the lobby to the dining room and immediately spotted Bob Wehr seated at a window table across the room.

The man looked up and waved, and Otto went across to him and sat down.

"Mr. Wehr. You're something of a surprise."

"I figured that either you or Mac would show up at the ranch, and when it was you, I wanted to know why, so I followed you here. And now we have a lot to talk about."

"We certainly do," Otto said.

McGarvey had let the phone ring five times, until the voicemail kicked in. It had been Dianna, and he had known that she would probably call, because he'd heard her cry out. She'd sounded stressed and almost certainly in pain. The bastard was downstairs with her.

"Anything from across the street?" he asked Pete, who was at the window.

"Nothing. She's a hostage?"

"Yeah, and I think he hurt her."

"So what do you want to do?"

"I'm going to call her back," McGarvey said. He hit the Return Call key. Dianna answered it on the second ring.

"Mr. McGarvey?" she asked.

"I was in the shower. Are you okay?"

"I don't know."

"Put your phone on speaker mode."

"Okay."

McGarvey heard the hollow sounds of the room. "Good evening, Nikolai," he said. "It seems as if we are at an impasse."

The line was silent for a beat. "I don't think so," Konev said.

"I know that you are a Spetsnaz shooter working for General Raskopov, that your name is Nikolai Shalayev, that you're considered very good, and that you have come here to assassinate me, my wife, and my friend."

"Let's meet face-to-face in exchange for the girl's life. I think that she's in love with you, and perhaps you with her. Come downstairs and see. I'll leave the door open."

"Leave the girl unharmed and we can meet outside."

"As you wish."

"In the back alley. We've spotted your shooters across the street."

"You'll still have to come down the stairs past me. What do you propose?"

"Send the girl out first," McGarvey said.

"I'm afraid that she is in no condition to walk on her own."

"He shot me in the leg," Dianna said. "And he says that he'll kill me if you don't cooperate."

"He means to kill us both, no matter what," McGarvey said. "But I'm going to kill him first."

"Call the police," Dianna cried.

McGarvey heard the silenced gunshot the instant before the phone went silent.

Wehr had suggested they have something to eat before they started because, he said, he never thought well when he was hungry. They had hamburgers and fries and a couple of beers, saying almost nothing to each other.

For one of the rare times in his life, Otto didn't know what to think. All of his instincts told him that Wehr worked for the Russians, that, in the beginning, he had been sent to watch Mac's parents and, afterward, to wait for someone to come out to the ranch for a follow-up investigation.

But that didn't add up either. The technology that Mac's folks had come up with was no longer relevant. Yet the SVR had expended a lot of resources to stop the probe.

"You work for the Russians, but I don't get why you guys are taking such a risk to beat a dead horse," Otto said. He wanted to hear what his darlings were making of this meeting—Lou was listening—but he didn't want to reveal that capability.

"The fact of the matter is, I'm not a Russian spy," Wehr said, and his conviction had the ring of truth.

"You're a field operative sent to cover up something that no longer matters, you motherfucker. And my wife is dead because of it."

"I'm sorry, Mr. Rencke, but I didn't have a hand in it."

"Then what the fuck were you doing working for Mac's parents?"

"It was just a job. I got to do what I wanted to do, at my own pace, and I loved to work on machinery—including that sweet Beech."

"Bullshit."

"I'd lost my wife to cancer, and I needed to get off the merry-go-round. Out in western Kansas—the boonies—seemed to be the right thing for me to do. And it was."

"Then why did you move to Sarasota after Mac did?"

"Because I knew that it was no accident that killed his parents. And I suspected that he knew that as well and would come calling someday to find out what actually happened and why. I wanted to be there to lend him a hand."

"How'd you know that I was at the ranch, and why the hell did you follow me here instead of just walking up and saying hi?"

Wehr smiled. "Because the last people who came out to say hi weren't very lucky. You shot them to death."

"Maybe I'll do the same right now."

"No."

"Why?"

"Because I'm going to help you."

"With what?"

"Get to Moscow. That's where you're going."

"To do what?"

"The same thing Mac intends doing."

"Yes?" Otto said.

"To assassinate either Vladimir Putin or Valeri Raskopov."

"You son of a bitch," McGarvey shouted, loudly enough that it could be heard through his partially open door and all the way down to the second floor. The single man in the front apartment on this floor, and the couple across from Dianna, were gone, so he wasn't too worried about any further collateral damage.

He hustled to the bathroom and, wrapping a hand towel around his pistol, smashed out the glass in the small window, then went back out to the living room.

"I'm going downstairs," he told Pete, keeping his voice just above a whisper.

"No way he fell for the bathroom window. He'll be waiting for you."

"Cover my back. But whatever goes down, don't let him get past you."

"I'm not going to lose you like this, Kirk."

"No, you're not," McGarvey said. He pecked her cheek, then took off his shoes and slipped out into the corridor, where he held up at the head of the stairs.

The building was mostly still. He cocked an ear, and he thought he could hear whimpering from below. A woman crying. Dianna wasn't dead. The shooter was covering the rear courtyard but was using the girl as bait. If she spotted McGarvey, she would almost certainly cry out.

McGarvey took the stairs very slowly, one at a time. At the turn, he could see Dianna's bare legs from the knees down, poking out into the corridor, and he stopped. There was a lot of blood on both legs and pooled up on the floor.

The girl wasn't moving.

FORTY-NINE

Konev waited just inside the door to Dianna's apartment. The breaking glass in back had been a ruse, of course. From what he'd read in McGarvey's extensive files, the man was almost certainly a Sir Galahad.

He'd lost his wife and daughter in an assassination attempt that had gone bad because amateurs had been sent. And he'd lost other women who had been important to him. And now his new wife upstairs was at risk.

The man had to know that if he lost his life, or at the very least was incapacitated, his wife would die too.

And the young girl, who obviously idolized the man as her superhero, was sitting in the corridor, her back propped against the door frame, bleeding from a severed artery in her right leg, where he had shot her the second time. She would bleed out in a matter of minutes unless McGarvey saved her.

From where he stood, he was only a couple of feet from the girl, who had begun to whimper, partially masking any noises that he was listening for from above. He was tempted to put a bullet into the back of her head to shut her up.

"Call an ambulance," McGarvey said from the corridor. It sounded as if he was halfway down the stairs.

"Do you want the cops, too?" Pete called back.

"The SWAT team, but have them concentrate on the roof across the street."

"What about Shalayev?"

"He'll be dead."

"He could bug out the back way."

"Cover it from the bathroom."

"Will do," Pete said.

"We'll wait now," McGarvey said. "Unless you want to make a deal."

"I'm listening," Konev said. It was exactly what he had expected McGarvey would offer. By the time an ambulance got here and police shooters had cleared Yuryn and Petr from their positions, the girl would be dead.

"Holster your gun, then come out and tie a tourniquet around Dianna's leg. I give you my word that I will not shoot you."

"How can I believe you?"

"For the moment, I want to save her life more than I want to end yours."

"The police are coming."

"I'll let the SWAT team take care of your two people across the street, but I'll let you walk free."

"Again, why should I believe you?" Konev said, assessing his chances. The girl's right leg, below where his shot had nicked an artery, had turned pale, and her whimpering was now so soft it was barely discernible.

"Your choice. Help the girl or remain here and die, either by cop or by me."

"Help is on the way," Pete shouted from somewhere inside the apartment above, her voice partially muffled.

"I'm coming out with a tourniquet," Konev said.

McGarvey didn't respond.

Something was wrong. There were no sounds of approaching sirens.

Moving fast, Konev leaped out of the apartment headfirst, keeping low and then dropping to his right shoulder and rolling away, his pistol in his left hand, sweeping the stairs for a target. But the American wasn't there.

In an instant he realized his mistakes. If the police were indeed coming, they had been instructed not to use their sirens. And the *pizda* wasn't on the stairs above. He had made his way in silence to the stairs below.

He brought his pistol around, firing four shots in rapid succession, when a bright flash burst behind his eyes.

McGarvey came up the stairs in a rush, his pistol trained on the Russian, who was lying on his side.

The man was dead or dying.

"Clear," he shouted up to Pete as he holstered his pistol and went to Dianna.

The girl looked up at him and smiled weakly. Her breath was short and ragged and her very pale face was drenched in sweat.

"A couple of SWAT team trucks just pulled up, the ambulance behind it, and cop cars are all over the place," Pete called from the head of the stairs.

"Get on the phone and tell the paramedics to hustle," McGarvey said. He pulled off his belt, and as he was strapping it around the girl's right leg, above the wound, she managed another smile.

"You're going to lose your pants," she croaked.

"Don't tell Tony."

"Cross my heart and hope to die."

An intense burst of firing out in the street ended almost as quickly as it had begun, and someone entered the front door.

"Paramedics," a man called from below.

"Second floor, clear up," Pete shouted from right behind McGarvey.

While Wehr went through his background, from his birth and upbringing in a small Minnesota town to his service in the marines, something else came to Otto's mind.

"Have you come up with anything yet?" he asked, his voice low.

"No," Lou said in his ear.

Wehr didn't seemed surprised that Otto was apparently talking to himself.

"How about his background, anything new?"

"A Robert Wehr, only child of Margaret and Sergeant Wehr, Hibbing, Minnesota, did exist. But I cannot confirm it is the same man as the one sitting across from you. Send me his fingerprints."

Otto slid his cell phone across the table. "Your index fingers."

Wehr hesitated for only a moment before he pressed his right index finger on the screen, and then his left.

"I'll do a precheck. Stand by, dear."

"You're communicating with your computer?"

"Yes, but how would you know something like that?" Otto asked.

Wehr smiled. "You guys really need to google yourselves."

"No matching fingerprints on file, including the USMC's database," Lou said.

"Deeper."

"I'm not in any database," Wehr said. "You could have asked and I would have saved you the trouble."

"Then who the hell are you?"

"My real name is of no significance for now. Let's just say that I am a friend of the McGarvey family."

"Let's not just say," Otto said. "Who the hell do you work for?"

"Trust me, I'm here to help you and Mac and Pete. I'm only sorry that I wasn't in a position to help your wife."

"*Pizda.*"

Wehr laughed. "No. I'm not a pussy," he said.

"*No par Russki?*"

"*Da,* I speak Russian."

"If you're working for the Russians, why the hell are you protecting the McGarveys?"

"I speak French but I don't work for the DGSE. I speak German but I don't work for the NDB."

"Then who do you work for, and what do you want?"

"Who I work for is not important, as I've said. As for what the people I work for want, it's the same as you and Mac: Putin's assassination. The rub is that it never be traced back to the CIA or any other U.S. agency. Which is why you and Mac and his wife have been identified as rogue operators. Warrants for your arrests are being processed as we speak."

For the first time that Otto could remember, he was at a loss for words, and Lou wasn't jumping in to help.

"Job one is to keep all of you out of custody, and my next is to get you to Russia without your being arrested over there, or shot to death. Though what the hell you think you're going to do when you get there is beyond me. Do I have your attention?"

FIFTY

The people in the two downstairs apartments had been evacuated, Dianna had been taken away in an ambulance, and Mac and Pete were seated in the rear seat of a Company Cadillac Escalade. A pair of minders, one of them the driver, stood outside talking to an FBI agent, leaving only one man, with a long, narrow face, seated in the front. He'd identified himself as Peter Gaston, a CIA special internal affairs investigator.

"Soon as we heard what was going down this evening, Mr. Waksberg asked me to come out and have a chat with you folks," Gaston said. His voice was soft, his manner diffident. Waksberg was the deputy director of operations, a position once held by Marty Bambridge.

"What's the word on the two shooters on the roof across the street?" McGarvey asked.

"Deceased. And before you ask, neither of them has been identified as yet, but their IDs looked first class."

"They won't stop, you know," Pete said.

"That's what the director said. But neither would either of you," Gaston said. "The problems that we're currently facing are what will you do next, and finding out Mr. Rencke's current location and his intentions."

McGarvey almost felt sorry for the man, who was only trying to do his job. He was a sacrificial lamb caught between a rock and a seriously hard place. If something went south, which everyone was sure would happen, he would take the blame for not stopping it.

"I don't know where Otto is, but if I did, I wouldn't let you guys go fetch him—if you were dumb enough to try."

Gaston started to say something, but Mac held him off.

"He's taken a big-time run on the SVR mainframe, as I'm sure you've already heard."

"From the White House, I'm told. And there's some serious heat coming down. Rumors are that the president might fire Mr. Taft if the issue isn't resolved very soon."

"Every director serves at the pleasure of the president."

"Yes, but in this case the issue depends on you."

"If you mean am I going to back off, the answer is no."

"Are *we* going to back off?" Pete said. "Same answer. A very good friend of mine was shot to death standing next to me. Makes me a motivated woman."

Gaston glanced outside as a member of the Bureau's forensics team, a man dressed in a white hazmat suit, came out of the building. Just behind him, a pair of techs wheeled out a body in a bag. Several news trucks and a small crowd of people were held behind police tape at the end of the block.

"The media has finally sat up and taken notice," he said. "And once they spot you, it's game over. Former DCI on the hunt, yet again, for more bad guys. Headlines wouldn't do your chances much good. Or ours."

"So right now your choice is simple: either arrest us or step back and let us get on with it," McGarvey said.

"Hell of it is, we can't afford to do either, although Justice has issued warrants—though right now no one is in a hurry to try to serve them. But it wasn't why I was sent here. Mr. Waksberg merely wants some idea what you folks are going to do next."

McGarvey looked at Pete who shrugged. "That'll depend on you people."

"Not us. The White House."

"Okay, it'll depend on the president."

"You'll back off if they insist?"

McGarvey shook his head. "Just how we go about it."

Gaston sighed. "They also told me that you'd say something like that. And of course the Bureau would like to talk to you again. I could just turn you over to them."

McGarvey changed tack. "How deeply were you briefed?"

"Just that you're investigating the accident that killed your parents thirty years ago and that someone—possibly the Russians—is trying to stop you, for reasons no one has figured out yet."

"The Russians wanted to stop them from developing an antimissile defense system."

"They wouldn't mount such a risky operation to protect what amounts to obsolete technology."

"No, but they might try to stop us from discovering how a spy ring penetrated Los Alamos."

"A valid argument, Mr. Director," Gaston said. "But I was told that you telephoned Mr. Putin and threatened him. Maybe it's in retaliation for that."

"They started it first," McGarvey said. "Twenty-eight years ago. I'm going to finish it."

By midnight, when he'd received no word from Konev or the other two, Zimin understood that they'd failed, completely failed, with only one hit—that of the wife of the computer geek.

Sitting alone in the apartment, he tried to telephone the New York number Yuryn had given him, but it came up no longer in service.

For a half hour he sat in the small living room, sipping vodka that Larissa had gotten for them. He was hungry, but he had no desire for food, and even the alcohol was having no effect.

He wanted to go home, but he had a fair idea what his reception would be when he did. Arrest, certainly. Possibly a long sentence in one of the several still-operating gulags in Siberia or in other even less desirable locations.

But at his age something like that would be a death sentence. It would be more humane, in his mind, for them to give him his nine ounces and be done with it.

He missed his wife especially, but he also missed some of the comrades he'd worked with over the years. And there'd even been the odd moment in this brief assignment when he found himself happy. Useful for the rodina again. Finishing his drink, he put the glass down and called the emergency number. The area code was 212, in New York, but it rang through to a blind number in Yasenevo. A woman answered in English after the first ring.

"Lighthouse Import, how may I direct your call?"

"I'm calling to follow up with my order."

"Please hold," the woman said, and she was gone.

Another siren sounded from somewhere here in Georgetown. It wasn't possible to say from what direction, or if it was coming closer, but he tensed nevertheless.

General Raskopov came on. "*Da.*"

"It's me," Zimin said.

"This line is secure for the moment. Make your report."

"I have failed. Only one of the subjects has been eliminated. What's left of my team, including the specialist I was sent, are overdue."

The general was brusque. "Give them time."

"Long overdue. What are my orders?"

"Follow your emergency extraction protocol. Report to me personally as soon as possible."

"Yes, sir," Zimin said. "I am sorry."

But the phone was dead.

The FBI had put crime scene tape all over the second floor and the stairway in their building, but Mac slipped under it, holding the tape up for Pete. Back in the apartment, she poured both of them a small brandy and they sat together in silence, seemingly forever.

"What's next?" she asked.

"Lou, I'd like to talk to Otto," McGarvey said. He didn't have to key his phone; Otto's programs monitored it as long as the SIM card was intact.

There was no answer.

"Goddamnit, talk to me."

"I'm sorry, but Otto is not available," Lou replied.

"I think that he's on his way to Moscow, or will be soon. Tell him I'll meet him there, at the Lotte Hotel, under our old work names."

Lou did not respond, but McGarvey knew that his old friend had been listening or would be given the message.

"I'm coming with you," Pete said.

"You're going to Los Alamos to put some pressure on their security people."

She smiled. "You're not taking me off the firing line."

"No."

"So you do trust me after all."

He had to smile, no matter how concerned he was for her. Down there, she would have a gigantic target painted on her back, but he didn't know what else to do. "You get killed, I'll never talk to you again," he said, borrowing one of her lines.

PART
FOUR

Beyond Moscow

FIFTY-ONE

□

Otto left his rental car with Hertz at Denver's airport and checked his single bag for the flight to Atlanta, from where he was supposed to fly on to Paris and then to Moscow—under the radar, because he'd thought that his Underwood papers were bulletproof.

His flight was boarding in twenty minutes, and he sat by himself at the boarding gate, well to one side, watching for the face or faces that seemed out of place. Basic tradecraft he'd learned over the years, most of it from Mac.

He had come up with the idea that a large part of what had been going on in Russia over the past year or so was a deepening rift between the president and the director of the SVR. Such things had happened since Putin had become president, and especially in his second term, after the brief reign of Dmitry Medvedev.

Most of the people who'd gone head-to-head with the former KGB colonel had either turned up dead, like Alexander Litvinenko, who was poisoned by polonium in London, or jailed, like the oil billionaire Mikhail Khodorkovsky, now in exile with several others in Switzerland.

He suspected that sending the SVR team to the States in a highly risky operation, plus Mac's direct threat to Putin, had upped the tension between the Kremlin and Yasenevo. And he planned to use that tension as a lever to cause even more damage to the bastards who'd murdered his wife.

First had been the SVR's mainframe, which, from what Lou had gathered, was in shambles, and next would be Putin and Raskopov themselves.

Mac had declared war on the president, but Otto was declaring war on both of them. Either a new Russia would emerge from the carnage or the country would slip into anarchy, as it had before in its history. Frankly, he didn't give a damn.

And then there was Bob Wehr.

Otto took the phone out of his pocket, but before he spoke he pretended to enter a number. "What is Wehr's location?"

"He is currently at Denver International," Lou said.

Otto scanned the faces of the people already lined up for boarding, He didn't see the man.

"I don't see him."

"He is at a Delta gate, waiting for Compass flight five seven one six to Albuquerque, New Mexico."

Otto was startled. "Under what name?"

"Robert Wehr."

"Are you finished with your search on him?"

"Yes."

"Results?"

"I retain a sixty-seven percent confidence level that the man is who he claims to be."

"Have you identified what agency, if any, he's working for?"

Lou hesitated, which rarely happened. It was an uncertainty response he'd programmed into all of his darlings.

"He has made no electronic contacts that I have detected in the past week. Anything off the grid would require HUMINT." She meant human intelligence—boots on the ground.

"Have you detected any stress levels in his voice?"

"None."

"Why is he going to New Mexico?"

"He is going to the Los Alamos National Laboratory."

Otto was not surprised. "Do you know why?"

"I believe that either Mac or Pete or both will go there, and Wehr wants to help."

"Your confidence level?"

"In total, forty-eight percent."

The boarding call for Delta SkyMiles and first-class passengers was announced and people began moving past the gate agent's check-in station and onto the Jetway.

"Have either of them booked flights or made any other travel arrangements?"

"Not under their names or any work names in my database."

"Have either of them attempted to make contact with me?"

"Mac has, four times in the past twenty-four hours."

"What is his current location?"

"He and Pete are at her apartment in Georgetown."

"Is there anything else?"

"Yes. An incident overnight involving what I believe was the Russian hit squad you had me warn them about has been successfully resolved."

Otto held his stress level in check as best he could. "Casualties?"

"Three KIAs, plus Mac's downstairs neighbor Dianna Miller, who will recover from gunshot wounds in both legs."

"Mac and Pete?"

"Neither was injured, though the DOJ has issued warrants for their arrests."

"Why wasn't I told?"

"I'm sorry, dear, but you wished not to be disturbed."

"I'm changing that instruction to include an override that should either of them be in developing danger I am to be immediately informed."

"Yes, dear," Lou said.

Otto could imagine hearing a slight note of dejection in her voice, and he had to remind himself of something he very often forgot: his darling was not Lou; it was merely a computer program. A sophisticated program, but nothing more than that.

"Let me talk to him."

"Yes, dear."

McGarvey answered on the second ring. "Hello."

"Lou just told me that you guys had a bit of an issue last night."

McGarvey sounded relieved but vexed. "I've been trying to reach you, but your machine said you weren't taking calls. Where are you?"

"Doesn't matter. Are you guys okay?"

"It does matter, goddamnit. And yes we're fine. A Russian hit man showed up with a pair of shooters as a diversion."

"The DOJ has issued warrants for your arrests."

"One of Waksberg's people came out and gave us a pep talk. The warrants won't be served for now. But apparently the White House hasn't lost interest."

"The president's in a tough spot with Putin. He doesn't want to upset the applecart."

"Then they shouldn't have sent someone after us."

"I agree," Otto said. "In the meantime, what're your plans?"

"Pete's already set up a VIP visit at Los Alamos."

"I know. What about you?"

"The same place as you."

"You might want to hold back," Otto said.

"I could give you the same advice."

"Putin and Raskopov are in the middle of a power struggle. I'm going to turn myself in, without making it too obvious, and see if I can't meddle."

"They'll shoot you, trying to escape."

"I have the keywords to the SVR's mainframe problems. And Lou is set to unleash another virus into the Kremlin's system if she doesn't hear from me every twelve hours."

"They might shoot first and ask questions later."

"Maybe," Otto said. "But I want to be there in person to see the look in their eyes when I stick it to the bastards. Not only for Lou, but for your mom and dad."

Mac had to laugh at his friend's naïveté, though it scared the hell out of him. "I'll cover your back."

"No."

"I have a vested interest."

"Your parents are dead. Lou is dead."

"I'm talking about a friend of mine," McGarvey said. "But how did you know that Pete was going to Los Alamos?"

"It was Bob Wehr who followed me from the ranch. He said that he knew I was going to Russia and that he wanted to help me. And he

apparently knew that either you or Pete was going to Los Alamos, because he's on his way there right now."

"Does Lou think he's working for the Russians?"

"She's not sure," Otto said. "But tell Pete to watch her six. Better yet,
go with her."

FIFTY-TWO

Pete had been in her bedroom packing a few things in a small bag, including her pistol and two spare magazines of ammunition, when Otto's call came in. Mac stood at the open door with the phone, still in speaker mode, in hand.

"The mysterious Bob Wehr materializes once again, when we least expect him," Pete said. "And even Lou can't figure out who he really is."

"I want you to go back to Serifos and wait it out there," McGarvey said. "At least until we get a better handle on who this guy really is."

"Which means what? You're going to follow Otto and at the same time check out Wehr? Neat trick if you can do it."

"I don't want to worry about you getting tangled up with him."

"And you don't think that I'm not scared out of my mind that you and Otto are going into badland?" Pete said, her voice rising. "They shoot people like you guys. Anyway, we don't have any business getting mixed up in some internecine war. Let 'em go to it."

"We know why they killed my parents, now I want to know why they're still so hell-bent on maintaining the cover-up."

"They have a spy ring at Los Alamos. We already figured that out. And me poking around might shake up a few things. Someone will make a mistake."

"You'll have an accident, or just disappear. Lots of mountains down there."

"Maybe Bob Wehr is the mistake."

"It's why I want you to back off for now," McGarvey said.

Pete shook her head. "None of this is making any sense, you know. Me at Los Alamos, you and Otto in Russia. What the hell are we thinking?"

"I don't like being shot at."

"Neither do I. So it'll be both of us backing off, and convincing Otto to do the same, or we're going at this full bore."

"Otto won't stop."

"He can wipe out their computer systems from here."

McGarvey had given that a lot of thought, ever since he'd stumbled onto the Russian plot behind the deaths of his parents. But the killing of Lou had changed everything. There was no going back. And yet, for one of the rare times in his career, he couldn't see any chance of success for any of them. Not for Pete in New Mexico, with Bob Wehr on her six, and especially not for him or Otto.

They were tilting at windmills.

Pete came to him and caressed his cheek. "I care about you, husband, even more than you can possibly imagine."

"I know," Mac said, but she put a finger to his lips.

"Let me finish," she said. "And this is the last time I'm going to bring this up, honest injun."

McGarvey knew what she was going to say, and the hell of it was that he agreed with her, against his better judgment.

"I know that you love me, no question in my mind. But it makes you blind to the fact that I am a trained CIA operative who's been on a number of operations. Even got my butt shot a couple of times. And now you have to get your priorities straight. Either tag along with me to make sure no one shoots me again—although that hasn't always worked in the past—or let me do my thing and I'll let you and Otto do yours." She shook her head. "And believe me, darling, I don't like sending you off any more than you like saying 'See you later' to me."

"I worry about you."

"Yup. But we're partners. Okay?"

McGarvey took her in his arms and held her close for a long time, a kaleidoscope of memories racing through his head, all of them about women he'd loved losing their lives because of him. He didn't know how he could stand another such loss. And yet, looking into Pete's eyes, he understood that there was more than one way to lose someone you loved.

He nodded finally. "Lou?" he said.

"Yes, Mac." Otto's program came back.

"I can't talk Pete out of going down to Los Alamos. Keep tabs on Bob Wehr, and if you come up with anything significant, get it to her."

"Will do."

"Thank you."

"And Mac?"

"Yes?"

"Otto is making a stop in Switzerland first. Kloten." The Zurich airport.

"Why?" McGarvey asked.

Lou did not respond.

"I'll go to the NH. Should be there by morning, under my real name. Would you book me a suite?" The NH was the five-star hotel near the airport.

"Yes," Lou said.

Pete's American Airlines fight to Albuquerque left just before three in the afternoon, and she insisted on getting out to the airport on her own. He saw her off in a cab at noon and walked the couple of blocks back to his own apartment. Traffic was normal for the time of day.

He'd not picked up a tail, and the police tape was gone from the building across the street and from the stairwell inside his building. Everything seemed normal. But just before he reached the second floor, he pulled out his gun and stopped to listen.

The building was quiet. The people downstairs had left and would probably spend the next couple of nights in hotels until the authorities assured them that it was safe to return home—which of course it wouldn't be, as long as he was here.

Upstairs, he let himself into his apartment, again taking care with his tradecraft, sweeping each room, his gun in hand.

In the bathroom, he holstered his pistol and stuffed a towel in the broken window, then went back out to the living room, where he checked the traffic on the street. No one was there. If anyone was left on the Russian team, they had backed off for now. But they would not be giving up. He and Otto and Pete were still their prime targets.

His flight to Zurich didn't leave until six thirty. He packed a bag with

his toiletries and a few items of clothing but no spare identification packages. Nor did he have any intention of changing his appearance. He was
going into badland under his real name and look. He also packed his
spare, disassembled Walther in the nine-millimeter version, along with
three magazines of ammunition and a holster, but no suppressor. If it
came to a gun battle, he wanted it noisy.

Setting his bag by the front door, he removed his gun from the small
of his back and took the holster off his belt, then laid them on the table
by the front window.

He sat down and closed his eyes for a moment or two.

"The trick is to bring yourself into the zone where you are fully
concentrated on all the parameters of your mission—the shit that could
possibly fall on your head and ruin your day—while at the same time
keeping your entire sensibilities tuned to your surroundings."

He remembered the senior instructor's face from his training at the
Farm, years ago, but not the man's name. It had been a good if nearly
impossible bit of advice. One of the students said that you'd have to be a
magician, and the instructor had overheard the remark.

"You're right. So you'd best start practicing now, *before* you get out in
the field and your arse is on the line."

Mac had worked for a time as the deputy director of operations, and
had even served a short stint as the acting director of the agency. He
hadn't liked either job, because he wasn't an administrator. He'd been a
field officer from day one. The major downside of the job, for him, had
always been the loneliness. And yet, when he was home and married, or
in a serious relationship, he had chafed at the bit to get back to badland.

The problem now was Pete. She was cut from the same cloth as he
was. And in his heart of hearts, he didn't know if he could live with it.

FIFTY-THREE

Otto, waiting at the Atlanta airport for his overnight flight to Zurich, telephoned Benjamin Church, the director of security for the Los Alamos National Laboratory. He caught the man at home.

"Mr. Church, my name is Leonard Goldberg. I am the senior executive assistant for Burton Webb, who asked me to give you a courtesy call with a heads-up."

Webb was the director of national intelligence, and Church was impressed. "What can I do for you, sir?"

Lou had done a quick backgrounder on the man, who'd come out of the military eight years ago as a full bird colonel, the number two man in the Marine Corps Intelligence, Surveillance, and Reconnaissance Enterprise. Working for the DOE at Los Alamos, he had built a reputation as a tough, no-nonsense man who worked less as an administrator than as a top cop.

"We've stumbled onto something that we have no way of verifying, but we want to bring it to your attention."

"I'm all ears."

"According to a walk-in at the CIA, you may have a foreign intelligence officer working there, in what may be a sensitive position."

"Do you have a name?"

"No, just that the informant has been deemed credible," Otto said.

"Could you send me a transcript of the interview or interviews?"

"The Agency is sending down one of its officers to have a chat with you; she may have some ideas. Her name is Pete McGarvey, and she should be driving up from Albuquerque either tonight or tomorrow morning."

"Any relation to the former DCI?"

"His wife. And his parents were scientists at the lab."

"They were killed in a car crash about thirty years ago. There's still talk that it might not have been an accident. This have any connection?"

"Anything's possible," Otto said. "But she's not on her way to conduct a review or any sort of an inspection. She's coming to give you a hand. But there may be a complication."

"There almost always is," Church said.

"The opposition, if there is such a thing, is aware that she's on her way."

"How the hell do you know that?"

"The walk-in said that it was probable."

"Great," Church said. "Can you give me Mrs. McGarvey's contact information?"

Otto gave him Pete's encrypted phone number and her flight information. "American Airlines, due in about an hour from Dulles. Eight oh three."

"I'll send a chopper for her. She can stay here, in the BOQ."

It was exactly what Otto wanted. The bachelor officer quarters. It would make it harder for Wehr to blindside her. If she wanted to meet him, she would be the one calling the shots. "I'll let her know."

"What if I need to talk to you?"

Otto gave him a number that was listed as belonging to the Office of the Director of National Intelligence but that would actually ring through to Lou.

Otto sent a lengthy text message to Pete's phone, along with a transcript of his talk with the LANL's chief of security. He didn't think that she would answer, but she did, five minutes after he sent it.

"We're already starting down, so I don't have long," Pete said. "Is there anything else I should know?"

"I'll send you the transcripts of the interview we supposedly had with the walk-in."

"Does anyone at Langley know about this?"

"Just us."

"If you meant to insulate me from Bob Wehr, it's exactly what I didn't want to happen. I wanted to push the man, to get his reaction. If I'm behind barbed wire, it won't be so easy."

"No, but it'll be safer if it's you calling the shots. You can meet him somewhere in public. If he's part of the opposition, it'd be a hell of a lot tougher for him to take you in plain view."

"Collateral damage?"

"If he's working for the Russians, he'll want to take you down with as little fuss as possible."

"Okay, I get you," Pete said. "Any word from Mac?"

"I'm going to make a stop in Switzerland, Mac wants to meet me in Zurich."

"Do it."

"I'll see."

"Goddamnit, Otto. You're okay with *giving* advice; how about *taking* some for a change?"

"Take care of yourself," Otto said, and he hung up.

Bill Fay was the lone pilot on standby this evening, and as soon as he got the call from Ben Church he left the ready room and began prepping the Airbus H120 VIP helicopter, releasing the rotors and tie-downs and then doing his walk-around.

The 120 was the smallest VIP helicopter in the fleet of four, with a capacity of one pilot and up to four passengers. But, with cruising speeds above one hundred knots, she was one of the most-used transports to and from the airport down in Albuquerque. And for Fay, who was tall and lanky, the pilot's seat, which could be slid back farther than in most choppers, fit him just fine.

He got aboard and had begun the start-up precheck when a Chevy Impala with government plates showed up and a stocky man in a business suit, his tie correctly knotted, got out and came across the tarmac.

"Mr. Fay, I'm Sam Maslik. I'm flying with you to pick up your passenger." He held up an open wallet, which had his photograph and an FBI ID.

"Did Mr. Church clear you?"

"Of course," Maslik said. He opened the rear door and climbed aboard. "She's due to land in less than an hour."

"We have plenty of time," Fay said. He contemplated phoning Church but decided against it. He started the Turbomeca engine, and as it warmed up he finished his preflight. At 7:45 he lifted off and swung toward the southwest, the night cool and dry, the wind light, the ceiling and visibility unlimited.

Pete got her single bag from the luggage carousel and had turned to head for the exit and the taxi stand when a man in a business suit walked up to her.

"Mrs. McGarvey?" he asked.

"Who are you?" Pete asked, her threat radar popping off.

Maslik took out his FBI credentials and identified himself. "I came down with your ride. I thought that we could start things off on the way back."

Something was wrong. Pete could feel it in her bones. Something about the way the man was dressed, how he talked, just didn't feel right to her.

"I have a car outside to take us back to the FBO," Maslik said, referring to the fixed-base operator that provided support for small carriers. "Let me take your bag."

"I have to use the loo and fix my face," she said, holding the bag away. "Just be a sec."

She didn't look back as she walked to the far end of the baggage hall and into the women's room, where she went into a stall and locked the door. Setting her bag on the toilet, she opened it and took out her Glock, loaded it, and stuffed it in her belt at the small of her back, beneath her jacket.

She thought about calling Otto, but if this was her first speed bump and she had to call for help, she might as well just return to Georgetown and hide under her bed.

This was just the start.

□

FIFTY-FOUR

Zimin, traveling under his extraction Swiss passport with the work name of Thomas Buerger, got out of the taxi at Baltimore/Washington International, checked his single bag at the JetBlue curbside station, and went inside, where he was passed through security.

He was an hour early, but he found his gate and took a seat with the few other passengers. All afternoon, since General Raskopov had ordered him to break off the operation and come home, he'd worried over the incomplete assignment and what the ramifications would be, not only for him but for the *rodina*.

Rencke's wife was dead, the latest op with the expert the general had sent had gone bad, and there would have to be some serious and immediate blowback.

Using his last burner phone, he called Raskopov's blind number. It was answered by the general's secretary after the first ring.

"Yes," she said in English, since the call had originated in an English-speaking country.

"This is a follow-up message."

"Go ahead."

"For the general's ears only."

"Go ahead," the secretary insisted.

"I would like a clarification of my orders. I believe that it would be for the best if I was sent a new team, to continue with my current assignment."

"You have your orders. No clarification is necessary."

"The primary subjects may be headed toward the primary objective."

"We know, and it is being taken care of," the secretary said. Her tone softened. "The general sends his regards for an assignment adequately handled, but now it is time to come home."

It made no sense to Zimin. "Very well."

The phone went dead, and he pocketed it. But then he took it back out, removed the SIM card, and walked to the other side of the terminal and then downstairs to baggage claim. He snagged a small piece of luggage from a pile that had been set to one side, to make it look as if he were an arriving passenger, and walked out the door.

He was fourth in line for a cab, and he told the driver to take him to a decent hotel within walking distance of Union Station.

"The Hyatt Regency on New Jersey Avenue, just down the block from the station and the Capitol and all that stuff," the cabbie said.

"The Hyatt it is," Zimin said.

The man who'd identified himself as an FBI agent was waiting at the door when Pete came out of the women's room and joined him.

"Just across the street," he said. He reached for her bag again, but she held it back.

"I got it," she said.

They crossed the busy driveway to a Lexus crossover, where he opened the passenger door for her—another red flag. FBI agents on assignment almost never opened doors for women, especially not for someone who was supposedly a fellow investigator.

"We're not far from here," he said, getting behind the wheel. "I have to ask you if you are armed."

"No need. I just came down on a show-and-tell."

"I'm sorry?" he said, pulling away from the curb.

"We had a walk-in who told us that he suspected there might be a deep cover agent inside the lab."

"Did he give you a name?"

"No. But I've brought the interview transcripts with me for Mr. Church," Pete said. "And could you tell me what the FBI is doing here?"

"Ben Church asked for our help. Actually, I'm the Albuquerque SAC, and we're called up from time to time to take a look at new hires. You know how it is. Put their feet to the fire, see how high we can turn up the heat. Never tell what might shake out."

Pete thought the man's English was too good, his accent possibly East Coast. "I'll bet you were born in California, or at least grew up there."

Maslik had to smile. "Does it show?"

"Big-time."

They left the terminal and headed south. "We're at Cutter Aviation," Maslik explained. "A bit more private, if you know what I mean."

"Sure do," Pete said. "This one of their cars, or yours?"

"Mine."

The guy was obviously not an FBI agent, but what bothered her was the speed with which the Russians—if that's who he worked for—had learned that she was coming here. The leak wasn't at Otto's end, of course, and her phone, like Mac's, which Otto had modified, was encrypted with a sophisticated 1.2-gigabit randomly shifting algorithm. It also was equipped with a built-in program that would alert Lou if someone had hacked the system.

Which meant that Maslik had to have access to the lab's security system, a possibility that she wanted to warn Otto about.

"I think I'm getting a call," she said. She took the phone out of her pocket and hit the power button. But then she looked up and grinned. "Nada," she said, and put the phone back in her pocket. Now it was connected with Otto's system. Lou would be monitoring everything in the car. "How long has your office been working with the lab?"

"Long before I was assigned here. How about you . . . how long have you been working for the Company?"

"Forever."

"It's a job."

"Same for you?" Pete asked.

"Yeah," Maslik said.

"Imposter," Lou said.

Pete drew her pistol and pointed it at the man before he could react. "What'd you do with the pilot?"

"What the hell are you talking about, and who's on the phone?"

"A friend. What about the pilot?"

"So far as I know, he's waiting on the apron for us," Maslik said. "And if you don't mind, please stop pointing your gun at me."

"You're an SVR field officer, here to stop an investigation into a pair of murders in Kansas twenty-eight years ago."

"Nonsense," Maslik said.

Pete hit him in the side of the head, just above the ear, with the butt of her pistol, opening a two-inch gash in his scalp that immediately began to bleed. The car swerved sharply, but he regained control quickly.

"I'll shoot you in the head unless you talk to me."

"We'll run off the road."

"I'll take my chances," Pete said. She switched aim and pressed the pistol into the man's crotch, her finger tightening on the trigger. "Maybe I'll shoot off your balls."

"You're dead, bitch."

Pete pressed the muzzle of the pistol tighter. "Five. Four. Three."

"Wait."

"Talk to me."

"I can't."

"I will shoot."

"From what I learned in my briefing, I have no doubt you will. But if I tell you what I know, it'd mean a death sentence. And I can do without my balls easier than my life. So, if I have a choice, I'll take a supermax here in the States."

"Lou, call the Bureau here in Albuquerque and have them come out to the FBO and take this guy off my hands," Pete said.

Maslik suddenly jogged very hard to the left, just missing an oncoming car, tossing Pete off balance.

He swung very hard to the right with one hand while reaching inside his jacket and pulling out a pistol.

Before he had it fully withdrawn, Pete switched aim and fired one shot point-blank into the side of his head.

They careered off the road, hit a ditch, and nearly turned over, but finally the car came to a rest in the sand and gravel fifty feet away.

"Are you okay?" Otto demanded.

"Just peachy," Pete said.

FIFTY-FIVE

As Pete was undoing her seat belt, she glanced in the rearview mirror and saw a red Jeep Wrangler with a black ragtop pull off the road and stop behind the Lexus. Bob Wehr, wearing jeans, jumped out.

Cars were already stopping on the road, and Pete had worried that she was going to get hung up with the cops. But Wehr suddenly showing up was an altogether different, and potentially very dangerous, matter.

She was still a little shaken up from the crash, but she brought her pistol around as Wehr yanked open the door.

"We need to get out of here, right now," he said.

She raised the gun. "How did you know I was here?"

Wehr glanced at Maslik's body. "I'll explain on the way to your chopper. But either shoot me or trust me, because someone has already called the cops for sure."

Pete hesitated.

Wehr yanked open the rear door and got her bag. "Can you walk on your own?"

"I think so."

"Then put away your gun and we'll get out of here."

Pete did as she was told, and Wehr hustled her back to his Jeep. No one on the highway was organized, and when Wehr held up what looked like a badge, it was enough to keep everyone back.

Once they were on the road and heading away, Pete took out her pistol and pointed it at him.

He glanced at her and grinned. "Are you in the habit of shooting everyone who drives you somewhere?"

"Only the bad guys."

Wehr glanced in the rearview mirror. "We're clean so far," he said, and he glanced at her again. "How'd you know that he was the opposition?"

"I was expecting someone like him to show up."

"And me?"

"Especially you."

"Mac doesn't trust me, and neither do you or Otto. Understandable. But I'm not working for the Russians."

"Prove it."

"I can't, at least right now. Maybe never. Really depends on how much trouble you guys manage to cause. I mean, declaring war, mano a mano, with Putin is over the top."

"They killed Mac's parents."

"Yeah, nearly thirty years ago, to stop them from finishing the project they were working on. Only by then it was too late, so the mokrie dela was a stupid waste of effort. But Mac is right about one thing: Putin was an officer in the KGB's First Chief Directorate, and possibly even in Victor, the old executive action department. They were the guys who planned and conducted assassinations. But they weren't the initiators. The orders came from above."

"The Kremlin," Pete said.

"In this case, yes."

"What do you mean, 'in this case'?" Pete asked. "Where did orders like that usually come from?"

"That depends on who's the flavor of the month. But those were days when the KGB had started its cyber infiltration and hacking unit."

"I'm not following you."

"Well, the one thing you guys got right is the power struggle thing between Putin and Raskopov."

"Why doesn't Putin remove him, or just have him shot?"

"The million-dollar question, which we'd rather you not try to answer. But as long as you're in the middle of it, I'll stick around to lend you a hand from time to time."

"If you knew something like this was going to happen when you went to work on the ranch, why didn't you do something about it then? Try to stop the murders, or at least warn them?"

"Because we didn't know."

"Who the hell do you work for?"

"Can't say for now, except we're the guys on your side."

They turned at the entrance to Cutter Aviation and drove around to the apron where the Airbus helicopter was parked. Wehr pulled up next to it.

"I'll keep in touch."

"Thanks for getting me out of there," Pete said.

"That was easy. The tough bits are just around the corner, and I can't be everywhere at once."

Pete got her bag from the back, and Wehr drove away as the pilot came out of the office at a run.

"Was that the guy who was supposed to pick you up?" he said in a rush. "He doesn't work for the FBI."

"A different one. The guy who rode down with you has been taken care of."

The pilot shook his head. "Are you good to go? Mr. Church is waiting."

"I need to make a call first."

"I'll stow your bag."

Pete walked a few paces away from the helicopter, and when she got her phone, Otto was already on the line. "I just left Bob Wehr," she said.

"Lou has pretty well eliminated him from the opposition."

"For sure?"

"Seventy-four percent. That's strong enough for me. But we just can't get a handle on who he does work for, except that apparently his first assignment was more than thirty years ago, when he first went to work for Mac's folks. It's the only real clue we have to work with, except that he has a damned good source of intel. It's driving us nuts."

"Who was the guy I shot?"

"The opposition, of course, and Lou is just about split down the middle whether he worked for the Kremlin or the SVR. But we're sure he won't be the last."

"Where are you right now?"

"On my way, or will be shortly."

"Mac will be right behind you."

"He wants to me meet in Zurich."

"Do it," Pete said. "Tell him, Lou."

"She's correct," Lou said.

The pilot started the helicopter.

"I can hear your ride," Otto said. "When you get up there, watch yourself. The opposition knows that you're on the way, and accidents do happen."

"Something like that right now would be too risky for them."

"That would depend on the risk–reward ratio. If it's high enough, they'll have to try to take you out."

Pete had thought about that on the way down from DC. "It's why I'm here," she said. "If they try something, it'll mean we're not tilting at windmills."

"If you're right, you could get killed."

"That applies to all of us."

Benjamin Church was waiting at the helipad when they touched down. He was a short, slender man with a long face, big ears, and a military buzz cut. Pete got out with her single bag, thanked the pilot, and went across to the lab's security chief. They shook hands.

"There was a shooting just outside the airport," he said. "Were you involved?"

"Yes. It was the guy who hitched a ride with your pilot. Said he was the FBI's Albuquerque SAC. And that was goddamned sloppy of your people, almost got me killed."

"I wasn't informed," Church said, stiffening.

"You should have been," Pete said. "Now, if you don't mind, I'd like to go over to your office for a little chat, and then I want to go to the BOQ for a couple hours of sleep. In the morning, I'll want to meet with your staff—all of them. Your operation is so sloppy, it's no wonder you have a spy here—maybe an entire network—for at least the past thirty years. Maybe from the beginning."

FIFTY-SIX

Putin's Russian-designed and -built Cortege project NAMI limousine glided to a stop in front of the Turandot on Tverskoy Boulevard a few minutes after seven in the morning. The restaurant was Moscow's most exclusive, and although it normally would have been closed at this hour of the day, the owner, Andrey Deloss, had gladly agreed to open it for the president and his one guest, the director of the SVR.

The morning rush hour traffic was already in full swing, but police had been stationed at every corner from the Kremlin to hold the streets open, and the ride had gone without a hitch.

Four of Putin's security detail, all very muscular men in tailored dark suits, escorted Putin from the limo and inside the ornately decorated restaurant, where Deloss himself was waiting.

"Good morning, Mr. President," Deloss said. He was dressed in a tuxedo. "General Raskopov arrived just a couple of minutes ago and I seated him in the restaurant-palace as you wished."

"Is he alone?"

"Yes. No bodyguards, as you also suggested. Will yours be joining you?"

"No," Putin said.

Deloss stepped aside, motioned Putin toward the extremely ornately decorated main salle, which was located in a round, colonnaded hall with a podium for an orchestra, and followed him to a table directly beneath the Malaysian crystal chandelier, where Raskopov was seated.

The highly decorated general, in uniform, rose at Putin's approach, and the two men embraced as if they were the warmest of friends.

When they were seated, a pair of white-coated waiters appeared, poured water and Krug champagne for both men, and then stepped away.

"Would you gentlemen wish to see menus?" Deloss asked.

"Leave us now," Putin said. "I'll let you know when we're ready to order."

"Very good, Mr. President," Delos said. "General." He withdrew.

"You have an operation in place in the United States," Putin said. "I would like to know how it is progressing."

"We have many operations currently in progress."

"The one involving Mr. McGarvey, the former director of the CIA."

"Interesting person."

"That's not what I asked, Anatoli."

Raskopov took a sip of his champagne. "A unique situation, that," he said. "An operation nearly thirty years ago that you may have been peripherally involved with resulted in the deaths of Mr. McGarvey's parents. It was one of the rare KGB wet affairs that actually had a good outcome. The McGarveys were involved in an important defense project that was deemed untenable for us."

"I was briefed earlier this week. But I just found out that the son not only has reopened an investigation into his parents' deaths but also is certain that I was personally involved, and that he means to hold me accountable."

"Extraordinary," Raskopov said, but it was obvious he wasn't sincere.

Putin smiled thinly. "He managed to get through to me on my private line. Told me that if I wanted a war, he would give me a fucking war. His words."

"Did he tell you how he planned to proceed?"

"No."

"He's on his way here, even as we speak."

"Good. Then I'll have him arrested the moment he shows up."

"Actually, he and his computer expert are en route to Zurich—for what reason, we haven't been able to find out—while at the same time McGarvey's wife showed up at Los Alamos."

Putin knew some of that. Like Raskopov, who had assets inside the Kremlin, Putin had a number of old loyal friends inside the SVR. It was the most important game of Russian chess. "Evidently your operation to eliminate them was not a success. Too bad."

"An embarrassment, because I underestimated Mr. McGarvey and his friends and overestimated my people. It's a mistake I will not make again."

"Mistakes," Putin said. "Among many."

Raskopov understood what Putin meant. "Don't threaten me, Vladi. You may have won the vote, but there are other, more important structures of power."

"Indeed," Putin said. He took the champagne from the ice bucket and filled Raskopov's glass. "Then let's not divide our power base."

The general sipped his champagne, before he answered. "Do we trade?"

"It's possible. What do you have to offer, and for what in return?"

"I'll deal with McGarvey and his friends."

"I'm listening."

Raskopov fiddled with his champagne glass. "You have developed a unique relationship with President Weaver."

"The man's a fool."

"No Russian curse is worse," Raskopov said. "But he believes, as most Americans do, and as many Russians do, that you have become a dictator. A neo-Stalin."

Putin chuckled "Your point?"

"No American curse is worse. But in this we may have an opportunity to salvage what you are on the verge of losing."

"And what is that?" Putin asked.

"I'll tell you," the general said. "But first I will assure you that McGarvey and his computer friend, Otto Rencke, will be taken care of in Zurich. And McGarvey's wife, now at Los Alamos, will be dealt with as well. And in case there are failures, one of my assets remains in place in Washington."

Church's unpretentious office had two large windows, looking east, which in the daytime would give a nice view of the Sangre de Cristo Mountains.

"Let's be frank, Ms. McGarvey—" Church began, but Pete held up a hand.

"Mrs.," Pete said.

"I'm not getting into an interagency dispute with you. This is a DOE operation over which the CIA has absolutely no jurisdiction, so if your intention was to come here and brief me on something you believe is important to our security, then proceed. Otherwise, go back to Langley; we neither need nor want your help."

"I could have used your help, but instead you choppered an assassin down to Albuquerque to take me out. So why don't we just start out fresh? I'll tell you what I have and you'll tell me what you intend on doing, if anything."

"Would you object to me recording this conversation?"

"Be my guest. But when we're finished I expect you would be better off erasing it."

Church hesitated for just a moment, but then touched a button on his phone console. "Proceed."

"We are almost one hundred percent certain that John and Lilly Mc-Garvey were assassinated by the KGB to stop them from finishing a satellite defense system they were working on," Pete said.

"That was never proven."

"Recently, my husband began looking into the possibility, along with my help and that of two others. Almost immediately several attempts were made on our lives, including the attempt on mine this evening. We managed to take out more than a half dozen operatives, during which a very close friend of mine lost her life. So please understand me, Mr. Church. You have a Russian spy or spies at this facility, and I am highly motivated to find them, with or without your help."

Church started to object, but Pete held him off again.

"I think that there's a good chance that your office is bugged, but I've told you nothing that the opposition doesn't already know."

"This space, along with my conference room, is electronically shielded. Nothing gets in or out. Try your cell phone. You'll find that it doesn't work."

"Lou," Pete said, not taking her eyes away from Church's.

"Yes, Pete."

Church's jaw tightened.

"Can you say if there is a bug in this room?"

"Not at this time, though I detect a white noise device."

"Thank you."

"You're welcome," Lou replied.

FIFTY-SEVEN

McGarvey was seated at the Moments restaurant in the NH Zurich Airport hotel, a few minutes before 10:30 in the morning, when Otto walked in. For just an instant, he didn't recognize his friend, but then Otto's face lit up when he spotted Mac, and he came over and sat down.

"I'm meeting someone for lunch in town, so I don't have much time to give you, except to tell you that you should go to Albuquerque," he said. "I think Pete's already in trouble."

McGarvey had suspected something would happen down there, but he held himself in check from overreacting. "Did it involve Bob Wehr?"

"Yeah, but he was the good guy," Otto said, and he gave McGarvey the information that Lou had relayed to him. "She and Church had a pull-no-punches meeting, and he agreed to help. It's the middle of the night now, and she's bedded down in the BOQ."

"Someone standing guard?"

"Besides the charge of quarters, Church stationed two of his people outside the front door. So, for now at least, she'll be okay."

"Someone will try to stop her."

"You need to be there," Otto said. "You don't want to lose her."

It had been McGarvey's constant nightmare since he'd said he loved her. "She'll probably be okay as long as she stays at the lab. If there's going to be more trouble, it'll come when she leaves."

Otto nodded. "One of us can call Housekeeping. Maybe Waksberg can send some muscle down."

It was something. McGarvey nodded. "Who are you meeting for lunch? And why here in Zurich?"

"Valeri Zhernov, because he and some other guys in the same boat live here in exile, after Putin drove them out of Russia. It was here or face a firing squad."

"What's his crime?"

"Same as all of them: they made too much money and didn't want to share a chunk of it with the president. Zhernov made his money in real estate, mostly in Moscow but also in Vladivostok. He was the fifth-richest man in Russia. So Putin nationalized his bank on fraud charges, took half his fortune, and let him escape with the other half, with the warning that if he ever set foot on Russian soil he would be a dead man."

"Accidents happen."

"Exactly."

"Okay, so he's a rich exile who's not in love with Putin. What's your connection with him?"

"I managed to pirate one hundred million and change for him and set up an offshore account in Jersey. I'm bringing him the password."

"He'll be grateful," McGarvey said, almost smiling.

"I believe he will be."

"What do you want in return?"

"Putin and General Raskopov are on the outs. But neither has made any sort of an overt run on the other. They just make enough noise, supposedly in private, so that it leaks out in bits and pieces. Putin could fire the man, appoint someone else to run the service, and Raskopov has the power to stage a putsch, maybe even have Putin assassinated, and call for another election."

"But they don't. Why not?"

"That's what I'm going to ask Comrade Zhernov," Otto said. "Maybe we'll stage our own putsch."

"If it happens, I don't see you riding into Red Square atop a tank."

"No, but I can soften Putin's response by screwing with their military communications systems. I have an untraceable malware program that'd have a back way out, once Putin and Raskopov are gone."

McGarvey sat back. There were only a handful of other diners having late breakfast in the dining room, none of them having any notion of what could be unleashed if Otto got what he needed from the Russian oligarch.

"Wars have started that way," he said.

Otto looked away for a long moment, but then nodded and turned back. "Now you sound like Lou."

"Your program?"

"My wife. And she would have been right. Both of you. But I'm not trying to start that kind of a war. I just want Putin, who ordered the attacks on us, and Raskopov, who directed them, to pay a heavy price."

"I'm coming with you."

"No."

"I'll stay in the background. But there's no doubt that Zhernov and everyone else like him is being watched. They see you talking to him, they might try to take out both of you. Anyway, I told Putin if he wanted a war, I'd give it to him. Today will be our opening shot."

"I have no idea where this is going, *kemo sabe*," Otto said.

"Neither do I."

Pete awoke from a light sleep with no idea why, except that her heart was pounding. She pushed the covers aside, sat up, and got her pistol from the nightstand. The room was small, with only two double beds, a dresser, and an en suite bathroom. The moon was low, but the soft light cast shadows.

She was fully dressed, except for her shoes, and she padded to the window. Keeping to one side, she looked down at the parking lot in front of the building. From this angle, she wasn't able to see the two guards Church had assigned to keep watch on her, but their government-issue Ford SUV was parked on the driveway directly across from the entryway portico.

Nothing seemed wrong, but she was spooked.

She started for the door, sure that she'd heard something. A very soft metal-on-metal sound. A key in the old-fashioned lock.

Stepping to the side, she found the light switch with her left hand, raised her pistol, and closed her eyes.

Whoever was just outside hesitated for several long seconds, but then she could feel the door open, a different sound and smell coming from the corridor.

She waited for another second, then hit the light switch and opened her eyes, just in time to see a man, blinded by the sudden glare, stagger backward, a pistol in his right hand.

Stepping forward, she grabbed his gun, turned it away, and jammed the muzzle of her pistol into his forehead.

"Jesus Christ," the man said.

"The goddamn *charge of quarters?*" she said. "What the hell are you doing here?"

"The two men Mr. Church sent are down," the man said in a rush, his voice low. "I just managed to get the hell away from my post to come up and warn you."

Pete pulled him inside and softly closed the door. "Did you see how many of them there were?"

"No," the CQ said. He was a younger man, in his late twenties, with a wild look in his dark eyes. Pete released her grip on his pistol, and he held it down to his side and out.

"Did you call for help?" Pete asked, going to the window.

"No time," the CQ said.

Suddenly, she had it. The CQ's pistol had a silencer attached to the muzzle, which was all wrong. And it was warm. He'd fired the weapon.

"Use the phone, call for backup," Pete said, as she started to turn back, leading with her left side.

"No need," the man said.

Before she was fully turned, Pete raised her left arm and brought the pistol in her right hand under the left.

The CQ was just bringing his gun to bear when she fired two shots, both of them striking him in the chest, and he dropped to the floor.

FIFTY-EIGHT

☐

They were meeting at the Kronenhalle, one of Zurich's oldest and most famous restaurants, not far from the lake. McGarvey went first and was seated at a table with his back to the bar and a good sight line on the front door. "*Un bière ordinaire,*" he told the waiter.

The place was only half-filled, many of the patrons obviously tourists.

Otto came in a couple of minutes later and went directly to join a slender man in his late forties or early fifties, of medium height, with blond hair. "Good morning, Mr. Zhernov. We talked by computer."

McGarvey heard everything from his cell phone, via a tiny, flesh-colored earbud that was completely invisible except by a very close examination.

"Sit down, Mr. Rencke," the man said, his British English accented only slightly with Russian. He'd been educated abroad. "Your reputation precedes you."

"As does yours, sir," Otto said, taking a seat across the table from Zhernov. "I'll be brief."

"Please be."

"You well understand the animosity between presidents Putin and Weaver."

Zhernov chuckled. "That's putting it mildly. Putin thinks your president is a fool."

"And Weaver believes Putin is positioning himself to become the next Stalin."

"He's nearly there."

"Yes. And his next logical step should be the replacement of General Raskopov."

"It might be in your country's best interest to have it the other way round," Zhernov said. "Tell me, are you here on what you would call a back burner mission for the CIA? Or is this something different?"

"I'm doing this independently, because the situation became personal for me recently. My wife was shot to death by agents working for the SVR."

"Is that why you offered to give me a rather large sum of money?"

Otto took a small slip of paper out of his pocket, laid it on the table, and pushed it across. "It's the account number here at a private Swiss bank, along with your password. The amount is one hundred million euros."

Zhernov didn't touch the slip. "In exchange for what?"

"Raskopov ordered me and my wife assassinated, along with two of my colleagues. I want to know if this was an independent operation on the SVR's part or if it was directed by Mr. Putin. And I want to know why."

"If this is a simple vendetta, you could use this money to hire a specialist, or a small army of specialists, to kill both men. Why come to me?"

"Because you know both men personally, and I believe that the real reason you were kicked out of Russia and not jailed or assassinated was because you made a promise to one or the other that you would keep your mouth shut."

Zhernov shook his head. "That makes no sense. If they believed that I knew something, they would have had me killed. A simple drive-by shooting."

"You have too many friends in Russia and elsewhere. Kicking you out caused less trouble than killing you—which they could do at any time. Unless you had an insurance policy."

"Which is?"

"Me."

Zhernov laughed softly. "You might be very good with money, Mr. Rencke, but you hardly fit the image of an assassin."

"As you said, a hundred million euros would get me a small dedicated army. But that's not what I want. I want to do it with my own hand."

"For that, you would need to know who directed the operation, why the order was given, and a lever strong enough to let you get close. A lever that you think I could provide you."

"I'm sure of it," Otto said.

Zhernov poured Otto a glass of mineral water. "Would you like to order something?"

"No, I have to get back to the airport shortly."

"Are you returning home?"

"I'm going to Helsinki, and from there to Moscow, with or without your help."

Zhernov was startled. "You're a fool."

"Da."

The Russian took a moment or two before he answered. "The first thing I learned, at the beginning of my career, was that knowledge is everything. But what I have to give to you is secondhand, very old."

"Twenty-eight years old."

Zhernov was startled again. "Then you know."

"Only some of it. I need to know the who—and why the operation still continues to this day."

"And who's to blame."

"Yes."

"Anatoli was just a junior officer, one grade beneath Putin, in the KGB's First Directorate. He was in charge of the scientific espionage in department one: the U.S. and Latin America."

"Los Alamos."

"Da, and Sandia, Lawrence Livermore, and all of NASA, but especially Goddard. I don't know why the last, except that for some reason it was fairly high on the list."

"I suspect it was because, of all the space agencies, Goddard might have been the easiest to penetrate."

"I don't know," Zhernov said. "Nor do I know the details, but Putin and Anatoli were in direct competition with each other."

"Enough to try to sabotage each other's work?"

Zhernov nodded. "It's the same in just about every agency in our government, as well as in yours. But you've come here to ask me about the assassinations of Kirk McGarvey's parents."

"Yes."

"Anatoli and I are friends—you know this. It's why you came to me. But my answer is that either of them could have been responsible, or neither of them. The McGarveys had apparently made a breakthrough in some satellite defense system, and it was important enough to catch the attention of the komitet's director himself."

"Putin could have arranged the assassinations to make the operation look like it belonged to Raskopov, who had made a large mistake," Otto said.

"Or Raskopov could have ordered the hit and somehow have the blame shifted to Putin," Zhernov said. "That's what Anatoli told me two days ago, when he warned me that someone like you would be coming to ask me that question."

"He could have been lying."

Zhernov nodded. "Don't all of you in the business lie for a living?"

Otto shrugged off the obvious question about the very nature of espionage. "Both he and Putin succeeded, so why are they apparently still worried about an operation that took place nearly thirty years ago? It can't make any difference now."

"General Raskopov wants to become the next president of Russia."

"And Putin?"

"Wants to be reelected, of course. So the rivalry still exists. And the attacks against you and Mr. McGarvey could have been ordered by either man, as I've said. Or both."

"They made a mistake," Otto said.

"All men do."

"One of them killed my wife."

"The fact is, you and Mr. McGarvey, seated across the room from us, have been caught up in the middle of a power struggle between the two most powerful men in Russia."

McGarvey spotted a dark blue Lexus SUV as it pulled up to the curb and parked in the no standing spot in front of the restaurant's entrance. The windows were tinted too dark for him to see anything except the driver and one passenger in the front, but neither of them made a move to get out of the car.

"So now he knows what I know," Otto said in McGarvey's ear. "He means to get to Putin. Will General Raskopov help?"

Zhernov laughed. "You'll have to ask him yourself."

"How?"

"Offer to return control of his computer system."

FIFTY-NINE

Two nondescript men got out of the back of the Lexus, waited for just a moment on the sidewalk, then headed for the front door. They wore dark suits, the sleeves the correct length but the cut over the torso loose enough to conceal large-caliber handguns.

McGarvey got up from his table and went immediately to where Otto and Zhernov were seated. Both men looked up.

"We need to go, now," he told Otto, who immediately got to his feet. "Company?"

"Coming through the front door," McGarvey said. "Mr. Zhernov, I suspect you may be safe if you remain here."

Mac didn't wait for a reply but took Otto by the elbow and headed him toward the doors into the kitchen. "Are you carrying?"

"The little Glock you gave me last year."

It was the 29 Gen4 model that Otto and Louise had practiced with on the firing range in the basement of the Original Headquarters Building at Langley. After a few incidents in the previous year or so, McGarvey had thought it prudent that his friend and Louise knew how to shoot, and to hit what they were aiming at. Otto was competent but Lou had been a natural.

The kitchen was very busy at this hour, but only a few of the chefs and several waiters bothered to glance up as the two intruders barged into the kitchen and raced toward back doors that led to three walk-in supply rooms, with shelving units for supplies. Beyond that was a receiving area, and from there, double doors that led to a back alley.

"Hold up," Mac said. He pulled out his pistol and eased one of the doors open just a crack.

A white panel van with a logo of a cow, a pig, and a lamb painted on the side, under an arch with the name of the supplier, Fleischmeister, had just arrived. Meat Master.

The driver and another man, both dressed in white coveralls, got out, pistols with suppressors on the muzzles in hand.

McGarvey fired one shot, hitting the driver center mass. He went down, but the other man ducked around the side of the van and fired three times, the rounds smacking into the steel service door.

Something was going on out front. A woman in the dining room screamed, a man shouted something, and then more people began shouting in what sounded like panic.

"Holster your gun," McGarvey said, and he hustled Otto back to the supply room, where a shelving unit along one wall was stacked with baggy white trousers, black-and-white-striped chef's jackets, and black beanie hats.

McGarvey pulled down one chef's uniform and tossed it to Otto, who began to put it on as Mac got another set for himself and got dressed.

They rushed back into the kitchen and reached one of the long prep tables just before the doors to the dining room swung open and the two men from the Lexus barged through and stopped, their pistols sweeping the room.

Mac looked past the two men and got a momentary glimpse of people racing for the doors, screaming in panic. Zhernov was slumped forward on his table, obviously dead or dying.

All work in the kitchen had come to a complete halt. The chefs, sous chefs, and others had all stepped back from what they were doing and were simply staring openmouthed at the men with guns and at the pandemonium beyond the dining room doors.

Otto started to go for his gun, but Mac reached out and stayed his hand. "Too many innocents here."

The shooters paused for only a second before they bulled their way past the kitchen crew and out the back door to the supply room.

"I want the driver out front," Mac said, the instant the shooters were gone.

"I'm coming with you."

"Stay here."

"Zhernov was Raskopov's friend, which means the shooters work for Putin."

"That's what I want to find out for sure," McGarvey said. "Stay here and keep your head down, goddamnit."

"Those guys will be coming back."

"Maybe," McGarvey said. "But keep your head down, because the cops will be showing up any minute."

He yanked off the hat and jacket and tossed them aside as he hurried to the dining room door, which had swung shut. He pulled out his Walther, eased the door open, and looked out.

The last of the diners and waiters had gone, leaving only Zhernov's body, slumped forward, his face in the middle of a large pool of blood on the white tablecloth.

The Lexus was still parked outside, but so far there were no sirens.

Pulling off the baggy white trousers, he stepped out into the dining room and crossed to the entry alcove, where he pushed the front door open. The people from the restaurant had scattered, some dodging traffic as they crossed Ramistrasse, others going down the block toward the lake, traffic on the Utoquai even heavier.

Concealing the pistol behind his right leg, Mac went directly to the rear of the Lexus, in a rush, as if he were the last of the people fleeing the restaurant and meant to cross the street.

At the last moment he turned back, yanked open the front passenger door, climbed inside, and pointed his gun at the startled driver's head.

"Drive away now or I will kill you," McGarvey said.

The driver hesitated for just a second, not knowing what he should do.

"Now," McGarvey said.

The driver slammed the gearshift lever into drive, but before he could pull away from the curb, the rear door on his side opened and Otto got in.

They accelerated away as the first three police cars, blue lights flashing, sirens blaring, rounded the corner at the end of the block.

McGarvey kept glancing in the door mirror as the police arrived and cops started jumping out, brandishing the submachine guns that just about every cop in Europe had been carrying over the past several years because of the rise in terrorist attacks.

"Where to?" the driver demanded.

"Peterskirche," Otto said. "There are lots of people there."

"Do it," McGarvey said. He glanced in the mirror as they were turning the corner and caught just a glimpse of one of the waiters pointing toward the Lexus, a cop right there with her.

Sirens were converging on the Kronenhalle from all over the city, but none seemed to be heading toward them. McGarvey directed the driver to park as close as possible to the side doors of the church with its spire rising high into the sky, away from the river bridge and the bulk of the tourist crowds.

They found a spot a half block away and the driver, a man about the same size as the shooters, and dressed similarly, pulled over and parked.

McGarvey reached inside the man's jacket with his left hand and pulled out an American-made Wilson pistol. He passed it back to Otto.

"Get the hell out, now. Ditch your gun and this one someplace and lose yourself in the crowd before the cops get here."

"First I want to know who sent the bastards," Otto said. He jammed the muzzle of the large .45-caliber gun into the back of the Russian's head. "And I'll blow your brains out if I think you're lying."

The Russian only hesitated for a second. "Mr. Sankov," he said.

"Who's that?" McGarvey asked, but Otto answered before the Russian could speak.

"Son of a bitch," he said. "Vadim Sankov, a top Kremlin go-to guy. Putin wants something done, and right away, Sankov is the man, especially if the SVR is to be kept out of it."

"Still leaves the question of what they want hidden after all these years," Mac said.

"The Los Alamos spy ring, for one."

A pair of sirens seemed to be coming from just across the river.

"Get the hell out of here," McGarvey said. "I'll cover for you."

"Let me shoot the bastard first."

"So far, you've done nothing wrong for the Swiss to hold you. Just go."

"I'm not stopping," Otto said.

"I'll catch up," Mac told him, and Otto slipped out of the Lexus and walked away.

In less than a minute he'd disappeared into the crowd, and immediately the first police car came around the corner, its siren blaring.

The Russian suddenly lurched to the right, momentarily knocking McGarvey's aim off.

"You're a criminal, holding me at gunpoint," the man shouted, grabbing for the gun.

It went off, the shot plowing into the side of the Russian's head at the same moment that a pair of police officers, their submachine guns at the ready, were at the Lexus.

"*Hande hoch! Hande hoch!*" they shouted. Hands up.

☐

SIXTY

Pete had been moved over to one of the VIP bungalows normally used for visiting dignitaries, usually from the DOE. It was a far cry from the dingy room she'd been given in the BOQ.

The place was on a slight hill, looking over much of the lab complex that had originally been built to develop the first atomic bomb, back in the forties. Now, at seven in the morning, the lab was coming to life with the day shift of scientists and technicians, most of whom had no idea that three shootings had occurred here this morning, plus the one down in Albuquerque.

She hadn't slept worth a damn last night, but now she was coming down from her adrenaline high and could scarcely keep her eyes open. But, all in all, she was satisfied with her progress so far. She had kicked the anthill and two bad guys had popped out. Two down, she thought, and she wondered how many were left here. She suspected a lot of them, all entrenched.

The landline phone rang. It was Church. "I'm on the way over with the FBI's Albuquerque SAC," he said. "Do you want me to send over some breakfast?"

"Just coffee."

"We're just pulling up. I brought some along, just in case."

"I'm getting out of the shower. Give me five."

"Okay."

Pete had taken the SIM card out of her phone, though it seemed silly in retrospect. The opposition had known she was coming to Albuquerque even before she'd landed. She put it back in and powered up the phone.

"Lou?" she said.

"Hello, Pete."

"May I talk to Mac or Otto?"

Lou hesitated for just an instant. "Not at this time. Do you need assistance?"

"Are there any bugs where I am?"

"Yes."

"Can you disable them?"

"I already have."

"Can you tell me if Mac or Otto are in any danger at the moment?"

"Otto is at the Zurich airport and Mac is in custody at police headquarters Zurich."

It was something. "Are either of them injured?"

"No."

"But I can't speak with them?"

"No."

"Could you contact Mr. Waksberg at Langley for me?"

"Yes, but he has already been apprised of your current situation and a team of investigators is being sent down, along with another team from the Bureau. They should be on the ground before noon and will take over from where you began. Would you still wish me to contact him now?"

"No, it's not necessary. Thank you."

"Otto would like to know if you are well."

"Tell him yes. And please keep me informed about my husband's status."

"Of course."

Church was at the door. Pete hung up, pocketed her phone in her jeans, and let him in, along with a taller, slender, serious-looking man in a business suit, his tie loose. Church identified him as Robert Baker, the FBI's actual Albuquerque SAC.

A security officer was stationed in front of the bungalow and another was in back.

"There's no need for you to say 'I told you so,'" Church said. "You were right all along."

"Have you identified the body at the airport?"

"His Florida driver's license lists his name as Edward Leon, but it's a fake," Baker said.

Church had brought a large cup of Starbucks coffee and a paper bag, which he set on the small table in the kitchenette. "I got you a couple of doughnuts."

"Thanks," Pete told him. "Let me guess: the guy's address was in Sarasota?"

"Yes, and we don't think that it was a coincidence," Baker said. "We're trying to reach your husband. Could you tell us where he is?"

"No," Pete said. "The man who I shot was the CQ; don't tell me that he was from Sarasota too."

"Dayton, Ohio," Church said. "And he's worked here for ten years, longer than me."

"You shot the imposter down at the airport, but someone helped you get away," Baker said. "Who was it?"

"I don't know," Pete said. "A good Samaritan."

Church wasn't pleased. "We're trying to help you. It would be a hell of a lot easier if you cooperated with us."

"Yeah, like choppering the shooter down to Albuquerque to take me out. Like assigning a CQ who wanted to kill me. Nice job of security, Church. You run a tight shop."

"We're not getting anywhere here, Mrs. McGarvey," Baker said, cutting off whatever Church was about to say. "You came here looking for a spy."

"A spy ring that's almost certainly been in place for at least twenty-eight years, and probably longer," Pete said. She was having a hard time keeping her temper in check. "I came here to find out just that, and as it turns out, I was right. I outed the bastards; now it's up to you guys to catch them. I'm going home, if you'll provide me a ride back to Albuquerque."

"The DA would like you to stick around. She has a number of questions involving the shooting death at the airport."

"I'm going home, Mr. Baker. This morning."

"I'm afraid that won't be possible," Baker said.

"Lou," Pete said, without taking her eyes off Baker or Church.

"Mr. Waksberg has been listening in. He is on a conference call with Mr. Taft, Mr. Kallek, and Mr. Spencer, and he asks that you stand by."

Harold Kallek was the director of the FBI and John Spencer headed the Department of Energy.

"Thank you," Pete said. "That woman is actually a computer program at Langley," she told the two men.

Church was furious, but Baker just shrugged.

Both his and Church's cell phones rang at the same time, three minutes later.

Pete got her coffee and a plain doughnut and took a seat in the galley kitchen as the two men separated—Church out the door and Baker to the front windows.

She thought about trying Lou again to see if she could make contact with Mac. The Zurich cops had him, probably on a weapons charge— but possibly on a murder charge if he'd gotten into a shoot-out and had to defend himself. But he had a history in Switzerland—not a particularly good one—and the Swiss federal police had very long memories.

But if he was in custody, he was safe for the moment. It was Otto she was more worried about, because she suspected that whatever had happened in Zurich, Mac had probably gotten him out of some jam, and he was now on his way into Russia. Badland.

Baker turned first. "You are free to return to Washington."

"Can I hitch a ride with you?"

"Of course."

Church came in, somewhat red-faced. "Get the fuck out of here, and don't come back."

"Thanks," Pete said.

The FBI's Albuquerque SAC had come up by helicopter, and he brought Pete back down to the airport and had a car take her to the terminal, where Lou had arranged a first-class flight back to Dulles for her.

"You need a little pampering," Otto's computer had said, and at that moment, Pete thought the machine had never sounded more like Louise.

Wehr was seated in the boarding area when she got through security and checked in with the gate agent. She walked over and sat down next to him.

"You ran into a spot of trouble at the lab, I heard," he said.

"Who the hell are you?" she asked.

He smiled. "A friend with a warning. Watch your tradecraft in Washington. The opposition wants you very badly, and I may not be able to get up there for a couple of days."

SIXTY-ONE

Zimin sat on a bench in Rock Creek Park, just a few feet from the slowly moving narrow stream. McGarvey's apartment, two blocks away, was still under surveillance by plainclothesmen, who he assumed were FBI. But the woman's apartment, just across the Parkway, was clean, so far as he could tell.

Over the past three days he had purchased four throwaway phones plus three sets of clothing—a blazer, gray slacks, and white shirt; shorts, T-shirt, and boat shoes; and jeans, a dark pullover, and running shoes—from five different establishments, including a shop inside Union Station.

He had called Yuryn's emergency number eighteen hours before and asked for help. Although the man had been surprised, even shocked, he'd agreed that McGarvey's wife was the only realistic possibility for them at the moment.

"She's in New Mexico."

"With Rencke?"

"No. But he showed up in Zurich, apparently with McGarvey, where there was some kind of trouble, and he disappeared again."

"What about McGarvey?"

"We think he's in custody," Yuryn said. "Where are you?"

"Washington. You?"

"Where I am doesn't matter, but now it's just the two of us, and whatever you plan on doing, I just hope the fuck that it works."

"I'm waiting for the woman to show up and I'm going to take care of her. But I'm going to need your help."

"I'm not a shooter; you people knew that from the start."

"I only need intel," Zimin said. "I want to know when she comes back to Washington."

Yuryn had paused. "Have you contacted Yasenevo?"

"*Da.* I've given them my full report."

"Can I reach you at this number?"

"No," Zimin said. He gave the man the number for the second throwaway phone.

Now, sitting in the early afternoon in the dappled sunlight that filtered through the trees, Zimin had an almost overwhelming urge to be back in his home in Moscow. Back in his comfortable routine with his good friends. And occasionally at times like this, he even fantasized about having his wife returned to him.

He was an old man, long retired, and he had the distinct feeling that he would never be going home.

It was a weekday, and traffic on the Rock Creek Parkway was steady. As he reached for the Styrofoam coffee cup sitting beside him, his phone burred softly in his pocket.

He answered in his excellent English. "Hello?"

"She lands at Dulles in one hour," Yuryn said.

"Is she traveling alone?"

"Yes."

"Thank you."

"She was involved in two shooting incidents. The CIA, FBI, and Department of Energy have sent teams to investigate."

"I don't care. She's coming here and I will finish the op and return home."

"You didn't hear me. She was *directly* involved. One of our people was sent to intercept her at the airport. Somehow she knew who he was and she shot him to death. And then, at the primary site, an operator was sent to eliminate her, but she shot him to death as well."

Zimin was alarmed. "She must have had help."

"Not at the primary, so far as we can tell, but someone helped her leave the shooting scene outside the airport."

"Is someone from the CIA shadowing her?"

"Unknown," Yuryn said. "But all I'm telling you is to be very careful.

The woman is a hell of a lot more capable than we gave her credit for being—just like her husband—and she has help."

"*Spasibo*," Zimin said. Thanks. And he hung up.

He sat for a minute or two, finishing his coffee. When he was done, he took the SIM card out of his phone. At this hour, not many people were in the park, but he made sure no one was around before he got up and threw the phone into the creek.

Up on the path, he found a trash barrel for his empty cup—and then for the SIM card, after he crushed it under his heel.

Pete phoned Otto's number. Lou answered on the first ring.

"Hello, Pete."

"Is Mac still in Zurich?"

"The police have him."

"Have you hacked into their computer system?"

"Otto has instructed me never to interfere with persons or institutions that mean us no harm."

Pete almost laughed out loud. Otto's darlings routinely hacked the mainframes of the CIA itself, along with the FBI and even some of the systems in the White House. But she let it go. "Then they've not lined him up in front of a firing squad yet?"

"No," the computer answered dryly. Humor very often escaped Otto, and it was no different for his darlings.

"Let me know if it happens."

"It is improbable under current Swiss law."

"At least let me know when he's released. I need to talk to him. In the meantime, I'm going straight home to get cleaned up and then I'm heading to Langley."

Lou hung up.

With the blazer folded and tucked under an arm, Zimin walked past Pete's apartment building, then slowly circled the block. He hailed a cab to take him to Gaston Hall at Georgetown University.

He'd gotten lucky and arrived between classes, and a lot of students were out and about.

Putting on his jacket, he walked down to Prospect Street, where, ten minutes later, he found a cab to take him back to Pete's building.

The front door was unlocked, and it took him less than three minutes to reach the top floor, pick her lock, and let himself into her apartment.

He made a quick sweep of the place, taking special care to check the landline phone, lamps, the television and stereo, and the bedside radio, as well as behind wall hangings, for any obvious signs of surveillance devices—cameras or microphones.

Finding nothing obvious, he took off his jacket, folded it neatly, and laid it on the bed. Then he pulled a chair from the table in the kitchenette and placed it in a corner that gave him an excellent sight line to the door.

He stood there for a moment, something spooking him. He let himself out and knocked on the door of the rear apartment across the hall. When there was no answer, he picked the lock and let himself in.

He checked the load and action of his Glock pistol, attached the suppressor to the muzzle, then waited with the door slightly ajar for McGarvey's wife to show up.

If he survived this encounter, and if he was successful, he would have a very good excuse for not having obeyed General Raskopov's orders. This part of the mission would have been accomplished, and all he wanted—all he'd ever wanted from the beginning—was to get back to his old life.

Coming this far, and sitting in this excellent position, he thought that his chances were better than fifty-fifty. He'd faced worse.

SIXTY-TWO

□

A uniformed guard came to the isolation wing for McGarvey after dinner. It was around eight, and although he'd not been formally charged with any crime, he'd not been allowed to make contact with anyone on the outside, not even an attorney. Nor had he tried to make contact with Lou.

"Where are we going?" he asked the unarmed guard. The man was old, his face round, his nose lined with broken veins.

"Someone wishes to have a word with you, sir," the guard said, his English passable.

"Who?"

"I don't know."

The central lockup at police headquarters was very typically Swiss, super clean and very quiet. He'd been held overnight, but the food was nearly as good as any decent hotel would serve and the bed was reasonably comfortable.

When he'd been here as an expat, years ago, someone had explained Swiss jails to him, which they said were very similar to those in Norway. The accused, as well as those found guilty and even those sentenced to long terms, were still human beings who needed to be treated with respect and kindness.

They took an elevator up to the administrative floor and then went down a long corridor to a small conference room, where the guard left him.

Dortmund Kelenbeck, the Swiss cop who'd handled the initial interrogation, was seated next to an attractive woman in her late forties, both of them in civilian clothes. They'd been talking, and when Mac came in they looked up, neutral expressions on their faces.

Kelenbeck motioned for McGarvey to have a seat across the table from them.

McGarvey sat down.

"Would you like a cigarette, Mr. McGarvey?" the woman asked in excellent English. Her face was round, her hair cut stylishly short, and her dark suit and white shirt, open at the collar, were obviously expensive.

"I don't smoke."

"Ah, then you finally quit. Good. And it's good to finally meet face-to-face."

"Do I know you?"

"No. My name is Renate Kroger, and when you were in Lausanne, years ago, I was a young NDB officer just starting out. And we were fascinated about you, and all of us felt genuine sorrow when Marta lost her life."

McGarvey was taken aback. After his first wet assignment for the CIA had gone bad and his wife had given him the ultimatum to quit the Company or leave, he had run to Switzerland. But the NDB—the Swiss federal intelligence service—had sent Marta Fredricks to keep an eye on him. Former CIA officers, especially shooters, made the Swiss nervous. She had been killed by someone for the opposition who was gunning for him.

"She was a good person," he said. "Am I being charged with a federal crime?"

"You are implicated in two shooting deaths," Kelenbeck said, with a little anger.

"Have they been identified?"

"No," Kelenbeck said, and he was about to say something else, but Renate held him off with a gesture.

"We're almost certain they were Russian intelligence officers, working on the same team that murdered Herr Zhernov at the Kronenhalle. And except for your restraint—under the conditions—the collateral damage could have been far greater."

"Zhernov was the target," McGarvey said.

"Can you tell me why?"

"He was talking to us."

"Us," Renate said. "You and Mr. Rencke?"

"Yes."

"About what?"

"An operation we're involved with," McGarvey said.

"For the CIA? Officially?"

"No."

"Then please tell me the nature of your operation."

McGarvey held his silence for just a beat. Everything that had gone on over the past days had been focused from the start—and now, at this instant—on the exact time he'd learned of his parents' deaths. That, and the loss of every woman who'd been important in his life, including Louise, rode with him like some dark cloud. Just over the horizon, but always there.

"My parents were scientists at Los Alamos. They lost their lives in a car accident twenty-eight years ago. I believe it was a KGB-directed operation, and as soon as I started to look into it, people around me have been getting killed."

Renate closed the file folder that had been sitting open in front of her. "I understand your pain," she said. She got to her feet. "As soon as you have completed your paperwork, please return Mr. McGarvey's personal belongings to him, and release him," she told Kelenbeck. "Someone will be along to escort him to the airport. He is being ejected from Switzerland this evening."

Kelenbeck simply nodded.

At the door Renate turned back. "Fredricks was Marta's work name. Her real name was Kroger. She was my sister."

Otto was having dinner in the restaurant at the Original Sokos Hotel Vaakuna, just a short walk from the train station in Helsinki, when Lou called him.

"The Swiss NDB have released Mac from custody."

"He must have been charged with two counts of murder."

"Self-defense. But they want him out of Switzerland as quickly as possible. They had him booked on a flight to Dulles, but he asked that I change it for him."

"Which you did?"

"Of course," Lou said.

"Here to Helsinki?"

"Yes. He is currently at the airport, waiting to board his flight. He wishes to speak with you."

"Put him on," Otto said.

"When are you leaving for badland?" Mac said.

"You should go back to Washington. I think the opposition isn't finished with Pete yet. She could use your help."

"Waksberg promised he'd have a minder covering her six. Right now, it's you I'm most worried about. They're going to want you to disappear, the moment you get off the plane."

"I'm taking the train in the morning."

"Jesus," McGarvey said. "You want Raskopov to reel you in."

"He'll keep Putin's gang away from me, at least until I can straighten out his mainframe. I'm sure that his techs are pulling their hair out now trying to undo the screw job I laid on them."

"Blowback," McGarvey said.

Otto chuckled. "Yeah, and if it comes, it'll be a dilly. All for something they did nearly thirty years ago. Something for which they could have apologized. 'Look, guys, it was an old KGB operation, you know. That kind of crap always tended to spiral out of control sooner or later. Happened on both sides. But we're a lot better now.'"

"Except there's more to it."

"Yeah, another coup d'état," Otto said. "And we're right in the middle of it. A show I don't want to miss."

"I'll be there later tonight. Where are you staying?"

"Go home, my friend."

"You know that isn't possible. This was my fight to begin with, remember?"

Otto was sick at heart, not just for Louise but for all of them, and for whatever was yet to happen.

SIXTY-THREE

Pete got her single checked bag from the carousel and used the bathroom to retrieve her pistol and holster it under her jacket on her left hip. Outside, she got a cab for her apartment. Before she could get in the backseat, a tall, solidly built man in maybe his early thirties, dressed in a business suit, his tie loose, got the door for her.

She automatically reached for her pistol as she turned toward him, but he was smiling pleasantly.

"No need for that now, Mrs. McGarvey. I'm Toby Patterson, your minder."

"Prove it," Pete said. She was jangly from everything that had happened over the past few days, especially Louise's death and the brouhaha in Albuquerque and at the lab.

"You wouldn't believe an ID if I showed you one, but Carleton Patterson is my grandfather, and he is a longtime friend of the family's, even going back to the first Mrs. McGarvey."

The man was sincere, but then so was Bob Wehr. "I'm not in the best of moods, Mr. Patterson, so you had best explain yourself in simple, easy-to-understand terms on the way into town, or I will shoot you."

Patterson grinned. "That'd be a hard one to explain to my boss."

"Who'd that be?"

"Van."

Pete relaxed just a little. P. Van Gessel, whom insiders called Van, was chief of security at Langley. "He and your grandfather are old fishing buddies."

Patterson laughed out loud. "Maybe I should check your ID."

The two men were like oil and water—the elder Patterson a

sophisticated, soft-spoken New York attorney and Van Gessel a rough-shod ex-cop from Missouri.

"Fair enough," Pete said.

The driver put Pete's bag in the trunk, and she gave him her address in Georgetown. Once they were headed away from the airport, she gave Lou a call. Even though they were separated from the driver by a Plexiglas window, Pete kept her voice low.

"I'm on my way to Georgetown. Anything I should know about?"

"Please point your phone at the man sitting next to you."

Pete did as she was told.

"Mr. Patterson. We're glad that you have been assigned to Pete. How is your grandfather?"

Patterson was startled. "Fine. Who are you?"

"A computer program," Pete said. "How's Mac?"

"He has been released from custody and is currently en route to Helsinki," Lou said. "But you have an issue of some concern that you and your minder need to address."

"What is it?"

"A man entered your apartment minutes ago, did a routine search, including for surveillance equipment—which he did not find—and then left."

"Did he plant any explosives?"

"No."

"What is his present location?"

"Unknown," Lou said.

"Can you identify him?"

"The system as it is set up at your apartment is of necessity primarily audio. I have only a forty-seven percent confidence that he is General Yevgenni Zimin, who entered this country from Moscow eight days ago."

The restriction on video had been due to Mac's concern for their privacy.

"You're certain he left nothing behind?" Patterson asked. "Perhaps an aerosol deposit on a doorknob, or something else that someone might come in contact with?"

"My audio equipment is extremely sensitive," Lou responded, and

Pete thought she could hear a note of indignation. But it was just a computer program.

"Do you suggest I call for backup?" Patterson asked.

"It would be advisable. At the very least, Pete needs to be moved to a more secure location."

"On campus?"

"I'm going to clean up and then go out to talk to them," Pete said. "But I'm not going to hide out. There's still work to be done."

"I can't guarantee your safety," Patterson warned her.

"That's not the real issue."

"What is?"

"Finding out who these bastards are and what this shit is all about. My friend is dead, and I'm getting goddamned tired of being shot at every time I turn around. I want it over with. I want my normal life back."

Patterson was looking at her, and even the cabbie glanced in his rear-view mirror, and she almost had to laugh. Normal life, indeed. But at least they could get back to Serifos and take up their vacation where they'd left it—late mornings, early swims in the pool with Greek coffee and French croissants afterward, hikes into town for lunch and retsina wine, afternoons in the hammock or making love in their bedroom near the top of the lighthouse, and evenings listening to music, maybe even watching an old movie on the television. Normalcy. No one shooting at them.

The next flight to Helsinki wasn't until first thing in the morning, on Lufthansa, and although the Swiss wanted him out of the country as quickly as possible, back to Washington, DC, they agreed to let him spend the night if he promised to stay put and not get into any further trouble.

His single bag had been held in storage at the NH Zurich. He rebooked a room and had the bag taken upstairs while he and Bernhard Vogel, the cop Kelenbeck had sent to bird-dog him, went into the Moments bar, busy at this hour of the evening.

Before they were seated, Renate Kroger, who'd ordered his release, walked in.

"I'm surprised to see you here," McGarvey said. "May I buy you a drink?"

"I'm surprised you didn't leave for Washington this evening," she said. "I thought you would have wanted to get home to your wife. But yes, I would take a drink with you."

"Would you like to me remain in the hotel until morning?" Vogel asked.

"You may leave. I'll vouch for Mr. McGarvey's promise to leave Switzerland."

"Yes, ma'am," the cop said, and he left.

Rather than sit at the bar, McGarvey got them a table in a corner, where he had a clear sight line to the entrance. She noticed it and nodded toward where he was looking.

"Old habits?" she asked.

"I'd rather be armed."

"You're safe here. In any event, your firearm, spare magazines, and even your suppressor have been delivered to your room in a sealed diplomatic bag. I suggest you don't tamper with the seal until you are gone."

McGarvey studied her oval face for a long moment. "You look like your sister."

She smiled. "Marta was ten years older than me, but when I was growing up my dad used to laugh and say that we were twin sisters born a decade apart. Truth is that she didn't leave home until I was eight, and that last year we fought like bitter enemies, though I always loved her and I was sure she loved me. She was my hero."

"I loved her then, as best as I could," McGarvey said, though when he'd found out that she was an NDB cop assigned to watch him, the love was a little tarnished.

"What are you doing here? Why the shoot-out with the Russians? And why was Mr. Zhernov assassinated? He was a very important man. Very rich."

"There could be some trouble brewing in Moscow."

"Political trouble?"

"It's possible."

"Because of your president?"

"I don't think so, at least not directly."

"What then?"

"A coup d'état."

The waiter came and they ordered a half bottle of dry Riesling.

"Their elections are coming up soon—or do they think Putin will have his way again?" Renate asked.

"We think it's more complicated, but that's part of it."

"Then who is the opposition?"

"General Raskopov."

"The SVR," Renate said. "My God. If you're right, it could well become a bloody coup."

SIXTY-FOUR

It was late, just before midnight, but General Raskopov was at his desk, talking on the phone to his chief of New York station, Sergei Yuryn, when his secretary barged in the door. He was angry because of what that fool in the States was telling him, but his ire spiked with the sudden interruption.

"What the fuck is it?" he shouted.

"The president has just arrived with a motorcade, General," his secretary said. He was a young man, just out of the intelligence agency's School 1, and very capable. "An armored motorcade."

He had known that Putin might make the first move, but he didn't think the bastard would be arrogant enough to try to take him here.

"I want the bitch dead! Resolve the issue now!" he screamed into the phone, and then he slammed it down.

"Shall I mobilize our strike force?"

Raskopov forced himself to calm down. Overreacting would accomplish little except to escalate the situation. Finesse, he decided, would be the better option, because he was in this for the long haul, and the stakes were very high and rising.

"Alert the duty officer to create a threat estimate and a measured response. Have him mobilize the necessary men and equipment, but keep them undercover."

"Yes, sir. What about Mr. Putin?"

"I want you to go down and greet him personally. Tell him that I would be most delighted to meet with him immediately, because I too have much to discuss concerning our country's future. And offer his men refreshments while they wait."

"Yes, sir," the secretary said, and he left.

Raskopov picked up his phone and dialed a number for George Thompsen, who was the Moscow bureau chief for Reuters. From time to time he had given the man exclusive first shots at developing stories. In return, Thompsen had given his word that he would hold a story until he was given the go-ahead for a release.

Every savvy politician the world over knew this trick for manipulating news breaks. Putin, too, had his newsman.

Thompsen answered his phone after four rings. He sounded as if he'd been asleep.

"Did I interrupt your sleep, George?" Raskopov asked in heavily accented English, even though his English was nearly good enough for him to be mistaken as a native speaker. But Russians were supposed to sound like Russians.

"Yes, General, but a call from you is welcome any time of the day or night."

"Liar," Raskopov said, and both men laughed.

"What can I do for you, sir?"

"I'm calling from Yasenevo, where an interesting situation is developing."

"I'm all ears."

"Mr. Putin has arrived and wishes to have a word with me."

The lateness of the hour was of no real significance; Russians often met in the middle of the night. But a call to a newsman in the middle of the night was significant.

"Any idea what the president would like to discuss?"

"A number of ideas, one of which is my job here. But what could be interesting is that he brought his palace guard with him."

"All presidents travel with security," Thompsen said. It was obvious he was playing devil's advocate.

"I'm told it's more than that."

"Do you think he could have come to arrest you?"

It was exactly the direction Raskopov had wanted to steer the newsman, but he laughed heartily. "I hope not. Vladi and I are the best of friends. Everyone knows this."

Russians had a long history of giving nine ounces to their friends out of political necessity. For the good of the *rodina*.

"I'd like to stop by, one of these days, for a one-on-one, General. Any time that would be convenient for you."

"The hour is late, but now would be good."

"I'll be there in a half hour. May I bring a cameraman?"

"Still or video?"

Any unscripted interview with the sitting chief of the Russian intelligence service was unprecedented, but a video interview was completely unheard of.

Video," Thompsen said.

Raskopov thought the situation was almost too easy. "Yes."

"Make it twenty minutes, sir," Thompsen said.

"I'll have an aide meet you at Post One." Post 1 was the main gate for visiting dignitaries. It also was the gate through which Putin and his entourage had just arrived.

"Yes, sir."

Thompsen had his wife phone Donna Myers at her girlfriend's apartment while he hurriedly got dressed. She was the bureau's top camera operator and, even better, she was hungry. She and her lover lived less than a block away.

"Got her," Charlene said, handing the phone to her husband.

"Get dressed and get your gear. I'll pick you up in five."

"Where we going?"

"Yasenevo."

"No shit?"

"No shit. Move your ass."

Raskopov's encrypted cell phone chimed once in his pocket. He didn't bother answering it. The chime from his secretary meant that he was on the way up.

He got the nine-by-eighteen-millimeter Makarov pistol from a drawer in his desk, checked the magazine and action, then laid the gun down within easy reach in front of him. On top of it, he placed a report, three pages stapled together. The Pistolet Makarova was an old friend, since the days when he'd graduated from the Frunze Military Academy as a second lieutenant and joined the KGB. An old, reliable friend that never missed, especially at an arm's-length range.

He heard them in the outer office and got to his feet, his right hand on the desk, inches from the pistol, as his door opened and Putin came in, Putin's aide and Raskopov's secretary right behind.

Putin waved the other two men back. "Anatoli and I wish to have our privacy."

"Of course, Mr. President," Raskopov said. "Please close the door," he told his secretary. "But inform me when our guests arrive."

Rather than moving to chairs next to each other on the other side of the office, Raskopov sat down behind his desk and motioned for Putin to sit down across from him.

"Guests?" Putin asked, a slight smile on his round face.

"A newsman."

"Russian?"

"Reuters. We have no secrets here this morning, Vladi, do we?"

Putin hid his anger, but it was obvious to Raskopov that his old friend had not expected such a thing. "Of course not. What will happen here will have far reaching consequences, as you must know."

"Have you come here to replace me?"

"*Da.*"

"May I know with whom?"

"Gresko."

"The Pacific Fleet's admiral. He's a good man. But then, I still have a few operations to conclude before I retire."

"In the U.S. I know."

"Important business for both of us."

"Let us be frank, Anatoli. What has happened over the past week has been a disaster for your people."

"It's not over yet."

"It is, and I have brought people to end it."

"I have people standing by, Mr. President," Raskopov said, his voice tightening. "If you want a war, I'll give it to you."

SIXTY-FIVE

☐

Yuryn had moved from the safe house in the brownstone near the university to the Georgetown Suites on Thirtieth Street Northwest, to give himself the chance to think in relative safety. No one, especially not the general, knew where he was in hiding. He was of two minds about whether to do what the general had ordered and get on with the original assignment or to go deep. Disappear forever.

But the world had become small since the internet, and especially since the cell phone, and finding a place to hide was not easy. Plus, it took a lot of money.

On top of that, there had been rumblings over the past year or so that President Putin and General Raskopov were in a power struggle. In America, such struggles usually ended with one of the parties losing a crucial election. In Russia, the number two man often ended up in a gulag or dead.

The key was picking the winning side and sticking with him, so that in the end he would remember who his friends were.

Going deep was, for all practical purposes, impossible, so it would have to be Raskopov.

He phoned his New York office again and got Tania Boyko.

She answered on the first ring and sounded angry, as usual.

"I need to know if General Zimin has returned to Moscow or is still here in the Washington area."

"I don't know, but I've had several queries from Yasenevo about him as well as you."

"I just got off the phone with Yasenevo."

"Good, then get back here. All hell has broken loose and I'm tired of covering for *pizdas* like you."

"Is Zimin on his way back to Moscow or not, woman?" Yuryn shouted.

"Not unless he took an alternate route. He missed his flight from Dulles and he doesn't answer any of his numbers. But that's something you should already know. This is still your operation."

"Then find him," Yuryn said, and he gave her his number.

"If he's still on point, then I would say either the McGarvey apartment or the apartment of his wife."

Yuryn's English was good, but he didn't understand the idiom. "On point?"

"Still working the op. McGarvey and Rencke are gone. Rencke's wife is dead, which leaves McGarvey's wife. Find her and you'll likely find Zimin. A good starting place might be her apartment. Or do I need to draw you a picture, comrade?"

The outgoing station chief had explained Tania Boyko when Yuryn had taken over two years ago. "She's a total pain in the ass, but brilliant at what she does. So just put up with her shit and you'll come out just fine."

"Thank you," Yuryn said into the phone, but the woman had hung up. "Bitch," he said softly, breaking the connection.

The cabbie dropped Pete and Toby Patterson off down the block from her apartment building. Her suggestion, and he approved. The street was not busy at this time of the day.

"Whoever tossed your apartment could be nearby."

"Unless he left something behind that Lou didn't pick up on," Pete said. She was hyperaware of her surroundings now, in part because the Company had sent a minder to watch her back but also because Lou almost never missed a thing.

"Still might be nearby to make sure whatever it was he left worked. They're not very good, but they're persistent."

Pete was impressed. "You've been briefed."

"Yes, ma'am. Extensively."

"The name is Pete."

Patterson nodded, but his head was on a swivel as they started down the block, him on the outside to take any possible fire from a roof or upper-floor apartment across the street.

"I need to clean up and change clothes and then we'll go out to Langley. I want to have a word with Mary Sawyer and the admiral."

"One thing at a time," Patterson said.

Pete looked up at him. "Spooked?"

"On duty I'm always spooked," he said. "How about we call for backup and wait till they show up?"

Pete pulled up short. They were only a few doors down from her building, but she too was feeling that something wasn't right. "Maybe that's not such a bad idea," she said, but Patterson was already talking into his lapel mic.

It was only a half dozen blocks from his hotel to the woman's apartment, but Yuryn had taken a cab. He'd told the driver that he wasn't sure of the exact address but that he'd been here before and he would recognize the building if he saw it.

They'd passed the apartment once, then circled the block back to the same street, when he spotted the woman with a man, at the moment they stopped short.

"Right here," Yuryn said. He passed a twenty-dollar bill to the driver as they pulled up.

He jumped out of the cab and, mindless of anything else, yanked out his unsilenced pistol as he ran directly toward the couple. The woman was definitely McGarvey's wife, but the man wasn't her husband. He was too tall. And a second, shorter, older man, was just coming around the corner to the left.

She started to look over her shoulder, her hand reaching under her jacket on her right side, but the man with her pulled out his pistol at the same time Yuryn began firing.

The distance was too far for him, and he was at a dead run, his gun hand jerking all over the place, all his shots going wide.

The man opened fire, hitting Yuryn in the hip on his left side. He stumbled and started to go down, when Pete fired twice, hitting Yuryn first in the left shoulder and then in his right eye.

For the first moments, Zimin did not want to believe what he was hearing, but then he understood that not only was a gun battle going on in the street in front of the building but also it had to be between the woman and someone else from the team. The only one left was Yuryn, and although the man might have been a good chief of station, he was an administrator, not a blooded field officer.

Downstairs on the ground floor, his pistol in hand, he cracked open the door just far enough to see out.

Pete McGarvey, her back to him, was approaching someone lying on the sidewalk about twenty meters away. She had a pistol in the two-handed grip.

A couple of meters behind, but just off to the street side of her, a large man was approaching the body, his pistol out. It wasn't McGarvey; Zimin was sure of it. Probably security from Langley. His head was down and turned slightly to the left. He was speaking into a lapel mic, calling for backup.

Zimin eased out onto the low stoop just one step above the sidewalk, raised his pistol, and pointed it at the man, whom he considered the primary threat.

But his specific orders were to take out the woman, and so he switched aim, concentrating on her back, center mass. If he could just knock her down first, he would deal with the man, and then return to her if need be.

But a man off to the left opened fire, the first shot missing. As Zimin turned to meet the new threat, a thunderbolt clapped inside his head.

SIXTY-SIX

☐

The DC Metro cops were on the scene first, one radio car to begin with and three others afterward. This was the second shooting in Georgetown in as many days, and people were frightened.

A plain Chevy Impala with government plates showed up with two FBI agents, but almost immediately a Bell Ranger came in low over the rooftops and hovered about fifty feet above the street, until the vehicles and personnel cleared a landing area.

The machine touched down and Van Gessel got out and came over to where Pete and Patterson were leaning up against one of the Metro cop cars.

"You two okay?" he asked. He didn't look happy.

"Yes, sir," Patterson said. "But there was another man, who took out the guy coming from Mrs. McGarvey's building."

"Who was it? One of ours?"

"I don't know. He just disappeared. One minute he was there and the next he was gone."

Van Gessel turned to Pete. "Did you see him?"

Pete shook her head. She had caught a glimpse of him as he turned the corner, and she knew who he was. "I didn't see anyone."

"You're staying on campus until we get the mess straightened out."

"My husband and Otto Rencke are heading to Russia and I'm going after them," Pete said. There was no way she was going to sit out the rest of the op on campus.

"No."

"Bullshit," Pete said, pushing forward. "It's my husband we're talking about."

"Yes, and he and Otto are walking straight into what's turning out to be the start of a Russian coup. All of Moscow is divided into two heavily armed camps—one side supporting Putin and the other supporting Raskopov."

"They need to be warned."

"It's been done, but they won't back off," Van Gessel said. "Now let's get the hell out of here before the media shows up. It's already become a three-ring circus. I don't want to make it four."

"I have to get to Moscow!" Pete shouted. She could feel what little control she had left slipping away.

"To do what, get yourself killed too?"

Pete turned to Patterson, who took her elbow. She was becoming dizzy and she didn't realize it, but he did.

"Let's go," he said gently. "It'll be okay."

"How?" she almost cried.

"Because Mac is involved."

"And so is the White House," Van Gessel said. "The president is talking with Putin, and Taft has been in contact with General Raskopov. It's up to them now, but no one wants a revolution over there."

McGarvey arrived at Helsinki Airport first thing in the morning and took a cab straight to the Sokos Hotel, near the train station. He asked at the front desk to leave a message with Mr. Underwood.

"I'm sorry, sir, but Mr. Underwood checked out at seven this morning."

"Did he say where he was going?" McGarvey asked. Otto wouldn't have, of course, unless he meant to verify what Mac already knew.

"No, sir."

McGarvey started to turn away. It was likely that his and Otto's paths had crossed at the airport. He turned back. "Do you know if he took a cab?"

"No, sir, he walked."

"How far is the train station?"

"Two blocks."

"Do you know what time the first train leaves for Moscow?"

"Oh eight hundred sharp."

It was a few minutes before that.

"Are they ever late?"

The clerk was indignant. "No, sir."

McGarvey hurried out the door and headed in a dead run to the train station, his single bag containing the diplomatic pouch with his pistol and extra magazines of ammunition in his left hand. He took out his phone with his right.

"Lou, I need your help right now."

"Yes, Mac."

"I'm in Helsinki. I want you to delay the eight o'clock train to Moscow. I'm just a few minutes away, and I think Otto is aboard."

"He is, but he does not wish you to come with him."

"Think about it, goddamnit. He's going to walk into a major mess, and he's going to need all the help he can get."

"You both will," the computer program said.

"Then do something!"

"A switch indictor at the control tower has been stuck in the closed position. Someone will have to be dispatched to check it out. You have your few minutes."

"Thank you."

"Good luck, Mac," the computer said. "He is in car four zero three, first class. Your ticket is waiting for you."

The train was the high-speed Allegro to Saint Petersburg, and it pulled out less than one minute after McGarvey boarded.

Otto looked up, not at all surprised, as McGarvey sat down next to him. "You cheated," he said.

"I wasn't going to let you go alone, and this time Lou agreed with me."

Otto's smile was sad. "I'll have to tweak a couple of her subroutines," he said. "Nothing ever stays the same does it?"

"*We* do," McGarvey said. Whatever they were running into would almost certainly happen even before they got to Moscow, possibly even at the Russian border.

The conductor came around to collect the declaration forms for the crossing, and he gave McGarvey the two copies that needed filling out.

The car was less than half-filled. "Where is everybody?" Otto asked.

"Could be some trouble ahead at the border," the conductor said indifferently. "It happens sometimes."

When the conductor was gone, Otto bent a little closer to McGarvey. "Us?" he asked.

"I was counting on it," McGarvey said. "Where's your gun?"

"In my bag."

"No matter what happens, don't try to reach it. Just go with the flow."

"What is going to happen?"

"You crashed the SVR's mainframe, so I'm pretty sure that Raskopov is going to want to grab you before Putin's people do. He might even have stationed someone on the train to take you before we get to the border."

"That's exactly what I want to happen. I'm going to offer him a trade: his mainframe for the spy network at Los Alamos, the predecessor of the one that killed your parents. What about you?"

"Putin wants me because I challenged him one-on-one, so I'm pretty sure his people are going to take me at the border, but certainly before we reach Saint Petersburg," McGarvey said. "At least I hope it'll go down that easily. I don't want us to get into the middle of a shooting war between the two sides. That'll come soon enough."

"Puts us on different sides of the coup, if that's what's brewing."

"I'm betting it is. And you and I are going to use each other for leverage. You to nail down the spy ring, and me to convince Putin to pick us both out of Russia before the sky falls down."

"I thought you wanted to kill him."

"No. Just to force his hand into finding out who killed my parents."

Otto shook his head. "Always a lot of losers in every revolution, so keep your head down, *kemo sabe.*"

SIXTY-SEVEN

□

It was a little past one in the morning, but Pete hadn't been able to get any sleep so far, even though she was dead on her feet. They had brought her to Langley, where she'd been set up in the Scattergood-Thorne house in the woods, not much more than a stone's throw from the George Washington Parkway and Highway 123, but still on campus. The rambling three-story colonial with a long, rich history was used by the Company as a conference center.

Van Gessel, Waksberg, and just about everyone else had been very solicitous of her. They had even sent over a doctor to see if she was okay. She was fit but run-down. Mentally exhausted, the doc said.

They'd also offered to have a female security officer stay with her, but she had declined, though several men were stationed around the house, some in static watchdog positions, others as rovers.

Carleton Patterson, Toby's grandfather, had stopped by at around ten for a glass of wine and a chat. "I'm here simply to hold a hand that needs holding," he'd told her, and he had taken her in his arms for a warm hug.

"I'm frightened," she admitted.

"We all are, every time the boy gets himself into these sorts of situations. But he always seems to come out of them."

Pete looked up at him and smiled a little sadly. "You almost said 'in one piece,' but that hasn't always been the case."

"You have a few scars of your own."

She nodded. "What have you heard?"

"Isn't Otto's computer talking to you?"

"Otto's shut her off."

"Didn't want you to worry," Patterson said. "Rightly so."

"They're in Russia?"

"From what we've learned, they arrested Otto at the border."

"The SVR?"

"Looks like it, but there was no mention of any physical violence."

"No mention by whom, Carleton? Who's giving this intel?"

"I don't know."

"What about Mac?"

"He's in a helicopter, en route, presumably, to Moscow."

"To the Kremlin?"

"Yes. The two of them have gotten themselves in the middle of what's shaping up to be a full-blown revolution. The president ordered our military to go to DEFCON 2, and the State Department has issued emergency lockdown orders to our embassies and consulates inside Russia."

It was all too much for Pete, and she turned away. "What the hell did they think they could accomplish?" she asked.

"Mac didn't go to kill Putin. Your husband's never been that crude. Nor, from what I'm guessing, did Otto do permanent damage to the SVR's computer system."

"Then what?"

"Only they know," Patterson said. "Now, get some sleep. I have a feeling they're going to want you at the White House sometime before noon."

"Sure," Pete said absently.

Patterson started to leave, but then he turned back. "Toby told me that he didn't shoot the Russian coming out of your apartment. Some man down the block did it. What'd you see?"

"Nothing," Pete said.

Patterson was obviously skeptical, but he nodded. "Get some rest," he said, and he left.

Pete didn't bother getting undressed. She just took off her shoes before she lay down on the couch in the living room. She put her pistol within reach on the coffee table and closed her eyes.

Sleep was a long time coming, and she dreamed that her minders outside had been killed and that someone had broken into the house and stood over her.

When that dream was gone, she worried about Mac, her heart racing, her stomach sour, sweat drenching her all over.

She woke suddenly, knowing that she was not alone in the house.

"Mac?" she said, sitting up and reaching for her gun.

"No. Just me," Bob Wehr said, from where he sat in a chair, across the room and near one of the windows.

The full moon was low in the sky, its light dappling through the tree branches, throwing eerie shadows like a Halloween nightmare.

"Jesus Christ," Pete said.

Wehr chuckled. "Not him, either, I'm afraid."

"It was you in Georgetown. You followed me from Albuquerque."

"I suspected that what was left of the Russian team here on the ground would probably want to take you, now that Mac and Otto are out of reach."

Pete had picked up her pistol, but she held it low and off to the right, her finger on the trigger. "Who the hell are you, and where are you getting all your intel?"

"My adopted grandfather was Wild Bill Donovan, the head of the OSS in the forties. I actually never met him, but my grandmother, before she died, told me that they'd had a brief fling during the war when she was young. My father wasn't his child—that was a lieutenant who got killed by a sniper in Berlin near the end. But Donovan never forgot her, and after I was born, he sent money every year for me until he died in fifty-nine."

"What about your father?"

"I never really knew him or my mother; they both died in a house fire when I was just a baby. That was up in Buffalo, and it was a neighbor who pulled me out. It was my grandmother who raised me."

"So where are you getting all your information?"

"When I joined the army, they put me in military intelligence right after boot camp, and I became the golden boy who everyone wanted to know."

"Because of your grandfather."

"Yes. Doors opened for me that wouldn't have ordinarily budged."

"At some point you were assigned to keep watch on the McGarveys."

"We weren't doing such a hot job of outing what we were sure was a spy ring working at the lab, so a number of us were sent out in the field, assigned to several key scientists. But I didn't do such a great job. They were killed on my watch."

"At which point you were assigned to keep tabs on Kirk?"

Wehr took a moment to answer. "Not directly."

"Otto couldn't find any reference to you in the army or any other branch of the government."

"That's because there isn't any. My real name isn't Wehr; my identification was assigned to me as a double blind. Nothing in writing, and my name was listed as dead of natural causes. The real me disappeared, and Wehr didn't exist until San Antonio."

"What's your real name?"

"Doesn't matter," Wehr said, getting up. "You'll be safe here now, and I suspect that your husband and Otto will find their way home before long."

"But you still haven't explained how you're getting all your information."

"My grandfather's name has always carried a lot of weight; still does, to this day."

"And?"

"President Weaver has been wrong about lots of things, but when he talked about a shadow government, he was right. The policy planners, the strategists, the senators and representatives are only the visible part. Ever wonder why, after Donovan, career intelligence officers were almost never appointed to head the CIA?"

"No," Pete said.

"Because presidents were steered in that direction. Gently nudged. It allowed everyone else—the aides, the fourths and fifths in command, the secretaries, the people who did the real work—to talk to each other. To compare notes without politics getting in the way."

"Otto should have been picked."

"I'm told that he was considered. But he, and your husband, were just too valuable where they were. All we could do was offer a helping hand from time to time."

"Like right now?"

"We'll see," Wehr said, and he went to the entry hall.

"Thank you," Pete said.

"You're welcome, Mrs. M.," he said without turning back.

SIXTY-EIGHT

□

The Mi-8 Hip military transport helicopter landed at three o'clock, under a gray, overcast sky, on the helipad inside the Kremlin walls. They
had touched down once to refuel outside the town of Bologoye, on the
main Saint Petersburg-to-Moscow railway route, and coming in over
Moscow from the south, McGarvey had watched from a window for any
signs of trouble.

Two beefy security officers from Putin's personal guard had come
to accompany him from the border. They had taken his bag with his
weapon in its diplomatic pouch, and had even taken his belt and shoe-
laces, which were considered useable weapons.

"There doesn't seem to be any trouble in the streets yet," he said, as
the rotors went to neutral.

"What trouble would that be, sir?" the one who'd identified himself
at the border as Valentin asked from across the aisle.

"The revolution."

The officer said something in Russian to the other unlatching the
door, and they laughed.

"I don't know what you are talking about, but there are no problems
here in Moscow."

"Maybe in Yasenevo."

Valentin shook his head. "Mr. Putin wishes to speak with you. I suggested that you be in restraints, but I was told that there would be no
trouble if you gave your word."

"You have my word," McGarvey said.

"Thank you, sir."

Only a few people were out and about as McGarvey was walked

the short distance over to the president's office, which was housed in a three-story yellow building with a front door flanked by tall evergreens. The national flag flying from the roof signified that Putin was here.

They were not challenged by the guard outside or by security inside the main entrance. The corridors were busy with people scrambling back and forth, but everyone moved and spoke in a quiet hush. National emergency or not, the president was at his desk, and everyone respected his peace and quiet.

Putin's secretary, a man in his thirties, wearing a dark suit, white shirt, and red tie, his thick black hair slicked back, got up from his desk in the anteroom and opened the inner door. "Mr. President, they are here," he said, and he stepped aside respectfully.

McGarvey's guards also stepped aside, and he walked into the office of the beleaguered president of Russia, who was on the phone.

Putin waved him to a chair on the other side of the desk, and McGarvey sat down, and crossed his legs.

"Thank you," Putin said, and he hung up.

For several long moments he just looked at McGarvey, his slight, enigmatic smile on his narrow lips. But then he nodded. "So you want to go to war with me, Mr. McGarvey. Here we are."

"You murdered my parents because of a breakthrough they had made at Los Alamos. Why the cover-up all these years?"

"To begin with, I don't remember that operation, though it was in my division. But I had the file pulled, and as the former director of the CIA, you must understand what our position was at the time. We had devised a system to defeat your surveillance satellites, and your parents were on the verge of building something that would nullify our work. It meant that we were vulnerable to a nuclear attack by the U.S. That could not be allowed."

"Why the attacks on me and my friends? Killing Louise Rencke made no sense, unless it was to stir up a hornet's nest, which it did."

"That was an SVR project, and it made no sense to me when I first learned of it."

All of a sudden it was clear to McGarvey, and it even made sense to him, in a horrible way. Nevertheless, he wanted to hear it from Putin himself. "And?"

"Outrage," Putin said.

McGarvey waited.

"One of your Atlantic hurricanes begins as what should be an insignificant ripple in the atmosphere coming off the coast of Africa. Your parents' deaths were not even important when they were ordered; apparently they had finished with their work. But it was felt, in certain circles, that, given the right nudge, you might reopen the investigation."

Still McGarvey held his silence.

"You have the reputation of taking anything that you do to the limits—often to extreme limits. Such a reaction was also expected, and of course it occurred. But like your Atlantic hurricanes, your storm needed feeding. Mrs. Rencke's death was a significant motivator."

"You want General Raskopov to go away."

"Yes, and he wants to take this office, so he planted the seeds to produce a storm that would result in a revolution, which of course has always been the Russian way of solving its problems."

"As simple as that?" McGarvey asked.

"Yes."

"But why the animosity between you two?"

"Lara Molev. She was an interpreter in our directorate. Anatoli and I were both in love with her. But she was a farm girl, and finally the pressure got too great for her and she committed suicide rather than have to choose between us."

"Revolution because of a long-dead woman?" McGarvey said, but he wasn't all that surprised.

"Smaller events have triggered larger storms," Putin said. "And, in the meantime, what to do with you?"

Otto, shackles binding his ankles and wrists, a small bandage on the side of his head above his right ear, was led into Raskopov's office, where he was given a chair in the middle of the large room. After the guards withdrew, the general got up, came around to the front of his desk, and perched on the edge.

"Here you are . . . so what to do with you," Raskopov said.

Otto raised his hands. "I don't need a keyboard to permanently fry your entire mainframe. Believe me, I could send your entire fucking operation back to the Stone Age."

Raskopov nodded. "I believe that you could have. But no longer." He touched a finger to a spot above his right ear.

Otto had been briefly drugged asleep on the way up from the border. He remembered falling forward, hitting his head on a metal support in the helicopter. He'd awoken with the bandage.

"Lou," he said. But there was no answer. He'd felt the pain in the side of his head, but he hadn't thought that the Russians knew about his implant, which allowed him to communicate with his darlings.

But Mac had told him once that if someone is shooting at you, shoot back.

"You're deaf and dumb," the general said.

"True. But how's it coming with your geeks trying to put your mainframe together?"

A quick flash of irritation crossed Raskopov's face, but then he smiled again. "The work is slow, but it's progressing."

"They haven't reached the first locked door. It's tough, but they get tougher."

"We'll see," the general said. "In the meantime, I can't kill you yet, in case we need you to help."

"Won't happen."

Raskopov shrugged. "But we're all a little bit busy here in Moscow, so I do need to get you out of sight and out of mind."

"A little revolution now and then is good for the spirit, isn't that what you people are fond of saying?"

"I have friends in Kazakhstan, where I might send you for a bit."

Otto wasn't quite so sure of himself now. Not all Russian gulags were located in Siberia. But he managed to smile, his mouth as dry as the desert Raskopov meant to send him to. "You'll never be able to let me loose. Because if you do, I will rain down a total shitstorm on this place."

"I know, and I hope that it gives you comfort."

SIXTY-NINE

□

Pete rode over to the White House with Admiral Taft first thing in the morning. They were passed through the northwest gate off Pennsylvania Avenue and parked at the main entrance to the West Wing.

"They've disappeared," Taft said, before they got out of the limo.

"What do you mean, exactly?" Pete asked, trying to dampen her worst fears.

"Bob Riley, our Moscow chief of station, said his people spotted them coming into the city—Mac by helicopter, directly to the Kremlin, and Otto out to Yasenevo. And that's it."

Pete took out her cell phone. "Lou," she said. Otto's darlings had not answered her all night.

The driver had gotten out and was about to open the rear door, but Taft gestured him to hold up.

"Yes, Pete?" the computer program responded.

"May I talk to Otto?"

"No."

"I'm told that our people on the ground in Moscow have lost contact with him and Mac."

"So have I."

Pete was stunned. "No. No. No. What do you mean, exactly?"

"His phone is off-line and his chip has either malfunctioned or has been removed. I detected a very slight change in position six hours ago, and then it went off-line."

"Keep trying, please."

"Yes. Mary Sawyer is in Otto's office now, and she's helping."

* * *

President Weaver, his jacket off and his tie loose, was on the phone in the Oval Office when his secretary passed them through. Charles Toms, his adviser on national security affairs, was seated on one of the couches, and Weaver gestured for Pete and the DCI to take a seat across from him.

"Yes, Mr. President," Weaver said. "I appreciate any help that you can give me finding my people. And good luck with your current situation. If there's anything I personally can do to help, call me."

He put down the phone and swiveled in his chair to look out the windows for just a moment, and then he turned back. "That was Putin. He assured me that McGarvey and Rencke were held briefly but then released overnight."

"He's lying," Pete blurted.

"Of course he is. But his hands are full at the moment, and he can't be bothered by either of them. They're probably in a holding cell somewhere, and if the situation between him and the SVR is resolved, they'll be released."

"There's nothing else the man could have done," Toms said.

"They'll never let them go," Pete said bitterly.

Weaver shrugged. "Going into Russia, after all that has happened over the past week, was a bad idea. But it was theirs." He turned to Taft. "What are you doing to find them?"

"Nothing," the admiral said.

"For now, leave it at that."

The twin engine Sukhoi Su-80 short takeoff and landing aircraft touched down on a dirt runway in the middle of nowhere just before six in the evening, local. Otto was seated at the extreme rear of the transport plane and McGarvey was seated at the front.

They were not shackled, but they hadn't been allowed to move around, nor had the four security guards who had accompanied them—two from the Kremlin, two from Yasenevo—allowed them to speak.

Nothing had been visible from the air in any direction—no towns, no lights, nothing, only what appeared to be desert terrain, or perhaps high steppes. Watching out his window, McGarvey guessed they were somewhere in the south, in the middle of Turkmenistan or one of the other stans.

The fact that Otto seemed unharmed, except for a bandage over his right ear, and that Putin and Raskopov had apparently cooperated in getting them out of Moscow together, meant something. For whatever reason, neither of them had been lined up in front of a firing squad or given a nine-millimeter bullet into the back of the head. Russian justice.

A man in army fatigues, his boots unbloused, was waiting beside a dusty Gazik—the Russian jeep—at the end of the runway, his arms folded over his chest.

"Home sweet home, as you say it," McGarvey's escort said. He got to his feet and stood aside.

A crewman came from the cockpit, opened the hatch, and lowered the stairs.

The engines hadn't been shut down, and the plane was filled with enough noise that McGarvey's minder had to shout for him to move forward.

He got out of the plane.

Otto stepped down the ladder and looked around. "Nice place," he said.

"How are you feeling?" Mac asked.

Otto touched a finger to his bandage. "The bastards took out my chip. I can't talk to Lou now."

The man by the Gazik waved them over, and one of the guards said something in Russian and laughed.

"Says 'Good riddance and good luck,'" Otto translated.

Mac and Otto walked over to the jeep. "Welcome to number twenty-seven," the driver said in English. He was grinning. "Distinguished guests," he added, laughing.

They got in the jeep, Otto in back, Mac in front. Once they had cleared the runway and headed down a dirt track, the airplane began turning around.

"You don't look like the typical lot we get down here," the driver said. He was a large, swarthy man, and Mac guessed he was Siberian.

"Where is 'down here'?" McGarvey asked.

"Right in the middle of Kazakhstan, a hundred and sixty K from the nearest town, road, or water." He laughed again. "The rockets are launched from over there," he added, pointing off to the left. "But out here, there's nothing. Better than the barbed wire these places are usually equipped with. You and other *pizdas* they send us have all the room you want to wander. And if you like to take hikes, be our guests. They all come back, sooner or later, begging for water—either that or, when we get around to it, we follow their tracks out to their bodies. Usually we bring shovels and bury them where they fell. Saves work dragging their sorry asses back to the camp."

"What kinds of people do you typically get down here?" Otto asked.

"The dregs, believe me. Perverts, child fuckers—one was even doing his own daughter, and she was only eighteen months old." The man laughed again, only this time it was with a dark humor. "You two must have really pissed someone off, because you'll be bunking with that fine specimen."

Mary Sawyer was seated at one of the monitors in the front room of Otto's suite on the third floor. She was a petite woman, in her early sixties, with a pretty, round face, a big smile, and short blond hair. She'd spent the better part of the last two days trying to make sense of the material stacked up just about everywhere. There were file folders, newspapers, and magazines in a dozen different languages—mostly Russian and Chinese—in large piles on the floor along the walls, maps and photographs on most of the half dozen tables, two trash cans filled with thumb drives, and even a large cardboard box filled with floppy disks, each with a code jotted on the memo lines.

"Have you been able to reestablish contact with Otto yet?" she asked, raising her head.

"No," Lou said, and she sounded sad. "His chip is off-line and his sat phone has been disabled, as has Mac's. May I call you Mary?"

"Yes, of course. It is a pleasure working with you, Lou."

"And with you, Mary."

"Now, let's start a new search program for Otto. And these will be the parameters, beginning with everything—no matter how seemingly unrelated to the current events—that he has been working on for the past seven days. If nothing turns up, push it back week by week."

"Make I make a suggestion?"

"Yes."

"I can do a global search of everything that Otto has worked on since I was born, primarily targeting programs that might be related."

"Then let's begin," Mary said.

SEVENTY

□

Gulag 27 was unfenced, as their guard had told them it would be. Driving up to what amounted to a main entrance of sorts, McGarvey wasn't surprised at how run-down the place was. With twenty or twenty-five low barrack buildings, all of them in almost complete disrepair—plus three smaller buildings that served as the guards' quarters and the camp administrative office, all of which were in only slightly better shape—this place had to be a hellhole for prisoners and staff alike.

It was nearing nightfall, but there was enough light, especially on the western horizon, to see that they were in the middle of an almost completely barren steppe. There were almost no hills, and only a dull yellow landscape was visible in all directions.

"You're too late for supper, but you'll love your breakfast," the guard said.

No one was out or about, and the camp, which was less than a hundred yards on a side, looked deserted.

"Prisoners are supposed to stay in their quarters from supper on, but nobody really gives a shit. Like I said, if you want to wander, be my guest."

"Are there work details during the day?" McGarvey asked.

"Only if someone dies, and then we send out a burial detail."

"I didn't see any graves on the way in."

"They're out there, we just don't bother marking them," the guard said. "Thing is, no one gives a fuck about anyone sent here, because no one is ever going to leave—or at least not get home from here. This place, or out there in any direction you choose, is your retirement dacha. As for me, I have only nine months to go."

They pulled up in front of one of the barracks near the rear of the camp, the one farthest away from the admin center and staff quarters.

"You have the entire building to yourselves, gentlemen, along with Mitrofan Semenov. We had to give him his own place, because the other guests would have killed him. No one likes his kind."

Mac and Otto got out of the Gazik, and the guard didn't bother to wait until they went inside before he drove off.

"We're getting out of here tonight," McGarvey said.

"Shouldn't we look around first?" Otto asked. "At least talk to some of the others? Maybe someone knows where we are."

"If the guard was telling the truth and we're in the middle of Kazakhstan, then this is a contract gulag left over from the Soviet Union days that Moscow is paying rent on."

"Which means?"

"We head due west to the Caspian Sea, and if someone picks us up before we get there, they won't be Russian."

"We're not going to make a hundred miles on foot without food or water."

"Just something to drink," Mac said. "We're going to use an old Spetsnaz survival trick."

"I'm listening."

"We're taking our roommate the child molester with us, along with something to cut his throat."

Otto blanched and stepped back. "Jesus," he said softly.

Mary had had a hamburger and fries in the cafeteria the night before and had gotten a few hours' sleep in Otto's office, and just before noon Lou announced that Pete was at the door.

"Let her in."

The door buzzed.

"Back here," Mary called.

Pete came to the rear office, where Mary was working at the large, horizontal flat-screen monitor, with newspapers, files, maps, and photographs littering the floor all around her. "Kind of a mess," she said, looking up.

"What are you guys working on?" Pete asked.

"Everything that Otto's worked on that might have any bearing on what's happened in the past week."

"Anything yet?"

"Aside from the fact that it's a Russian operation—something we already knew—and that it involves spying at Los Alamos and Mac's personal relationship with Putin, nothing of any significance yet."

"I met with Weaver at the White House yesterday, and something that he and Putin talked about stuck with me. Putin said Mac and Otto were released. But Weaver said he was lying, and he told me that he thought they were being held somewhere."

"'Somewhere' covers a lot of territory," Mary said.

"My guess would be somewhere out of Russia. If Putin got rid of Mac and Raskopov got rid of Otto, both of them would want the boys out of the country. They'd be too dangerous to either side if this comes down to an actual coup, with shots being fired."

"A gulag somewhere," Mary said.

"Give me a moment, please," Lou said.

"You don't look as if you've been getting enough sleep," Mary said.

"Neither do you."

"Not counting prisons inside Russia, there is currently only Gulag Twenty-Seven in Kazakhstan," Lou said. "Under contract with the government. There is pressure to dramatically raise the rental rate or close the installation down. Currently, the gulag has an estimated population of seventy-five prisoners, all men and all convicted of various crimes under Russia's perversion laws."

"Can we get a satellite pass over the place," Mary asked.

"It's dark, so it would have to be an infrared-only look down."

"That's exactly what we want," Pete interjected. "If Mac is there with Otto, they're going to get out of there ASAP. Nighttime is best."

"Can you do that?" Mary asked.

"Yes," Lou said. "I have Louise's procedures and passwords."

"They change almost daily."

"Yes," Lou said. "This may take up to five minutes for a retasking."

Mitrofan Semenov was a small man, about forty years old, with a narrow face, small dark eyes, and a birdlike manner. His attention constantly flitted back and forth, as if he suspected he would be attacked from any direction at any moment.

He'd been sitting on his bunk at the far end of the barrack when McGarvey and Otto walked in, and it was at least a half hour before he spoke up.

"I'm supposed to be alone in here."

"We know," Otto said in Russian. "But we're getting out of here tonight. And if you want to come along with us, it's okay."

"What if I don't?" Mitrofan demanded.

"Then stay."

"I didn't say that."

"Do you have a knife?" McGarvey asked, and Otto translated it.

"I'm not ignorant. I speak English."

"Good," McGarvey said. "Do you have a knife? A sharp one? Something you stole from the mess kit, maybe sharpened on a rock?"

"Why do you want to know?"

"We're getting out of here, and there may be animals or people who want to stop us."

Mitrofan thought about it, but then nodded. "I have such a weapon."

"Good," Mac said. "Then you're coming with us."

"When?"

"Now."

"There," Lou said. "Three figures, heading directly west."

"Three?" Pete asked.

"If they're moving west, they're trying for the Caspian," Mary said. "That's more than a hundred miles. They'd need something to drink."

"What?"

"My specialty, besides computers, is Spetsnaz tactics."

"We need to get the Kazak air force to pick them up before that happens," Pete said. "Lou, get me Taft on the phone."

"Yes, Pete."

Taft came on a minute later. "Mrs. McGarvey. Do you have something?"

"We think we've found them, heading away from a Russian gulag in Kazakhstan. They're on foot, and we can provide the coordinates. We'd like you to give Mr. Berliner a call and ask him to ask the Kazak air force to pick up our people and deliver them to a neutral port or airport." Leonard Berliner was the secretary of defense.

"Where is this gulag?"

Pete gave him the location.

"I'll see what I can do," Taft said. "But, for your information, the situation in Moscow seems to be calming down. Apparently, General Raskopov committed suicide. Shot himself to death."

"His nine ounces."

"Something like that," Taft said. "I'll get them back."

PART

FIVE

Serifos

SEVENTY-ONE

The weather on Serifos in early winter was warm and brilliant, as usual. It had been only a month since the business with the investigation into the deaths of McGarvey's parents, the abortive coup in Russia, and everything that had happened in between. But it seemed like another lifetime.

Mac was doing laps in the pool when Pete came out of the kitchen with a bottle of Krug and two flutes. She was nude, and her body looked absolutely perfect to him, as it always had. She sat down on the first step, her feet in the warm seawater, and she filled both flutes as he swam over.

"Krug, not Dom. I'm not a millionaire," he said.

She laughed, the sound musical to him. "Yes you are, so stop griping."

He took a glass and they clinked.

"A toast to what?" he asked.

"Us."

He nodded and they drank, a moment of thoughtful silence between them.

"Questions asked and questions answered," she said.

Mac smiled. "Have I told you yet this morning that I love you and that I couldn't have done much of anything without your help?"

She smiled and brushed a finger on his shoulder. "And Mary's."

"Yeah."

"She and Otto are coming for a few days, and they're bringing Audie."

"When?"

"Not till noon."

McGarvey grinned. "Gives us plenty of time."

"I hoped you'd say that," Pete said, and she put down her glass and reached for Mac's hand.